THE ...... EK THEIR
DESTINY AND THEIR DREAMS ON THE BANKS OF
A RIVER THEY CALLED . . .

THE BRAZOS

Jon Tallman—He knows the Brazos and its dangers. Rumors say he's a spy and maybe even worse, but only Tallman knows the truth, and the tragic past that has shaped his life.

Nancy Stafford—She lost her husband and her son on the treacherous trek through Texas, but this strong-willed and stubborn woman refuses to lose the last thing she has left: her pioneer spirit.

Jacobs—Arrogant and reckless, he thinks he knows it all, until he finds himself stranded in a hostile land where one mistake could be his last.

Alan—A young boy brutalized by the Apaches and Comancheros, he's found a new home—and he'll fight to the death to protect it.

Redford—A brutal and sadistic outlaw, he always gets what he wants—and what he wants most is a woman he'll have to kill to possess.

Montes—A Mexican Army captain sent on a mission of protection, he is torn between his desire for glory and his contempt for the Brazos settlers he is sworn to defend.

RIVERS
WEST

THE
BRAZOS

Jory Sherman

BANTAM BOOKS

NEW YORK • TORONTO • LONDON • SYDNEY • AUCKLAND

THE BRAZOS

A Bantam Book / April 1999

ISBN 0-553-56797-7

Published simultaneously in the United States and Canada

Bantam Books are published by Bantam Books, a division of Random
House, Inc. Its trademark, consisting of the words "Bantam Books" and
the portrayal of a rooster, is Registered in U.S. Patent and Trademark
Office and in other countries. Marca Registrada. Bantam Books, 1540
Broadway, New York, New York 10036.

PRINTED IN THE UNITED STATES OF AMERICA

WCD   10 9 8 7 6 5 4 3 2 1

This, the last of the novels in the Rivers West series, is dedicated to Greg Tobin, who first shared my vision, and to the writers who made the vision a reality: Win Blevins, Gary McCarthy, Don Coldsmith, Richard S. Wheeler, Frank Roderus, and Fred Bean.

I have travelled near five hundred miles across Texas, and am now able to judge pretty near correctly of the soil, and the resources of the Country, and I have no hesitancy in pronouncing it the finest country to its extent upon the globe.

Sam Houston's Report to the
President of the United States, 1832

THE

BRAZOS

Chapter One

The man on the dun horse, a surefooted animal with a coat gray as steel, still shiny from winter, heard the far-off cries of pain and fear. He reined up to investigate the sounds and separate them into pieces that he might understand. The dun horse held its ground, its head still high, ears coned to twisting listening posts, with the fine hairs inside quivering like hundreds of tiny tuning forks.

And Jon Tallman, a wanderer and adventurer, a man gorged on wild country as if the wildness in him needed feeding and nurturing, heard the other sounds that seemed chilling beyond measurable degrees in such a warm climate, the yips and throaty cackles of warring Comanches with fleet horses and deadly weapons, gloating with the blood lust of savage children turned loose on the world. Tallman twisted his head to stare over the dun's twin ears, which now held rigid on a straight path to the commotion, and tried to judge the distance across the harsh land dotted by mesquite, clumps of prickly pear, scattered oaks, and broad carpets of short stubborn grass that grew where it could, where rain sometimes ran along the ground and wild deer fed nervously on stark open range.

That's when Tallman heard the ripe crack of a rifle, the stubby bark of a flintlock pistol, the sounds interspersed like peppery snatches of dialogue between screams and fighting yelps in frantic powder and lead punctuation. These sounds registered on Tallman's brain and formed a picture of people caught out of time in a strange land fighting off a maddened hornet horde of painted redskinned centaurs suddenly risen from mythological origins to become flesh and blood and dreamless nightmare.

From the sounds he measured and weighed and sorted, Tallman reasoned that the band of Comanches was small and ambitious, perhaps a hunting party that had stumbled on serendipitous treasure in the midst of nowhere and envisioned opportunity and sport. The distance, he thought, was probably deceptive, measuring anywhere from a quarter mile to a mile or so, well beyond his short horizon. His straining vision probably stretched less than a thousand yards, since the land was gently rolling in that part of unmarked Spanish territory.

There was more gunfire, *pop, pop, pop,* as if those under attack had clumsily reloaded rifles and pistols or had waited until the bravery of the Comanches had brought them in closer to the muzzles of the metal weapons. And, even in that revelation, there was a picture of Comanches with bows and arrows. The shots from firearms seemed fixed and static, rather than from moving men on horseback.

The dun dipped its head, then jerked it back up quickly to express impatience, perhaps, and consternation, since Tallman noticed its coat quivering in excitement along its legs. He pulled gently on the reins to hold the horse in check and spoke to it in a soothing tone. "Steady, boy," he said to the gelding who had carried him many miles with no complaint.

As Tallman listened, the shrieks and yelps faded away and the gunfire died out with one last rifle crack. The sound seemed to linger on the still air, as if to test Tallman's hearing and memory. He continued to listen and to wonder if he had imagined everything, if the sounds were not just some aural mirage, a trick played on him by the desolate and empty landscape and his own solitary state of being. He strained to listen for the sound of hoofbeats or one last savage screech, but the slight breeze was just a whisper in his ears, almost like the dead sound heard in the graceful folds of a seashell.

But there were no pounding hoofbeats, no sounds of voices. Tallman heard only the soft rustle of the breeze in the dry grasses and the plaintive chirp of a bird, as if that avian creature was unsure that the shooting was finished. Tallman clucked to the dun and touched the knobby tips of his spurs to the horse's flanks, setting the animal into motion.

The silence was disturbed by the muffled plod of the dun's hooves, an eerie sound that was almost deafening now that the voices and rifle shots had stopped. The dun's ears were no longer pricked, but relaxed, as if all danger was past.

The dun covered the distance to the horizon, Tallman holding the horse to a slow cautious walk and frequently stopping to listen for sounds of movement or life. At the distant point he had marked mentally, Tallman stood up in the stirrups to peer ahead. He saw a line of cottonwoods and willows alongside the Brazos River that wound through the land from the northwest. He had known the river was there, for he had crossed it before.

Nearly a thousand yards away, Tallman saw the wagons moving northeast, away from the river, five of them, two covered, the others open, laden with furniture and tools, pulled by winter-haired mules that plodded under heavy harness. A lone man rode in the front, leading the way, a buckskinned man on a big bay, pistols dangling from his saddle horn, a rifle laid across the pommel, the brass fittings—butt plate, patch box, trigger guard—gleaming golden in the sun. White smoke still lay among the grasses like folds of cotton batting, wisps of it breaking off and curling in the air like ghostly tendrils of some decimated spirit.

Tallman scanned the ground for pony tracks as he rode closer to the departing wagon train. He had seen settlers coming into Spanish territory before, but always headed south. These people were moving to the northeast, back towards the treacherous Red River and territory where Comanches and Kiowas held reign, often exacting tribute from those pilgrims wanting to cross the Red. There apparently had been no casualties, for he saw no dead men on the open plain. But as he rode on, he saw another wagon down close to the cottonwoods that grew along the banks of the Brazos, and movement there, a swirl of cloth that disappeared behind the stationary wagon.

Tallman turned his horse to intercept the wagonmaster. He was conscious of being observed by those in the wagons and those who rode behind, young men from the looks of them, and another riding flank, an older man who was also carrying a rifle. Tallman waved, but the wagons did not stop, and one of the men at the rear unlimbered his rifle and pointed the muzzle in Tallman's direction.

Tallman did not jog the dun, but held his steady pace so that he would not alarm those who were suspicious of him.

As he drew closer to the head of the train, he saw the roiled, roughed-up ground, crisscrossed by unshod pony tracks but giving no sign of where the redskinned marauders had gone.

Tallman saw three young men guarding a half dozen cows and wondered if the Indians had been after the stock, so zealously were the youngsters watching after a few scrawny head. He angled the dun toward the man riding in the lead, more out of curiosity than any wish to involve himself in whatever troubles these pilgrims might have.

He could feel their eyes directed at him in dour and silent suspicion. He did not wave a greeting, nor did any of their number hail him. He felt, as he rode across the empty prairie, that he was about as welcome as a leper. He closed to within fifty yards or less.

Then, the leader held up his hand to stop the small caravan. The wagon train lurched to a halt. The leader swung his rifle off the pommel and aimed it in Tallman's direction.

"You there," the wagon master called out, "hold up a minute."

Tallman reined the dun to a halt.

"You wouldn't be no comanchero, would ye?" asked the man.

Tallman shook his head.

"You got some business here?"

"Just passin' through," Tallman replied. "I heard shooting."

"You're damned right you heard shooting, mister. And there's liable to be a hell of a lot more till we get out of this damned godforsaken country."

"Anybody hurt?" Tallman asked.

"Hurt? Not unless you count dyin' as hurtin' real bad."

"Pardon my asking," Tallman said, a hint of sarcasm in

his voice. He sat there, wondering if the wagon master was going to shoo him away or bid him to ride up. There was a silence as long as a man took to change clothes. Tallman slumped in his saddle as if to show that he didn't care one way or another.

"Hell, I reckon you can ride up, if you've a mind, but we ain't stoppin' and we're bound to be on our way afore somethin' else happens."

Tallman waited more than a decent interval before clucking to the dun and moving toward the wagon train. The wagon master barked an order, and his horse stepped out. Those in the wagons snapped their reins, and harness creaked and wood groaned as the wagons began to overcome inertia and follow their leader.

"I ain't a-gonna ask you your name, feller," the front rider said. "You ain't gonna be here long enough to strike up a friendship. Mine's Jacobs."

"I'm Tallman," Jon said.

Tallman brought the dun up alongside Jacobs, who looked the stranger over, regarding his buckskins, the powder horns, the possibles pouch, the flat-crowned hat he wore that appeared to have been forged out of tough buffalo hide. Jacobs especially looked into Tallman's deep-set pale blue eyes, the high cast to his cheekbones, the hard-set lips, the creases in his face around the mouth.

"You want to know what happened back there at them cottonwoods?" Jacobs asked.

"I got some time," Tallman said.

He looked back toward the cottonwood trees. Again, he saw a flicker of movement, the brown hide of a cow with patches of white.

"Wonder what that is back there?" Jacobs asked.

"I am some curious."

"Damned crazy woman, that's what. Lost her man up on the Red when we was jumped by Injuns. Then, her boy got killed back there. He warn't no more'n eleven or twelve, I reckon. Then, two gals who was ridin' with us was captured away by them red niggers. They come after the womenfolk, I reckon, but they got 'em some of our cows, to boot."

"And you're riding away?" Tallman asked.

"Look, mister, we got other folks to think about. Them gals was warned to stay close. The one was just a young gal with no more sense than a goat. Neither was more'n eighteen, or just abouts, and warn't nothin' none of us could do about it. Them savages had us surrounded and if we left the wagon to go after 'em, why, we'd of been kilt, sure enough."

Tallman said nothing. Jacobs had told a grim story in a few words, and Tallman knew the pilgrims had been whipped bad, so bad they could no longer reason or use good judgment. From the looks of the people there, they were good folks, caught up in something they couldn't handle or fully comprehend. They had run into a situation no schoolbook nor growing-up advice could prepare them for; they were lost in a world of which they had little or no understanding.

"You think we should go after them red niggers?" Jacobs asked.

"How many Comanch'?"

"A good dozen, I'd say. They was quick and they moved around a lot. Gawd, I never seen men ride like they did on them little paint ponies."

"How many able-bodied men you got?" Tallman asked.

"Four, maybe five, and one of them's no more'n a boy."

"What about the two girls? They have any kinfolk with you?"

"Sara Jane Wells, now, she was just taggin' along for the adventure, hooked up with the Lomax family back there. They took her in, but they don't feel no responsibility toward her. As for the other gal, Lorena Belton, she claimed she didn't have no family. She just wanted to go West and find herself a man. I reckon there ain't much we can do for either one of them gals."

Tallman could see that Jacobs had made up his mind. He wondered, though, how any of the men in the party could justify leaving a lone woman to fend for herself, especially after a Comanche raid.

As if reading Tallman's thoughts, Jacobs said, "I reckon she wants it this way."

"What way is that?" Tallman asked.

"Her wantin' to stay behind and not hightail it for civilized parts."

"Maybe she's not thinking straight."

"Oh, she's thinkin' straight, all right. Means to go on and do what she and her husband planned to do. Get 'em a little farm and grow kids and food. Don't look like she's gonna have no more kids, though."

Tallman had heard enough. Jacobs and the others were not going to wait around for a lone woman to change her mind. They meant to save their own skins. Tallman didn't have the heart nor the meanness in him to tell Jacobs that any way he ran, he'd likely find more trouble of the same kind they'd just gone through. He gathered that they had run into Indians up on the Red, and if they went back, they'd have to cross that muddy river again. And the Comanches would be there waiting for them.

"You take care," Tallman said.

"You leavin' us?"

"I reckon so. I been north."

"Well, suit yourself. We're headin' back to Kentucky."

Tallman raised his hand in farewell and cut the dun away from Jacobs.

"That river ain't fit nohow," Jacobs said as Tallman rode away. "Full of salt."

Tallman nodded.

"Don't know why anyone'd want to live in this place."

Tallman swung the dun around to head for the river.

"Arms of God, they call it," Jacobs yelled. "Arms of the devil, I'd say."

Tallman let Jacobs and the wagon train pass from his mind. His thoughts turned to the lone woman down in the cottonwood stand along the Brazos.

He did not hurry the dun. The sounds of the wagons and stock gradually faded from his hearing. Then he heard a canyon lark down in the river bottom, a sign that the noise and the furor were over, perhaps. The plaintive call did not give him any reassurance, however. Two white women captured by Comanche, if Jacobs had told it right, and another all alone, abandoned, possibly by choice, and left to the fates.

The dun pricked up its ears as it drew near the cottonwoods. A cow bellowed low, and Tallman heard the rasp and slide of metal on gravel. The wagon loomed up in his vision first, its bed cowled in canvas, but it was no Conestoga. From its ungainly appearance and the size of it, it appeared to be homemade. The wren stopped singing, and a crow cawed from somewhere downstream. Suddenly the sound of the shovel ceased, and Tallman grew wary as he approached the wagon. The dun began to sidle as if it did not want to go forward, as if it sensed danger.

Tallman gave the dun twin prods from his blunt spurs

and the horse leveled out, its ears still pitched forward, its neck arched as if about to do battle with unseen forces.

"You can just stop right there, mister, or I'll blow your head clean off."

A woman's voice, and no timidness in it, either.

"Whoa up," Tallman said to the dun. The horse stopped without Tallman's touching a rein.

"Ma'am, I mean no harm," he said. "The name's Tallman. I just wondered if you need any help."

"How come you didn't join up with that sorry wagon train?" the woman asked.

"I spoke to Jacobs."

"Jacobs's got the backbone of a garter snake."

"Yes'm," Tallman said.

"I am not needing any help."

"You might."

"What kind of help?"

"You aimin' to stay in this country, maybe a heap."

"Are you one of those comancheros I heard about?"

"No'm, I don't reckon."

"Well, you ride on down here real slow, Mr. Tallman, so

I can look you over. This rifle's primed and cocked and it shoots straight as a carpenter's string."

"Yes'm," Tallman said.

He rode down to the river bottom and still did not see the lone woman. But she had a cow that looked to be carrying a calf, and an ox that pulled the wagon. The cow was hitched behind the wagon, a big brindle with moon eyes and a flicking tail. As he pulled up in front of the wagon, the woman stepped out from behind a cottonwood. She was carrying a rifle, and it did not look strange in her hands. She had it aimed straight at Tallman and it was, indeed, fully cocked.

Tallman looked down from his horse, past the woman to a shallow depression in the loamy ground. A shovel lay next to it, and beyond, a small figure wrapped in what was either a blanket or a house curtain. There was a stain on the covering where the blood had soaked through.

The woman followed the line of Tallman's gaze and sucked in a jaw-tightening breath.

"I'm might sorry, ma'am," Tallman said softly.

"That was my boy, Alan," she said. "I hate to bury him here but there's no other place." There was bewilderment in her voice, an unbelieving cast to the expression on her face.

"Let me dig for a spell," Tallman said. "You need some time to think about your son."

Startled by his statement, the woman let out a small gasp and her eyes widened in further disbelief.

"You don't know us," she said. "You don't owe us nothing."

"Kindness is a free gift, freely given," he said.

"My name's Nancy Stafford. Why don't you get off that horse and we can shake hands."

Tallman swung his leg over the cantle and stepped down

from the dun. He tied the reins to a wagon spoke and walked over to the woman. He held out his hand. She looked at it for a long moment before she put out her hand and they shook.

"Your hands are rough," she said. "The hands of a man who is used to work. What do you do?"

"I just come off a scouting job," he said. "But I work at other things. Cattle, mostly."

"That's what my husband, Randall, wanted to do. Raise cattle."

Tallman dug the grave deep as Nancy spoke her prayers silently, her lips moving over the soundless words, the light breeze ruffling her hair and stirring her skirt with invisible fingers.

When he had finished, Tallman turned to the woman.

"I'll help you with the lifting," he said. "Whenever you're ready."

"I hate the finality of putting my boy in the ground."

"It's something that can't be put off much."

"No. I-I'll hold his head; you take his feet."

Together, they lowered the boy's body into the grave. Tallman laid the feet down gently a moment after the boy's head touched the earth. He stepped back, waiting.

"I can't bear to see him covered up," Nancy said. "Do you mind covering him?"

"No ma'am."

Nancy walked away, holding her hands to her ears so that she could not hear the dirt strike her son's body. She went behind a cottonwood and stayed there until Tallman was finished. He put rocks over the mound before he called to her that he was done.

Nancy walked from behind the tree and over to her son's grave. A tear bubbled from her eye and glistened on her cheek like a tiny jewel. She stared down at the mound of earth and sighed deeply, then shuddered with a visible spasm of emotion.

"Good-bye, my son," she breathed and wiped the vagrant tear from her cheek. She turned away from the grave site and walked toward the wagon.

"Where will you go now?" Tallman asked.

"I will look for a good piece of bottomland and build the farm my husband and I dreamed of," she said.

"You'll have to go a long way downriver to find good land."

"Look at my stock," she said. "They're tuckered. We can't go far."

"The Brazos is a long river. It goes all the way to the sea. There's better land farther down, a better place to start a farm. Safer."

"Safer?"

"Yes'm."

Nancy laughed wryly, startling Tallman.

"Ma'am?"

"Safer from whom?"

"Comanches. Comancheros. Not to mention Kiowa and Apache."

Again, she laughed. "Mister, did Jacobs tell you that there was another wagon train?"

"No'm, he didn't."

"We started out with one," she said. "After we crossed the Red River, there was a lot of arguing. One of the men said Jacobs was a bad wagon master and should be discharged. When most of us spoke up, this man said he was going his own way and asked if anyone else felt as he did." Nancy looked off in the distance, recalling that day.

"Go on," Tallman said.

"Several wanted to go with this man and they pulled their wagons out of the caravan and went with him."

"You decided to stay with Jacobs."

"Yes," she said, wincing. "I didn't trust this other man. He had been forward with me."

"Forward?"

"He had made crude advances to me—even while my husband was still alive."

Tallman said nothing.

"His name is Tom Redford, and he said he'd see me again. He said this when he was leaving."

"Where did he go?"

"He headed south, toward the Brazos river, but took a different course than Jacobs."

"So, you think this Redford might be farther down-river," Tallman said.

"I'm almost certain of it."

"Are you afraid of this man?"

Nancy looked Tallman square in the eye. "I'm not afraid of any man," she said.

"But you dislike him."

"He's a despicable man. I don't trust him. He took more money from the people he led away and reduced our strength by almost half."

"Does Redford know the country?" Tallman asked.

"He said he did. He said Jacobs would run into trouble going the way he planned." She added wryly, "I guess he was right about that."

"There is no sure way to come into the Brazos country without running into Indians," Tallman said.

"I feel sorry for the people who went with Redford," she said. "And I'm heartbroken about the two girls who were captured. I fear for them. I wish there was something I could do."

"Yes'm. There's nothing you can do, though."

"But Jacobs and the others could do something."

"Not likely."

Nancy grimaced. "No, I suppose not. It seems a shame that no man would try and free those poor girls."

"Comanches put high stakes on white women captives, ma'am."

"Well, so do I," she said, and there was a definite muscle-flex of challenge in her voice. "If I were a man I would go after those Comanches and free those women."

"Not much one man could do," Tallman said. "He might buy them back if he had enough ponies."

"I would give all I had to set those women free."

"Yes'm." Tallman felt the brunt of her accusing stare, but he had no call to rescue two women who had the bad luck to get captured by marauding Comanches. In a short while, those women would be reduced to slaves, mounted by every buck in the bunch, treated with contempt by the Comanche women and children. It was a sad fate, but no less a tragedy than life offered all creatures hunted every day.

"Well, there's no need to discuss this further, I can see," Nancy said. "You'll be leaving now."

"Yes'm," he said.

"Where are you headed, Mr. Tallman?"

"South, along the Brazos. I'm supposed to check on a man who put himself a homestead on the river a few miles from here."

"Well, I'm just going to look for a good place around

here," she said. "I'll find a place to cross the river and put down stakes."

"There's quicksand in this part of the river. All along it, matter of fact."

"Quicksand?"

"It'll suck you and your wagon down sure as anything. You might lose your stock."

"Do you know a place to cross?"

"Some. Not here."

Nancy brushed a lock of hair away from her face, regarded Tallman with a critical eye. "I don't trust you, either," she said.

Tallman shrugged. "You have no reason to, ma'am."

"I thank you for your help and courtesy, Mr. Tallman. Now, I must ask you to leave me be while I go about my business."

"I wish you well, Mrs. Stafford. I hope you find good land for your farm. Be careful of the quicksand and the hostiles who claim this river as their own."

Nancy nodded, tight-lipped, and Tallman put a foot in his stirrup as he grabbed the saddle horn with his left hand. He swung up into the saddle and sat straight, then took one last look at Nancy Stafford. He raised a pair of fingers to the brim of his hat in a farewell salute and told her one more thing before he touched spurs to the dun's flanks and rode out of the cottonwoods. "Keep your stock away from the river. Wait until you find a clear creek. River's full of salt."

He did not look back as he rode downriver, letting the dun pick its way along an old game trail.

Tallman thought about the woman, all alone, her husband and son both killed by Indians. Stubborn as a Missouri mule, maybe tough as a hickory stump inside, but frail and soft as any female on the outside.

The river was pale and milky and there were pieces of branches floating in it, a sign of weather passing through to the north and west. It was running almost full and would be treacherous to cross even if he swam his horse and didn't have to reckon with quicksand.

The Brazos was a crooked river, winding like a snake through rough country that changed more often than a woman's mind. No more than a big creek in that section of Texas, a stream born of rough country off to the west in New Mexico, the river ran for some eight hundred miles to the Gulf of Mexico. It looked like a river now, but Tallman knew that in high summer it would return to its lowly status as a creek. Only during the spring and autumn rains did it swell up this far to the north.

As he rode along, well clear of the marshes and soft shoreline, he saw the unshod pony tracks coming into the game trail. Some sense of memory prickled his senses, and he stopped to dismount and examine the spoor as he lay on his belly.

The tracks were fresh, moments old, and they marked at least a dozen riders and a half dozen head of cattle. He pulled himself up to his haunches and drew in a deep breath.

He read Comanches in the soft loam, probably the same bunch that had attacked the wagon train. Evidently they had circled the settlers to mislead them for some reason and doubled back to the south for the same or still another reason.

Slowly, Tallman stood up and climbed back on the dun, working the puzzle over in his mind. The Comanches never did anything without purpose. Why would they return to the river after leaving it? And why had they given up on the small wagon train so easily? It didn't make much sense.

Tallman waited, not wanting to track the band of Comanches too closely. He rode to higher ground, toward some low-lying hill, seeking shade and concealment. He rolled a smoke, held a glass against the sun to send a burning ray to the tip where the tobacco stuck out like brown straw. He inhaled deeply, willing his mind to calm down, think things through.

He wondered if the lone woman, Nancy, would ride his way, and perhaps farther, right into the band of Comanches. If so, then he had given her bad advice. Or would she rest and make camp to start afresh in the morning? He did not know and he knew he would not be welcomed if he returned to warn her. She had already told him that she didn't trust him, and that made for a powerful barrier between them.

After he finished his smoke, Tallman rode back toward the river to pick up the trail of the Comanches. It was not difficult to follow. Ten minutes later, he saw a splash of color on a small bush and rode over to it. He saw that it was a small piece of red cloth. He snatched it up and held it in the palm of his hand. Something moved inside him, a stirring that made his blood run hot. He lifted the cloth to his nose and sniffed it. There was a faint scent of perfume in his nostrils that made his stomach churn. He felt a twinge of something like anger as he stuffed the torn cloth into his pocket, where it burned into his flesh, haunting, accusing, taunting.

What he had found was a torn ribbon, velvet soft and crimson as blood.

Chapter Three

Nancy Stafford watched the man on the dun ride away, out of sight, and heaved a gentle sigh of resignation. Perhaps, she thought, she had been too short with the stranger, too critical of his motives. But she had learned in the past weeks and months that few men were to be trusted. When her husband had first read the notice in the St. Louis newspaper that a man named Moses Austin wanted settlers to accompany him to a new land, Texas, he had been excited. He had gone to a meeting and met someone who said he was one of Moses Austin's agents. They had given this man their hard-earned money, saved up over a year's time, to sign them up for the expedition.

Later, they learned that the man was a scoundrel and did not even know Moses Austin or his son. The wagon train had left St. Louis without them, and they had fretted that they had been left behind. Then Nancy's husband had met Redford, who said another expedition was being formed by Jacobs, who was authorized by the Mexican government to bring American citizens into Texas to settle some of the sparsely populated regions.

All the plans, all the dreams, all for nought, she thought, as she picked up the shovel and put it inside the wagon. That was not where it belonged, but she was tired, exhausted of mind, spirit, and body, and she did not want to bend down and put the shovel in its proper place beneath the wagon, in a storage bin her husband had built to carry the larger tools.

Wearily, Nancy climbed up on the wagon seat and unwrapped the reins from around the brake. She clucked to the ox and shook the leather straps. They made a sound like brittle rain on a wooden roof, and the ox jerked against the traces and plodded forward.

The ox took to the higher ground against its will as Nancy guided it away from the river. She didn't want the ox to drink and founder if the water was indeed salty as Tallman had said it was. That was a worry now, too. Water. She had ten gallons, perhaps twelve, and that would not last long in such desolate country.

I'll find a sweetwater creek, she thought as she listened to the creak of the wagon, the jingle of the harness rings. She looked back to see her son's grave, but it was hidden by the cottonwoods. Just as well, she thought, he's gone and I must accept that as I accepted the loss of my husband. My life. My everything. She fought back the tears, tried to stop the quivering of her lips as emotion swept through her like a mountain torrent. It was all she could do to keep going, not to turn the wagon around and return to the grave and weep out her heart, let herself die of grief atop her son's grave.

"No," she said aloud, then gave the reins a ripple with a

flex of her wrists; the ox picked up its lumbering gait. The
rope to the milk cow trailing the wagon tautened on the cow's
collar, forcing it to lope along through a scrim of pale dust.

"I am Mrs. Randall Stafford," she said aloud, as if to es-
tablish her identity to the harsh landscape. "My son, Alan
Stafford, has been buried and prayers said over him. I'm going to go on and find a place to live out my days and remember my boy and my husband." The ox trudged on, its yoke
creaking with every twist of its body, and the cow bawled in
protest at being dragged through unbreathable air. "I'm going to live on in the memory of my men who died to bring me
this far."

The words seemed to comfort her, to stay the tears that
welled up in her eyes, and she fanned herself with a limp kerchief that was still sodden with the dregs of tears already
shed. When the sun was high and her stomach raw from
hunger, she stopped and let the ox and cow find the shade of
some cottonwood trees. She set the brake, then climbed
down from the wagon and wrestled a wooden pail loose from
its slanted dowel on the back of the wagon. She filled the pail
from a tapped barrel and watered the ox first, then the milk
cow, before she filled her cup from the barrel and drank it
empty. Nancy climbed back into the wagon and opened a
hamper filled with dry sourdough bread and dried beef and
cut into both, swatting at flies that circled the food. She
munched on the tough beef and the crisp bread and swallowed the food with water that wet the morsels smooth, as the
midday heat bore into the wagon through the canvas.

After eating, Nancy dug out some dried apricots from a
flour sack hanging on the sideboard and plopped one in her
mouth. She climbed out of the wagon and searched for a long
stick among the cottonwoods. She found one that resembled

a shepherd's staff and walked the two hundred yards to the Brazos. She took off her shoes and stockings, folded up her dress and waded out three or four feet. The current hummed against her feet and ankles, stirring up grains of sand that tickled her toes and squished through them like the blessed touches of healing fingers. Poking ahead with the stick, she waded into the middle of the shallows. A water moccasin swam past, hugging the opposite bank, its wriggles leaving little curlicue wakes in the cloudy water. Nancy watched it furrow out of sight as it dove under the water. She made a semicircle with the end of the stick and then felt it sink so fast she almost toppled over into the water.

The sand sucked the stick downward so that Nancy had to jerk it free while bracing herself. Gasping, she waded back to shore, somewhat shaken by the experience. She had never seen quicksand before, and she conjured up horrible images of stepping in it and being swallowed up and suffocated. She shuddered in the wan sunlight as she tossed the stick away and stepped into the shade of the wagon to regain her composure.

She replaced the empty water bucket and climbed back onto the wagon seat, unwrapped the reins and released the hand brake. She flapped the reins and the ox stirred. It started to turn towards the river, and Nancy jerked hard on the left strap.

She looked at the bluffs ahead and wondered if she would ever find a place that was safe to ford. A pair of green-winged teal flew past, low over the water, and disappeared around a bend in the Brazos, their whistling wings making a plaintive flutelike melody.

"Giddap," Nancy yelled at the ox, which had no effect on the animal's speed. The ox settled into a serviceable gait that paralleled the thin river's course through trees and underbrush, past limestone bluffs that seemed forbidding after the open prairie. Nancy kept seeing Indians on horseback atop the ridges, and every alien sound sent shivers up her spine.

She knew, without any formal education, that none of the land she passed would do for a farm. It was too wild, too rugged, too rocky, and she was sure that there must be better sites farther downriver. She kept looking at the opposite side of the river, to the south and west, realizing, without knowing, that the good land would be found there. She wondered if she might not have some instinct for finding fertile land, if her intuition might not lead her to the best place, land where she might grow a garden to sustain herself and find wood for building. She had all the tools that Randall had bought, many of them almost new, and she had helped build houses before, had watched barns being raised when she was a small child, and had seen her father use the resources of land for shelter while she was growing up in Pennsylvania.

She wished her father were alive now and with her, her mother, too. But they had both died of the fever along with her sister. She had long since lost track of her older brother, who had left to seek his fortune after they buried their family, leaving Nancy with a couple of strangers to live out her budding years. Finally, she had left those faceless people to head west, subconsciously seeking her brother, but looking for adventure, too, a life away from crowded Philadelphia, where it seemed all of life passed her by, going and coming from the east and west, north and south. She had come to St. Louis, where she met and fell in love with Randall when she was too young to know what love was, and thought, perhaps, she might eventually find her brother among the many who came to the frontier seeking a better life for themselves.

The wagon floundered in the rough roadless country along the Brazos, tilting and rocking like a vessel in a storm-rumpled sea. At times, Nancy had to climb out of the river bottom and travel atop the wooded bluffs, find paths wide enough to allow the wagon to pass. There were no tracks to follow, no defined trails to show her the way. A deer rose up from its bed and startled her, flashing its white-lined tail as it bounded out of sight through wind-gnarled oaks, its hooves clattering on small stones and cracking dead branches in its flight.

Someday, she thought, I'll have to hunt one of those beautiful creatures and kill it. I'll have to butcher it for my food and maybe cure its hide so that I can use it for a rug or to cover the furniture I'll have to make. Randall said we'd do such things, and I wonder if I can.

When she descended to the river again, it had changed, was even muddier than before. Ducks and geese rose off quiet pools and headed south, their pinions straining as they lifted off the water. Small birds flitted from bush to tree, and the river twisted through a silent, hostile land like some trace of memory in her mind, a remnant of her childhood view of the Ohio.

She began to question the wisdom of going on, of leaving the wagon train and its comparative safety to enter such a desolate, unpopulated, uncivilized land that was so unlike any place she had ever been. She had never felt as alone as she did now, nor so lost as when she looked upward at the immense blue sky with its small puffs of clouds that seemed as abandoned and lonely as she was.

A wave of melancholy flooded through her thoughts as she listened to the monotonous groan of the wagon over scrambled talus and uneven stones. She found herself thinking about her husband and talking to him in her thoughts. Before her son had been killed, she had spoken to him, and now he was gone and there was only herself, and no one else.

There you go, she thought, feeling sorry for yourself again. She looked down from the sky and back to the wending river, then gazed beyond at the land on the other side, imagining where she might build a house on good soil, one protected on all sides from a sneak attack by Indians. It was discouraging, as the wagon trundled along, that she saw no such place. Instead, there were only thickly wooded patches that afforded no view of the land beyond the littoral scape.

As the day wore on, Nancy found herself having to push forward on high ground, well away from the Brazos, and the desolation there was more intense, almost palpable. Empty land stretched as far as her eyes could see. There was no shade where she might build a house, no creek for water, no protection from the interminable wind that was beginning to build even as the sky began to fill with large gray clouds lumbering in from the Gulf of Mexico like massive leviathans heavy with moisture.

Maybe, Nancy thought, I'll have to leave the wagon and walk the entire river in order to find a place. Then she thought of the cow, heavy with calf and due to give birth any day now, and a sense of urgency possessed her.

She found another ravine that led back down to the river, a place worn through the earth by flash floods over eons. The wagon creaked its awkward way through the fissure, and she gazed upon the Brazos once again. The sky darkened as she worked the wagon along the driftwood-littered shore. Then, the first patter of rain began to beat a light tattoo on the canvas covering the wagon.

She looked around for a place to draw up and find shelter. It was then that she realized someone was following her. She caught just the faintest glimpse of a dark shape, enough to chill her blood. But the shoreline narrowed at that point, while it opened up on the other side of the river. There, less than two hundred yards away, were trees and shelter and safety. The river was shallow and wide, but there did not seem so much water between her and a better path for the wagon, some shelter from the oncoming storm, and protection from approaching danger.

The rain began to hurl itself at her with a sudden fury and the wind picked up with savage momentum.

It was at that moment that Nancy knew she must cross the river, quicksand or not.

Chapter
Four

Tallman followed the pony tracks, which crossed and recrossed the Brazos several times. He noticed that the Comanches always forded where the bottom was hardpan, and so he did not encounter quicksand. He marked those places in his mind for future use, looking for the permanent landmarks, since he knew that rivers often changed course and sometimes disappeared beneath the soil in times of extreme drought.

The Comanches were moving steadily, seemingly in no hurry, but when he came to a rocky stretch of shore, the tracks disappeared. Only an experienced eye could discern which way they had gone, but Tallman saw enough pebbles overturned, wet side up, to follow them. When the tracks appeared again, they were fewer, and he knew that at least two Comanches had separated from the main body, perhaps to watch the backtrail or lie in ambush. That was when he left the trail and sought shelter from prying eyes in a copse of oak and cottonwood trees, surrounded by dense thickets of second growth and cactus. As he waited, the sky darkened, and ponderous black clouds unfurled across the sky, blotting out the sun and erasing all traces of blue.

The rain would wash away the tracks, Tallman knew, but there was nothing he could do about it. A storm would also force the Comanches to halt and take shelter. And surely they knew the country well enough to find high ground, where there was no danger of their being swept away by a sudden flash flood. The same, he thought wryly, held true for himself.

Tallman prodded the dun to a faster gait, wanting to close the gap between him and the main body of Comanches before the storm struck. At the same time, he knew he had to be careful that he was not surprised by those braves who had left the band, perhaps to protect those who went on from surprise attack by anyone who might be following them.

As he rode on, the tracks grew fresher, and Tallman observed that the Comanches had picked up the pace. The hoofprints of each horse were farther apart and the ground more disturbed. Where were they going in such a hurry? Tallman wondered as he spurred the dun to a fast lope.

He was not surprised when the tracks moved away from the Brazos. Rains, especially very heavy ones, could turn the river into a raging torrent. He had seen it at such times, in the spring and summer, when the usually placid, meandering, lazy stream changed into an avenging water god, ripping out banks, gutting new land, uprooting trees, devouring plants, gorging on sand and limestone, desecrating old graves of creatures long since gone to bone and dust.

Tallman rode through that thick hush that seems to come

before every storm, rode through a midday twilight that
played eerie tricks on his eyes. Colors shifted and changed,
softened and blurred, as though some master dauber had the
earth on a palette, mixing and blending light and shadow, yel-
lows and browns, ochres and delicate vermillions, grays and
blacks and whites, casting hues where the shadows had been
washed away by a light that had no shape nor form, a ghostly
light cast down from some sallow unseen sun, a sun that had
smothered and died in the crushing embrace of billowing
clouds.

The wind picked up, blowing tumbleweeds and dust
ahead of him, filling in tracks, smoothing what had been a
clear trail moments before into a boneless erasure of all signs
of life, as the earth does to all scars and marks upon its face
over time, blotting out signs of all presences that have walked
or ridden its immense surface. Tallman pulled up the collar of
his shirt as fine grit stung his bare neck and felt the wind bear
down on him from still another direction.

The sky turned fully dark as the clouds thickened, blown
in from the northwest, piling up on one another until the air
filled with static and lightning began to flash in the distance,
so far away the thunder did not reach Tallman's ears. The
horizon shimmered with the faint glow of electricity as if gi-
ant mirrors were flashing signals between gods.

Tallman knew the oncoming storm would be a dangerous one. He did not want to be caught out in the open where
he might become a human lightning rod, nor did he want to
be close to trees that might explode or catch fire if lightning
struck. The charge could travel through the ground, frying
any living thing unlucky enough to be near such a spot.

The truth was, he knew, there would be no safe place in

such country. To be near the water might prove more perilous than anywhere else. He wondered if he could find a sheltered ravine or gully on such short notice, yet these were also perfect places for sudden floods. He thought he might ride uphill and perhaps find an outcropping of dirt or rock that could shelter him until the storm had passed.

He rode through the stand of trees, climbed to higher ground. As he came out into the open again, he heard the first faint rumbles of thunder, and when he looked to the northwest, he saw the black clouds become illuminated with jagged forks of lightning.

Scattered raindrops began to pock the dirt, glaze the leaves of trees, splatter the rocks. Tallman felt the gouts on his face, heard them tattoo his hat like the faint taps on a snare drum. The dun shook its head, bowed its neck. Its leg muscles quivered, sending little ripples beneath its coat coursing to its hooves. A small bird folded its wings as it dove into a bush, and a sudden gust of wind blew the falling rain at a ninety-degree angle against horse and rider.

Tallman turned the dun so that its rump was to the wind and headed for a tall, leafy oak, its leaves quivering, standing atop a small knoll. A flash of scorching lightning burned a silver path to the sky, and the thunderboom followed in a fraction of a second. The backlit tree left an afterimage on the retinas of Tallman's eyes.

The dun humped its back and ducked its head as if struck by a fist. Its ears stiffened to rigid cones and twisted to a fixed position slightly to the left of the tree. Tallman moved his head, startled at what he saw in that brief moment of brilliant light.

The darkness that followed the lightning flash obscured

what Tallman had seen or thought he saw. As he drew nearer
the tree, he smelled the odor of burnt wet wood. The storm in-
tensified its electrical display. Lightning bolts connected the
earth to the sky in ragged lattices of silvered shafts and
stitched the black clouds with complex lacings of mercury.
Thunderclaps shook the very ground like batteries of mighty
artillery on some olden battlefield of the gods. The rain began
to beat down without mercy, hurled earthward by ferocious
winds that whipped the dun's mane and tail and blew the
brim of Tallman's hat flat against one side of his face.

Tallman turned the dun away from the wind once again,
straining to see through the slanting, quavering shrouds of
rain. A sense of danger prickled like nettles in his mind, and
the dun was now fighting the bit, wary of approaching closer
to the smoking ruins that had risen up from the prairie seemingly out of nowhere, a grim apparition of some horror that
Tallman had not yet defined or determined. He spoke sharply
to the dun and ticked its flanks with the tips of his spurs, wondering at the same time if he should not trust the horse's instinct, which was not so different from his own. A feeling
of dread was starting to build in the pit of Tallman's stomach,
as if he had just swallowed something raw and alive and
clawed.

The dun seemed to prance as it sidled toward the smoking ruins of something that once had been, still fighting the
bit but responding to spur and rein as it had been trained to
do. The closer Tallman got to the wreckage, the more he
wanted to give the dun its head and ride around whatever it
was he had glimpsed in the stark flashes of lightning.

Again, the sky whitened and shivered with streaks of
lightning that broke the clouds like veins running with silvered blood. In between static charges of electricity, Tallman

glimpsed the ruins of an overturned wagon, the corpses of horses and mules, a tattered flap of canvas whipping in the wind like a sundered battle flag. .

Underneath the aroma of woodsmoke, Tallman smelled the scent of fresh blood, a cloying tang that was unmistakable. And he heard what sounded like a loud moan, a human cry of pain indicating someone was still alive in that terrible wreckage.

Warily, Tallman rode still closer, the dun fighting the bit and bucking under the prod of his spurs. Tallman rested a hand on the stock of his sheathed rifle, ready to jerk it free of its scabbard at the slightest indication that he was riding into some kind of ambush. He saw no sign of Indians, but it was his guess that Comanches, Kiowas, or Apaches had been at this spot just before the storm broke.

Tallman came within twenty-five yards of the burned wagon, halted and waited, trying to see through the rain and during the flashes of lightning. A chain of forked lightning strung white-hot vines of luminous silver through the clouds, backlighting the entire scene. Though brief, the illumination lasted long enough for Tallman to see that there were other wagons strewn across the plain, their oxen and mules dead hulks still in their traces. He saw a woman, her dress blowing like an obscene banner above her naked white loins.

He saw other things too: two children draped over the side of a wagon, arrows jutting from their sides, the body of a man lying atop a dead mule, clothing scattered like rags all over the place, chairs, churns, and broken toys, books, flour sacks, and feed bags.

He rode on, past the bodies of braves, their war paint ghastly under the searing blaze of lightning streaks that seemed never to end. His instincts told him to turn the dun and ride away. There was nothing he could do here. He saw no signs of life, and there was nothing in the wreckage that he wanted.

The dun balked at going any closer to the ruins of the wagon train. It stopped and began to back up. Tallman spoke to the horse and dug his spurs into its flanks. The dun responded and stepped forward, its back humping up as if it wanted to throw its rider. Tallman patted the dun's neck and spoke soothing words, "Come on, boy, settle down."

As he rode up to the shattered and burned wagons, the dun whickered. To Tallman's surprise, there was an answering whinny from a horse that was apparently alive. Tallman swung the dun toward the sound, then he heard a deep groan from somewhere in the maze of wreckage.

"Hello," Tallman called. "Where are you?"

A peal of thunder drowned out any reply. Tallman saw the horse as more lightning lit the dark skies. The animal was standing next to a wagon that was lying on its side. Again, he heard a low groan from somewhere close. He determined that the groan was coming from the other side of the tipped wagon, near where the lone horse stood.

"You there," Tallman called, "can you hear me?"

"I hear you. I'm over here by this wagon."

Tallman rode around the wagon and through the scrim of sheeted rain he saw a man leaning against the bed, a rifle across his lap. There was another man there, too, but he was dead, lying on his back, mouth and eyes open, raindrops bouncing off his face.

"Stranger," the man said, "I need help pulling out this arrow."

The man moved slightly, and Tallman saw the feathered shaft jutting from the man's calf, toward the rear of his leg. A good four inches deep, Tallman figured.

"Can you stand the pain?" Tallman asked.

"I reckon I can stand it a little while longer. You gonna help me?"

Tallman swung down from the saddle. He tied the dun to a wagon wheel and stood over the wounded man. "Anyone else alive, besides you?" he asked.

"I reckon not. Onliest thing what saved me was this damned rain. We got jumped by a bunch of Comanches."

"Not Comanches."

"Huh?"

"Mister, those are dead Kiowa out there. If Comanches had done this they would have done you in before they left."

"Kiowa, Comanch', it's all the damned same."

"Roll over," Tallman said. "Let me have a look at that arrow."

The man shifted his weight slightly, grimaced in pain.

"Do you want a stick to bite on?"

"No. Just pull the damned thing out, will you?"

Tallman shrugged and bent down to examine the arrow more closely. The shaft was buried in the fleshy part of the man's calf and did not appear to be near a major artery. When the lightning flashed again, he saw the blue-black bruise around the entry hole. Blood oozed from the torn flesh.

"Brace yourself," Tallman said. "That arrowhead is going to tear a bigger hole when it comes out. I'll have to put a tourniquet on so you won't bleed to death."

"There's some rope in this wagon. You can cut what you need."

Tallman stood up, went to the rear of the wagon and rummaged around in the darkness until his fingers touched a coil of hemp rope. He pulled it out of the wagon, cut off a three-foot length. Then he turned his attention back to the injured man. He knelt down again, set the section of rope nearby on the ground.

"Ready?" Tallman asked.

"You go on and do it."

Tallman grasped the arrow shaft in both hands. He wanted to pull it out straight and fast, otherwise the man would likely jerk his leg and scream from the pain and the arrowhead might sever too many veins, or it could hang up on a bone and have to be cut out with a knife.

"Here goes," Tallman said.

The wounded man clenched his teeth as Tallman grasped the arrow.

Tallman pushed the arrow in slightly, then gave it a hard jerk. He felt the arrow slide as the man screamed in pain. The arrow came free, ripping out a small hunk of flesh as it cleared the wound entrance.

"Jesus," the man swore.

"It's out," Tallman said. He heard a click and turned his head. He felt something hard and cold press against his side. He knew, without thinking, that it was the barrel of a pistol.

"Mister," the man said, "I better not bleed to death, cuz if I do, I'm takin' you with me."

"There's no call for that."

Calmly, Tallman picked up the length of rope he had cut and slipped it around the man's calf. He pulled it tighter than he should have, but the tourniquet did work to stop the flow of blood from the wound. Tallman jerked the pistol from the man's hand.

"This'll do until I can find a stick," he said, and he set the barrel on the rope, made a loop, then twisted the barrel to keep the tourniquet tight.

"You bastard," the man said.

"You're not going to bleed to death right off," Tallman said, "but if I don't clean out the wound you could sure as hell get gangrene and lose that leg."

"The damned tourniquet's too tight."

"Can you get on that horse?" Tallman asked.

"I don't know."

"Well, you better," Tallman said. "Because one or both of us has to get the hell away from here."

"How come?"

"Because as soon as this storm lets up, those Kiowa are coming back here to pick up their dead."

"You reckon so?"

"I damned well know," Tallman said, as he stood up. "And they'll want our scalps."

Lightning stabbed the sky and Tallman saw that the man's face had blanched. Whether it was from pain or fear, he did not know.

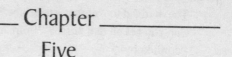

Nancy braced herself on the seat and reached for the light buggy whip. She cracked the whip's tail over the back of the ox. The wagon lurched down the bank and plunged into the Brazos. She could feel the tug of the water as it flowed against the spokes. She snapped the whip again when the ox faltered, and gritted her teeth. The wagon swayed as one of the wheels sank in soft, clutching sand.

The wagon swayed sickeningly, and Nancy felt herself sliding off the seat toward the water, the dangerous quicksand. The ox struggled, pulling hard against the traces, and the wagon wheel pulled up, rolling onto bedrock. The wagon swayed back to level and Nancy slid to the center of the seat, her stomach roiling with a queasiness born of fear. Lightning flashed in the sky; thunder pealed across the heavens, a sound like boulders rolling around on a room's bare wooden floor.

Rain began to spatter Nancy's face and tap on the canvas cover of the wagon. She heard it above the din of the pots and pans and pewter dishes that were rattling inside the jolting wagon. She chastised herself silently for not having put on her husband's rain slicker, which was buried in a wooden box under a pile of bedding.

The ox staggered to the opposite shore, summoned its strength to climb the bank, which was quickly turning to mud. Nancy cracked the whip, and the noise of it was drowned out by the ear-deafening roar of a thunderclap.

"Go on, go on," Nancy shouted, as she felt the rear of the wagon sway with the surge of the current. So close, she thought, and so far. The whip handle turned slippery in her grasp, and she threw it down at her feet, preparing to jump if the wagon did not clear the river.

The ox strained at the harness, its shoulders nudging the single yoke high on its back. Its hooves tore through the mud to dry footing and the animal edged forward and upward. Finally, its momentum carried it to the top of the bank, where it halted, spent from exertion, its tongue lolling from its open mouth, its lungs heaving as it drew breath.

Nancy's stomach twisted in fear. The reins were stretched taut, as were the traces, and she feared the harness would break under the weight of the wagon. She screamed at the ox as lightning stabbed between earth and clouds and the thunder rocked the air with explosive fury.

The ox began to lose its footing. Its wet hooves turned slippery, and the sand underneath slowly eroded. The ox moved its forelegs to obtain better footing, but the ground gave way and its weight descended on its rear hooves. Frantically pawing at the earth, the ox lost more ground. The wagon rolled back into the river, careening sideways on the uneven bed.

Nancy half stood as if to pull the wagon forward. She

jiggled the reins, slapping them against the ox's hide, but it was too late. The ox slid sideways down the bank, snaring itself in the traces. The milk cow, tied to the rear of the wagon, its eyes bulging from their sockets, whirled around in a frantic attempt to escape but only floundered into quicksand. It bawled as it struggled to free itself from the suction, but the effort caused its forelegs to sink even deeper in the mire. It arched its neck to keep its mouth above water, and then its hind legs slid into more quicksand.

The rain pelted down with a ferocious velocity, hurled by the high winds, and lightning danced across the sky in gigantic zigs and zags, scrawling incomprehensible hieroglyphics beneath the jet black clouds. The ox, now thoroughly entangled in its harness, fell on its side and pulled the wagon along as it struck the rushing waters of the Brazos, now a maelstrom from the rains feeding it from miles above.

Nancy grabbed for the side of the tilting wagon, but she was flung backward as the rushing waters caught it broadside. She tumbled topsy-turvy inside as the wagon swirled in a circular motion. She no longer heard the terrible sound of the cow bawling, and she thought instantly that it must have drowned.

The rear end of the wagon swung into the current, dragging the ox with it. The lead rope tied to the cow held the wagon in place, preventing it, for the moment, from washing downstream. The current was so strong it pulled the cow from the quicksand, and she swam free. But the river carried her down to the tailgate of the wagon. Nancy heard a crash, but was unable to see, since she was buried under foodstuffs and utensils on the bed of the wagon. The wagon swung to midstream and began to float with the ever-increasing current.

The ox tumbled in the rushing water and the harness

straps broke, setting the animal free. The wagon tongue swept around and gouged its tip into the bank. The wagon swirled around on the fulcrum until the tongue snapped. Then, caught in an eddy, it swirled around until the main current caught it and sent it shooting at high speed over rocky rapids.

Nancy, inside the wagon, rocked and tumbled by the jolting, grew dizzy and disoriented. She tried to brace herself with her hands, but she was helpless as long as she was in motion. She cracked her head against the sideboard and smashed an elbow on something else, pain shooting through her like electric current. She moaned softly, knowing there was no one to hear. She knew she would have cuts and bruises to show for this storm.

The wagon righted itself in the stream long enough for Nancy to brace herself by jamming her feet hard against the sidewall and tailgate. Then, she grunted and managed to sit up. She reached for the rifle in the right corner of the wagon nearest the seat. It seemed the only tool worth saving if she were to survive. Stretching out again as the wagon lurched into another spin, she grabbed the straps and strings of her husband's possibles pouch and the two powder horns. She lay the heavy flintlock rifle across her lap and struggled to sit up again.

She felt the wagon moving more swiftly downstream as she doubled up and leaned forward, trying to grasp the tailgate. Through the rear opening, she saw the black bulging clouds laced with ragged streaks of lightning, and she cringed when the thunder followed on the heels of every electrical discharge. As her fingers draped over the tailgate, the wagon dipped, as if falling into a hole, and she felt herself flying through the air. The rifle jarred against her forearms and she grasped it like a straw. The rifle turned slightly so that it did not catch on the wagon, and Nancy tumbled through the opening and dropped into the raging water.

Instinctively, she held her breath, but did not go under. Instead, her feet touched bottom and a rush of water knocked her ashore. She let out her breath and watched the wagon and ox drift into the darkness downstream. Then, all that she owned in the world rounded a bend and was out of sight.

Nancy lay sprawled on the shore for a moment as the rain battered her with relentless lancings. She felt defeated, completely hopeless, and she half wished that the river would rise up and take her down into its depths and blot out all reason, all mental pain. But something deep inside her, some feeble spark rose up and turned fiery and she shook off the shroud of despair.

Summoning a strength she scarcely believed she had, Nancy gripped the rifle and used it as a staff to pull herself up to her knees. She wiped the rain from her eyes and stood up. Her knees were jellied, her legs shaking as she surveyed her surroundings. She was lost, she was alone, but some scrap of determination in her put iron in her backbone and steel in her resolve, and she took the first steps toward finding shelter.

By the time Nancy reached a small copse of trees, she was wet to the skin. The cold wind made her shiver and there was no warmth in the tree she leaned against, a young oak with few leaves. Exhausted, she clung to the tree for support and some measure of comfort. It was the only living thing, she thought, in miles and miles, and she wished it could speak, for she was sorely in need of conversation. The thunder was so deafening and absolute, she thought it bespoke anger from God, and each flash of lightning seemed closer than the one before, as if God's ire were reaching out for her, as if His hand wished to strike one last blow to her hope, her desire to go on living. She cowered under the tree as a lightning bolt struck a bush near the river, setting flame to it.

The bush blazed for a few moments before the rain extinguished it. Was that, too, a sign? she wondered. Before the fire went out, it flared high and bright. In that brief illumination, she thought she saw a figure just beyond it, not in the river, but walking alongside. She rubbed her eyes, and then the fire was out and she was plunged, once again, into darkness.

Then, she heard a voice call out.

"Woman, stay where you are."

Nancy's heart seemed to freeze in her chest. She lifted the rifle while thinking somberly that the powder in the pan was thoroughly wet or washed away, and perhaps the powder in the barrel as well. The rifle was useless, but she lifted it, even so, determined to fight to the last.

"Leave me be," she said, straining to see the man striding towards her.

A streak of lightning sizzled the air a hundred yards beyond the approaching man, and she could not see his face, only that he, too, carried a rifle. He was wearing buckskins, she knew that much, and she imagined his face was hideous, evil—that it was the face of death. Death come for her on that dark and terrible day when the earth was in upheaval, when God had taken everything from her and now wanted her life and her soul.

The man spoke no more, and Nancy did not scream. She waited for what she hoped was a merciful death.

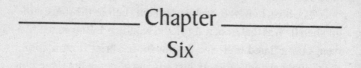

Chapter
Six

Tallman helped the wounded man to his feet. Together, they walked to the horse tied to the wagon. It wore a bridle, nothing more.

"Saddle's somewhere in the wagon," the man muttered.

"You'll ride him bareback, mister. There's no time to run him under a saddle."

"Hell, the Kiowa ain't comin' back in this storm."

"I'll help you up," Tallman said.

"Bareback ain't my idea of forking a horse."

"Suit yourself. If you're not up on this critter right quick, I'll leave you for the buzzards."

"You're one hard bastard, ain't you."

Tallman did not answer. After a moment, the man shrugged and grabbed the horse's mane. Tallman locked his hands together, held them palms-up for the man to use as a step. The man put his boot in Tallman's hands and pulled on the mane. Tallman lifted upward, and the man swung a leg over the horse's rump and sat.

Tallman walked over to his horse and stepped into the saddle. He rode back to find the man slumped over, the bridle in his hands.

"You going to make it?" Tallman asked.

"Just a passin' pain. Where to?"

"Follow me. First, though, you got a name?"

The man hesitated. "Call me Bud."

"I'm Tallman."

"Lead out, Tallman."

The two men rode into the brunt of the rain, through an eerie landscape of lightning and thunder, barely able to see, and every bush and tree appeared like alien apparitions, lit by staggering light and then turned to char in the thundering darkness.

Tallman rode to a place he knew, high ground where trees grew. He wondered how long Bud could last with that wound throbbing. The blood wouldn't clot fast in the rain, he knew, and while Bud seemed to be sturdy of limb and strong, he knew the pain must be stabbing through him like a thousand knives. When they pulled into the trees, Tallman looked back. Bud was loosening the tourniquet.

"We'll stay out the storm here," Tallman said.

"Good enough," Bud said. He stayed on his horse for a few moments, then Tallman noticed that he was tightening the tourniquet again. The man had some brains, he thought.

The two men dismounted, using their horses for partial shelter, wedging their bodies between them and the tree trunks. By the intermittent light of the flashing lightning, Tallman became aware that Bud was staring at him with an intensity that was more than just idle curiosity.

"Tallman," Bud said, finally. "I've heard that name."

"Maybe so."

"Wasn't you in Nacogdoches with Gus Magee?"

"Nope. I wasn't but a boy when Magee captured Nacogdoches."

"But you know him." It was not a question.

"We've met," Tallman said.

Augustus W. Magee was a career soldier who had graduated from West Point. During Mexico's long war against Spain for independence, which lasted from 1810 to 1821, Magee had entered Texas with his Republican Army of the North in August of 1812. This after José Bernardo Gutiérrez de Lara, a Mexican revolutionary, had come to Natchitoches, Louisiana, where, with the help of U.S. agents, he had organized an expedition to wrest Mexico from Spain. Magee took over from there and marched on Nacogdoches, a town he took easily.

There, Magee recruited men for his "army," a ragtag assemblage of Mexicans, Americans, French, and other nationalities, willing to help Mexico get out from under Spain's yoke. Most knew, however, that the United States had its eyes on Texas, which had been neglected by Spain to the point where it was considered ripe for the taking.

At La Bahía, Magee was besieged, but withstood it and marched on to San Antonio, where he was again victorious. There, in April of 1813, he issued a proclamation declaring the existence of the First Republic of Texas, hoping thereby to separate Texas from Mexico's fight with Spain. But in taking such bold action, Magee stirred up a hornet's nest that proved disastrous.

A few months following that decree, Magee's army was

soundly defeated by Spanish troops at the Battle of Medina River. Many of his men were captured and taken back to San Antonio. Later, to set an example for Mexican revolutionaries and Americans alike, Spanish royalist general Joaquín de Arredondo executed three hundred republican prisoners. Present at that execution was a young lieutenant who had already proven himself to be brave in battle, Antonio López de Santa Anna.

"Well, Mexico finally got its independence," Bud said.

"And that's about all."

"They got Texas, too."

"Maybe. For the moment," Tallman said.

"What do you mean by that? We came here as colonists."

"An expediency. There's too much Texas for Mexico to govern. They'll use people like you until they get a foothold, then kick you out."

"That ain't the way I understand it. Look what they gave Moses Austin."

"Moses is dead," Tallman said.

"Dead? Hell, he just come down here."

"He was sick when he left St. Louis."

"So you think the Mexicans are going to boot us all out?"

"Not right away. Stephen Austin is in charge now. He's got a colony here on the Brazos."

"Hell, that's where we was headed, to hook up with Moses. Might as well be Stephen, I guess."

"I doubt if you're on his list, Bud."

Bud stiffened. "What do you mean by that?"

"You didn't come down with Moses, obviously. So you're in Texas illegally."

"Possession is nine-tenths of the law."

A thundercrack followed Bud's last statement. Tallman laughed.

"What's so funny?"

"Think about what happened to Magee and his army. Think about those three hundred men in San Antonio, put to the sword for all to see."

"Them was Spaniards what done that," Bud said.

"And the Mexicans won't forget it. Ever hear of a man named Santa Anna?"

"Nope."

"Well, Santa Anna is ambitious, and he's greedy. He hates gringos and hates the U.S. government. If he ever comes to power, he'll stamp out any ideas of Texas becoming a U.S. republic. And that's what Austin wants."

"How do you know?" Bud asked. "Did you know Moses?"

"I did."

"And you know Stephen."

"We know each other," Tallman said.

"Well, I've heard your name somewheres," Bud said, wincing as he reached for his calf. "I'll recollect where it was directly."

"Don't trouble yourself, Bud."

Bud loosened the tourniquet and breathed heavily for a few moments before he twisted the pistol barrel and retightened the cloth. The rain blew at them from the north, but the trees and horses offered some protection.

"How long do you think this will last?" Bud asked, after some moments.

"The storm? Hard telling. Seems to be stalled right over us."

"Never saw no storm like this in June."

"Well, you get the warm air coming up from the gulf and when it meets the cool air from the north, you get rain in Texas."

"A hell of a place," Bud said.

"Who was wagon master of your party?" Tallman asked.

"I was."

Tallman said nothing, but he was thinking that this man had been responsible for all those lives. He looked pointedly at Bud, who seemed to understand what he was thinking.

"We had no damned warning," Bud said. "Them Kiowas come at us out of nowhere."

"They came from somewhere."

"One minute we was goin' along just fine and then the stock smelt the river and we had our hands full keepin' 'em all from boltin' and runnin' off to drink."

"Didn't you have scouts out?"

"I had me a scout up front."

"And the Kiowa came up on your rear," Tallman said.

"That's right." Bud paused, as if reflecting. The rain washed his face so that it looked like a waxen mold whenever the lightning glazed it with a silvery sheen. "They seemed like they rose up out of the dirt," he continued. "I mean, one minute we was goin' along just fine, and next, we was bein' swarmed over by a passel of yellin', screamin' savages."

"What did you do?" Tallman asked.

"Me? I was as surprised as anybody. Feller in the rear wagon, name of Jenkins, he hollered and his lady screamed to high heaven. I thought one of their kids had fell out of the wagon and got run over. When I turned around, I saw them painted savages shootin' arrows into Jenkins and his woman and then everybody else was hollerin' and screamin', and by the time I brung my rifle up I could see people lyin' on the ground dead as doornails and blood all in puddles. I seen Injuns pullin' kids from the wagons and women and hackin' at 'em with stone clubs and little store-bought hatchets, just hackin' 'em up like meat, God, and I'm shootin' off a shot from my smokepole and fumblin' for my wipin' stick after I shot and pourin' powder down the barrel and scratchin' for another ball and wagons goin' ever' which way and horses screechin' and goin' wild and gettin' tangled in the traces. It was bloody and quick. They was savages on the ground peelin' scalps and hackin' at bawlin' kids, mincin' 'em up like butchers choppin' at hogs. Christ, I never seen such doin's, and before I could get off another ball, three or four of them Kiowas was all over Baldwin, my scout, like flies on shit. Then I felt something sting my leg and seen an arrow stickin' out. I go down and a wagon rolls over me and falls over and I'm knocked cold as a duck."

Tallman said nothing. He mulled over Bud's account of the attack and thought of the swift raid of the Kiowa on a small wagon train. Such things had happened before, no doubt, but he wondered why Bud hadn't seen it coming. And why was the attack so brutal? Had Bud done something to stir up the Kiowa? He had a lot of questions, but they could wait. He still didn't know who Bud was and what he was doing in this part of the country. He had evidently come into Texas illegally, like Jacobs. The Spaniards had gone to a lot of trouble to control immigrants, and he was sure that the revolutionaries were not going to change that policy right away.

But, for the moment, that was not his problem. There was something about Bud that he didn't like. His story, for one thing, lacked a lot of detail that made him think Bud was hiding something besides his name. Before he could think things through, Bud started talking again.

"Tallman, Tallman. That name," Bud said. "I know it. Is Frank your Christian name? Or James?"

Tallman stiffened. Bud had struck a nerve. He had not said those names to himself for a long time.

"No," Tallman said. "Frank was my father's name."

"James, is that your name?"

"I had a brother by that name," Tallman said, his voice low and husky.

"I know I heard of them. They was with Magee, wasn't they?"

"That's right," Tallman said.

"They was U.S. agents. Jacobs told me about them. He knew 'em. They rode to San Antone with Magee. So, you're Frank's son. And James's brother. I'll be damned. What happened to them?"

Tallman sucked in a breath, held it for a long moment. He stared hard at the man who called himself Bud. He studied his face in the dimness of the darkened day, glared at the rain-drenched mask of it as if trying to find meaning in its eyeless enigma.

"They're both dead," he told Bud, "slaughtered at San Antonio, murdered by the Spaniards."

"Jesus," Bud said, "I . . . I guess I didn't know. I'm right sorry."

But Tallman didn't believe him. For he saw something on Bud's face when the next ripple of lightning shimmered over its contours.

Bud had known his father and brother, he thought, he had known them at San Antonio. And, Tallman was sure, Bud had known they were dead.

Chapter
Seven

In the dim light of a distant streak of lightning, the man's face appeared hideous, almost grotesque. Nancy trembled in every limb, and she thought she would faint from fright. Still, she held the rifle to her shoulder and even cocked the trigger.

"Now, woman, you know that rifle ain't goin' to go off in this rain. You put it down, hear? I don't mean you no harm."

"Who . . . who are you?" she asked.

"A friend, I hope. Name's Ottmers, Virgil Ottmers, and I been seein' your track nigh half a day whenever I put in."

"Put in?" she asked, a querulous curl to her voice.

"I been on the Brazos in my canoe," Ottmers said. "Took it out when that storm come up on me."

Slowly, Nancy let the rifle sink. It seemed to weigh a thousand pounds. She eased the hammer down, fighting back the flood of tears that threatened to break through the dam of her eyes. The man stepped closer to her and grabbed the rifle by its stock before it could fall from her hands.

"There, now," he said. "You go on and have yourself a cry. I seen what happened to your wagon. Tied your cow up on high ground 'bout a quarter mile or so back upriver."

"You found Flossie?"

"That her name? She's belly big with calf, she is, and in a mite better spirits than you are right now, I reckon."

"My ox . . ."

"Now, now," Ottmers said, a soothing quality to his voice, "don't you fret none about your belongings. When the storm lets up, you'll just have to see what you can salvage. Likely that wagon's all broke up and your goods scattered for a good ten mile down the Brazos."

Nancy crumpled, just thinking about it, and Ottmers caught her in his sodden arms. He let her lean her head on his shoulder and sob it all out as he patted her hair with a fatherly touch.

She thought of her clothes and pots and staples lying out in the rain, washed up on the banks of that raging river, all the mementos of her life with Randall and Alan. She wished now that she had not shooed that man Tallman away. Perhaps he might have been able to keep her from losing the wagon, the ox, and all of her possessions. Perhaps. She wondered how he was faring in this awful, awful storm.

"Were you following me?" Nancy asked when she recovered enough to speak.

"I was behind you. Saw you a time or two, but I wasn't following you, ma'am. We were both just going the same direction. Down the Brazos."

Nancy found Ottmers's words comforting, in an odd

way. It was not often one found a Good Samaritan in these
parts. He could have taken her cow for himself or stayed with
his canoe, but he had not. Instead, he had come to help her,
and she was touched by his apparent concern. She stopped
trembling, and her legs ceased to shake.

"I feel better," she said. "Thanks to you. How long is
this storm going to last?"

"I've seem 'em last," Ottmers said. "Rest of the day,
most of the night, probably."

"Do we just stay here?"

"I have a tarp with the canoe, but with the wind blowin'
like it is, I doubt I could put it up. We're safe enough here for
the time being."

Just then, a massive display of lightning etched the clouds
with a metallic and incomprehensible structure, a monolithic
diagram of connecting angular lines. The thunderclap followed almost immediately. Nancy jumped from the sudden
fright that galvanized her muscles.

"That one scared me," she said.

"It's a fearsome storm, all right."

In the skyborne light, she saw Ottmers's face clearly for
the first time. He wore a battered hat, old and moth-eaten,
soggy from the rain, which funneled down the creases in its
brim. He appeared to be bald, or at least had a high forehead,
and his face was round, his eyes wide apart and not deep-set,
brown, she thought, and he had thin lips, a narrow chin. He
wore buckskins with fringes that shed the rain, with no beads,
quills, or other decorations. The buckskins were rumpled and
wet through, and she thought he must be very uncomfortable
wearing them.

"Do not worry, ma'am," Ottmers said, as if probing the

deepest recesses of her mind, "this storm will blow over like all the storms that have ever been, and you will have a memory for your grandchildren."

"I have no children," she said. "No husband, either."

"And you out here all alone?"

"My husband was killed near the Red River, and my son met the same fate this morning."

"Redskins?"

"Yes," she said, her voice so soft she could scarcely hear it herself. "Different tribes."

"Fate is the word," he said. "It's God's way of playing tricks on his creation."

"I don't like such tricks."

"Ah, but the Master has a plan for you, ma'am, else He would not bother."

"A plan? The most precious things in my life were taken from me. What, pray tell me, could be left for me but heart-ache and sadness?"

"Well, I am your fate, as well. Things in this old world don't just happen, don't you know? What are the chances, do you figure, that I should happen along this way during one of your darkest moments?"

"I have no idea," she said, starting to pout. She had almost decided that Virgil Ottmers was slightly crazy. Maybe more than slightly. When the lightning lit his eyes, they did seem to have a mad cast to them.

"Ah, then you must accept fate, and whatever it brings to you. Some call it by different names, but it is all the same thing. We cannot see into the future. We cannot see around corners, but when we see fate rise up and confront us, then that is how we test our mettle."

"Our mettle?"

"Courage. Backbone." Ottmers no longer seemed mindful of the storm. Rather, he spoke with a degree of intensity that was neither overbearing nor argumentative, but more like a schoolmaster's recital to a pupil, of history or mathematics or even music. His voice did have a lulling effect on her.

"Are you a schoolmaster?" she asked, with a blunt abruptness.

Ottmers laughed. "No'm. Not I. I am a farmer, a trapper, and a hunter. I have me a farm down the river a ways, fair bottomland, and I make gewgaws out of silver I buy or trade for in far Santa Fe when the sun shines upon the land and the winds blow fair."

"The winds are not blowing fair today," she said.

"No, but Santa Fe is a place where winter comes to dwell, and in the spring, the trappers and hunters and tradesmen meet there to hawk their wares, and I go among them after the thaw, even though I've lived in a warm clime while many have frozen their feet and hands in snow and ice."

"If you have silver with you, isn't that dangerous? To travel, I mean."

"It's dangerous, sometimes, to travel without silver and such. Just livin' is dangerous now and then."

"Don't you think you ought to be with your canoe? Someone might rob you while you're gone."

"We'll go back there by-and-by. Soon's the storm lets up some. Walkin' around water when they's lightning in the sky is mighty dangerous."

Nancy believed him. She had never seen so many lightning strikes before. At times, the entire sky cracked open with jagged streaks of light that shimmered bright as day. And the thunder was loud and frequent, the rain relentless.

Ottmers did not flinch when the lightning struck or the thunder pealed, but Nancy jumped every time there was a flash or a rolling boom of thunder. Standing there with Ottmers, she had the odd feeling that everything was unreal, that she was living in a dream. If she had not been wet through and through, she would have thought she was dreaming. Still, there was an air of unreality about being there under a tree with a man she did not know.

"Do you know a man named Tallman?" she asked abruptly, as if trying to bridge reality to the dreamlike trance she seemed to be in.

"Jon Tallman?"

"Yes, I . . . I think so. Yes, that was his name."

"You know him?" Ottmers asked.

"He . . . he helped me bury my son. This morning. He wanted to stay, but I sent him away."

"Hmm. Well, now, wonder what he's a-doin' up in Brazos country. Last I knew, he was in Mexico."

"Mexico?"

"He spends a lot of time down there."

"He said he was a rancher."

"Oh, he has him a spread on the Brazos. Mexicans working for him. But he's a man of many parts, he is."

"What do you mean?"

Ottmers did not answer right away. He seemed to be mulling over what he was going to say. Finally, he said, "Some say he's in cahoots with the royalists, the Spaniards. Others say he's in league with the Mexicans. And others . . ."

"Others?"

"Well, some say he's a man what works for the U.S. government. That he's a kind of spy."

Nancy sucked in a breath as the sound of thunder roared in the distance.

"A spy?"

"Well, there's some wants Texas to be a U.S. republic, maybe a state someday. The old colonists, them what was here before the Spanish allowed immigrants in to the upper part of Texas, like me, want to break off with Mexico and kick 'em back down south."

"And Tallman is on whose side?" she asked.

"Nobody knows, for sure. He don't talk much, but he's got him land give him by Spain, and the Mexicans say he can keep it."

"So you think he's on the side of the Mexicans," she said.

"He could be, ma'am. By the way, you didn't tell me your name."

"Nancy Stafford."

"Well, Mrs. Stafford, out here you don't ask too many questions. You just listen and hope you can tell which way the wind's a-blowin'. Mexicans is mighty changeable people. One minute they're nice and polite, but I think they learned a lot of bad habits from the Spaniards. And the Spaniards could be a mighty cruel bunch."

"It all sounds so complicated," Nancy said, and they spoke no more about politics as the storm eased up and the lightning and thunder became more distant.

"We can go back to the canoe now. I'll build a fire to dry us out."

"That sounds wonderful," she said.

"I think the worst of it's over. At least we're not likely to get cooked by lightning." Ottmers laughed, but Nancy was not reassured. The sky was still black and it was still raining.

She followed Ottmers blindly, not knowing where she was nor where she was going. The wind still gusted and dashed her face with rain, stung her eyes. But finally they left the open plain and descended to a place where she could hear the roar of the Brazos.

To her surprise, she saw a fire blazing, and Ottmers's canoe overturned and raised as a shelter on sticks.

"There's already a fire," she said.

"Yes, I see."

"But who?"

Before Ottmers could reply, she saw someone emerge from under the canoe. A boy stood up, and her heart fluttered and fell like a wounded bird. In the firelight, the boy looked like her son, Alan, and she opened her mouth to call out to him before she realized that the boy could not be her son.

"Oh, I forgot to tell you about the boy," Ottmers said. "He's some bright, startin' a fire and all in this rain."

The fire sputtered and crackled, but it blazed high, throwing light, a golden light, all around the place where Ottmers had portaged his canoe. The boy turned to look at Ottmers and Nancy. Then he held up a hand and waved.

Nancy felt her legs give way. The boy smiled and her heart melted. At that moment, he looked exactly like the son she had buried that morning, a son alive and happy, with that same bright smile.

Chapter Eight

The wind lessened for a moment, and the rain slackened off long enough so that Tallman knew the storm was blowing itself out. The sky no longer danced with electricity, and the thunder was only a vague throb beyond the horizon. When the wind picked up again, it lacked its former force but none of its coldness as it winged southward from the north.

"We ought to go back long enough to get us some grub," Bud said.

"That might be your last meal."

"I bet them Kiowa are far away by now."

"They're scavengers," Tallman said. "They'll want to pick over the bones of that wagon train."

"I'm mighty hungry."

"I've got some grub," Tallman said, "but you'd have to

eat it cold. I don't want to send out any smoke smells just yet."

"Seems to me you're mighty fidgety over Injuns you ain't even seen yet."

Tallman did not reply. He knew the Kiowa as he knew the Comanches and the Lipan Apaches of that Brazos country. And, to the north, the Cherokees had also made an impression on him with their ways. A man who paid no attention to Indians was a man destined to pay a high price for his ignorance. This Bud might have been in Texas before, but he had a lot to learn. His ignorance had already cost him a wagon train, the lives of people in his charge. There was more to Bud than met the eye, and before he decided what to do about him, there were some questions he wanted answered.

"What you got to eat?" Bud asked.

"Hardtack. Jerky. Some dried apricots and burnt corn."

"Pig food," Bud said.

"Hogs get fat."

"Well, the way my stomach's shrinkin' I could eat the south end of a northbound nag."

"Let the hardtack get some rain on it and it won't go down so bad," Tallman said.

The two men chewed on dry food as the rain pattered on leaves, trying to stop as suddenly as it had started. There would be no sun that day, Tallman knew, and he regretted that he would lose the track of the Comanches. He would have to guess where they went, taking along their young women captives.

"This is where we part company," Tallman said, as he wiped his mouth and picked up his reins.

"Where you goin'?" Bud asked.

"I got places to go."

"I could go with you."

"No, I don't think so."

"I ain't got no place to go."

"Where were you headed?" Tallman asked.

"I'm lookin' for someone."

"In Texas?"

"Yep. She was with Jacobs, and I got to find him."

So, Tallman thought, Bud was with the original wagon train, most likely. He would have to drag it out of Bud, though. He wasn't going to give him any information or let him know what he already knew.

"Where would this Jacobs be?" Tallman asked, feigning ignorance.

"Upriver, I think. They's a widder woman with him I got to talk to."

"Why didn't she go with you?"

"She made a mistake," Bud said.

"A mistake?"

"She listened to the wrong person."

Tallman didn't want to press Bud. It was clear that Bud didn't know what had happened to Nancy Stafford and the two girls. Nor did he know that Tallman had met Jacobs. He debated on whether to take Bud with him or leave him to his own devices.

"I'll find her one of these days," Bud said, as if the conversation had not ended.

"Who?" Tallman asked.

"Nancy Stafford," Bud said, and there was a shining in his eyes that Tallman didn't like, a salacious tone to his voice. "That's her name. Widdered up on the Red by Cherokee.

Damn fool husband tried to be a hero. She ought to be over her pining by now. She's got a kid who needs a man to be his daddy."

Tallman now thought it might be a good idea to take Bud with him. That way, he could keep an eye on him. There was little chance he would know where Nancy Stafford was or find her easily. She ought to be way back upriver, and maybe she'd found a place to settle by now. The last thing she needed was an animal like Bud preying on her. And her son no longer needed a daddy.

"You want to come along with me, Bud?" Tallman asked. "It could be a mite dangerous."

"Where we goin'?"

"You'll see."

"Big secret, huh? I reckon I'll go along. You got the grub and I'm still bleedin'."

So, Tallman thought, Bud was an opportunist. And, he didn't mind a little charity, either, evidently. Without saying more, Tallman turned his horse and headed for the Brazos, toward the point where he had left off tracking the Comanche. He still wanted to go back to that wagon train Bud had been with and look it over after the Kiowas finished with it. There was something suspicious about all those people getting wiped out and Bud being the sole survivor.

The two men rode through a smattering of rain and the day continued to darken as it lengthened into late afternoon. Tallman found the place where he had broken off the hunt for the Comanches and stopped several yards from the river.

Bud reined up when he came alongside. "What you lookin' at?" he asked.

"Just trying to figure something," Tallman said, without

explanation. He wondered where the Comanches might have gone to ride out the storm. Would they have holed up somewhere or ridden on despite the thunder and lightning? They might have, if they had a place to go to, a camp, for instance, where their women were waiting. If so, it would be someplace near the river, someplace easy to guard, someplace safe from their enemies.

"You're studyin' on somethin'," Bud said, after a time when Tallman did not speak.

"I am."

"Might be I could help."

"No, I don't think so. This is something I have to figure out for myself."

"You're lookin' for somebody, ain't you?"

"I'm looking," Tallman said.

"Who?"

"Comanches." He saw the muscles on Bud's face ripple, and there was a slight blanching of color on his skin.

"Whooee, Comanches, eh? Now, there's a hand I wouldn't want to draw to."

"You can go your own way," Tallman said.

"You're trackin' Comanches? What in hell for?"

"That's my business."

Bud kept his mouth shut for a few minutes. Tallman thought about the river, about its many bends and meanderings. One thing he was almost sure of, the Comanches had not far to go. They had not hurried to this point, and they had not changed direction. They most likely had a large camp somewhere along the Brazos and were taking their prisoners back there to show them off and brag about their attack on the wagon train. That was their way, he knew.

Now he was wondering if their path would cross that of

the Kiowa. That put an entirely different perspective on the matter. Comanche and Kiowa were kissing cousins, but he doubted they were all living in the same camp. No, he decided, there was no connection between the two wagon train raids. Or was there?

That was a puzzle, he admitted, but there was no need to solve it now. If he managed to find the Comanche camp, he would know soon enough if the Kiowa were there, too, like visiting relatives.

Just before dark, after riding another hour and a half, Tallman picked up what he thought might be the tracks of the Comanche war party. There were no visible hoofmarks of unshod ponies, but the muddy ground was moiled and wide. The tracks were about two hours old, filled with water. There was enough sign to tell him that a large party on horseback had passed through there, heading away from the river, into hilly country where trees grew in profusion.

"You track pretty good," Bud said.

"A blind man could read that sign."

"It just looks like a lot of dirty water to me."

"I could be wrong."

"I doubt it."

"We'll make camp," Tallman said. "Maybe the wind will come up again and dry those tracks out so I can make a head count."

"You want to know how many Comanches rode by here?"

"I have a pretty good idea now," Tallman replied, but, again, he didn't want to give away too much. If he was right, he'd find other signs when the land saw daylight, places where the riders had stopped to relieve themselves and allow their captives some comfort as well.

The two men made a dry camp, no fire, and chewed on cold, dry food. Tallman rubbed down the dun while Bud tended to his leg, which had stopped bleeding. That, Tallman thought, could be a good or a bad sign. If the wound scabbed over and did not get infected, the injured man might live. If not, then he'd lose his leg or his life in a very short time.

"Gonna be hard to sleep with no bedroll," Bud said, after supper.

"You can cut yourself some boughs and keep off the ground."

"You got a bedroll."

Tallman did not reply. He didn't feel sorry for Bud, nor did he feel guilty about his lack of bedding.

"Lend me your knife," Bud said.

"There's a hatchet in my saddlebags," Tallman said. "Help yourself."

"Aren't you afraid I might use it to take all you got?" Bud asked.

"It would be the last thing you ever tried."

"That's what I figger."

Tallman did not sleep much. He kept a wary eye out for Bud during the night, but the wounded man slept like a water-soaked log. Tallman roused him before dawn broke, but he had already rolled up his bedding and saddled the dun.

"Pretty damned early, ain't it?" Bud asked.

"Wind came up in the night, and I think we'll find some tracks to read."

"What are you going to do when you find these Comanches, Tallman? Surround 'em?"

"I told you. I'm going to make a head count."

"What are you, anyways? A damned census taker?"

Tallman let it go. It was obvious that Bud's leg had stiffened up on him during the night and he was going to have a rough day. He helped Bud mount his horse and then set out to follow the trail of the Comanches. An hour later, he was on it, and by noon, the tracks were dried out enough to read. The two Comanches who had cut away from the band earlier had rejoined the main party. That was what Tallman wanted to know. But there was more to the reading than just that.

Bud saw it, right after Tallman came to the ominous conclusion.

"Another bunch joined this 'un," Bud said.

"Looks that way," Tallman said.

"More Comanches?"

"Hardly."

"Kiowa?"

"No," Tallman said, his jaw hardening. "Those are shod horses. Five of them, I make out. Tells me something, though."

"What's that?"

"I'll let you know when the time comes," Tallman said.

"So, who joined the Comanches, if not more Injuns?"

"Comancheros," Tallman said. "White men. Renegades."

"Hell, for all I know, you might be a comanchero yourself. That's what I been thinkin' this whole time."

"Me?"

"Yeah," Bud said. "Why else would you be trackin' Comanches? One white man wouldn't stand a chance against a bunch that big."

"True," Tallman said, "but I'm no comanchero. If I was, you wouldn't have gotten this far."

"I reckon that makes some sense."

Tallman continued following the track, Bud bringing up the rear. The two men did not speak, but Tallman stopped every so often to check his backtrail.

The comancheros didn't seem to be carrying heavy on their horses and they had no pack horses with them, so they weren't joining the Comanches to trade with them. But they might have come to buy, he thought. Many of them, he knew, were slavers, and two young white girls might interest them.

Whatever their reason was for coming to the Comanches, Tallman reasoned, he knew that he had to try and rescue those captive women. If the comancheros got to them before he did, they were as good as dead.

An hour after the sun climbed to the center of the heavens, Tallman smelled woodsmoke. The wind had shifted to the south. That could mean but one thing, he knew. The Comanches and the comancheros had run to ground; they were in camp.

And the worst thing was, Tallman had no plan on how to free the two captives. Not in broad daylight, and not against an entire encampment of Comanches.

But he knew, with every breath he took, that he must try if it was the last thing he ever did.

It promised to be one hell of a long day.

Chapter Nine

Nancy felt her knees turn to quicksilver and start to buckle. She swayed for a moment as a wave of dizziness assailed her.

"Alan," she murmured.

Ottmers caught her in his arms before she fell. She felt her head strike his buckskinned chest as the dark sky spun overhead and sank down on her as if she were in the vortex of a whirlwind.

"What's the matter with her?" the boy called out. "Is she dying?"

"No, she ain't dyin'. I reckon you reminded her of someone." Ottmers struggled to stand upright as his moccasined feet slipped on the muddy ground. "Give me a hand, boy."

"Yes, sir," said the lad and started running toward

Ottmers. The smile faded from his face, leaving a worried look on his visage, a slight frowning curl to his lips.

"Lordy, she's a big woman," Ottmers grunted as he regained his footing. The boy grabbed Nancy's right arm and put it over his shoulder, letting some of her weight sag on to him.

"She is a mite heavy," the boy said.

"Help me carry her over by the fire," Ottmers said. "She's wet and cold."

"Yes, sir."

Together, boy and man carried the swooning, nearly unconscious Nancy to a place near the roaring fire. While Ottmers held her, the boy fetched a dry blanket from under the upturned canoe and brought it to his master.

"Good boy," Ottmers said. "Help me wrap that around her. I'll scoot down and let her head lay in my lap."

"How come she called me Alan?" the boy asked, after Nancy was resting peacefully.

"She buried her son just this mornin'," Ottmers said. "Maybe his name was Alan. I don't rightly recollect if she told me his name or not."

"Maybe I am her son," the boy said.

"Well, I reckon you could be. You said you don't remember your mama."

"Not real well. I can't put no face to her."

"Well, she didn't say nothin' 'bout havin' two boys."

"Where's her husband?"

"He was kilt, too," Ottmers said.

"I see," the boy said, and hung his head. Then, he walked over close to Nancy and looked down at her face. "She sure is pretty."

"Yep, she is that."

"What's her name?"

"Nancy."

"Pretty name, too."

"You don't recollect your own name yet?"

"It's . . . it's Alan, I think."

"Oh, pshaw, boy. That ain't your name."

The boy's face shadowed, then lit with his smile. "Well, I think it's Alan. That's a good name, isn't it, Virgil?"

"Yes, it's a good name, I reckon. You shush now and let this poor woman get some rest. She's been through a passel this day and is plumb tuckered out."

"Yes, sir," the boy said, and walked to the overturned canoe. He sat in its eave as the rain pattered lightly on his head. He seemed to be thinking; Ottmers noticed this and wondered about the boy as he had wondered about him for the past two months since he had found him.

The boy didn't know his own name, or couldn't remember it. Ottmers figured it had probably been beaten out of him by the Lipan Apaches or the Mexicans. He didn't remember his parents, or said he didn't. In fact, the boy had never said much, but he was a likable sort, despite being afraid of every stranger, suspicious of every shadow. But he had attached himself to Ottmers and didn't seem to want to run away.

After a time, Nancy's eyelids fluttered. She opened her eyes to see Ottmers's hand shielding her face from the drizzle. She blinked several times, then tried to sit up. Ottmers helped her to stand up. She stood there, eyes still blinking, staring at him, then at the boy, who was now straightening the tarp he had put up, stringing it from a tree to the bow of the canoe. Then she looked at the blazing fire and held out her hands to warm them.

"I fainted," she said.

"Yes," Ottmers told her. "You slept for a little while. It was needed."

"Where are we? Who is that boy? You didn't tell me you had a son."

"This is where I put in this morning. That boy is not my son. I didn't tell you about him because it's a long story and you had your own troubles."

She looked at the boy again.

"Amazing," she said.

"That he looks like your boy?" Ottmers asked.

"Yes. What's his name?"

"He doesn't know. Now he says it's Alan."

"Alan? That's my son's name. Was."

"I know. He's a motherless child," Ottmers explained. "He might be a little teched in the head."

"What do you mean?"

"He doesn't remember his own mother. He thinks you might be his mother."

Nancy heaved a deep breath, touched a hand to her forehead as if to absorb the information Ottmers was giving her. She looked again at the boy. He smiled at her and she felt a melting in her heart. The boy looked so lost and forlorn, and something inside her, something motherly, reached out to him, wanting to make some kind of connection.

"Come here," she said to the boy. He leaped up from his seat and ran to her. He looked up at her adoringly.

"Hello," he said.

"Do you think I'm your mother?" she asked.

"No'm, I don't know. I don't remember my real mother."

She turned to Ottmers. He didn't avoid her gaze, but he

didn't volunteer any information, although she guessed he must know she had a lot of questions to ask him.

"Where did this boy come from?" she asked.

"I found him, sort of."

She looked back at the boy. "What's your name?"

"Ma'am, I don't know. It might be Alan."

"Well, I'll call you Alan. But you're not my son, you must understand that."

"Yes'm."

She said the words, but her heart tugged at telling him the truth. Up close, he did not resemble her son very much, but he was about the same age. She thought of Alan, dead in his grave, so cruelly cut down by Comanches, so young and alive, with so much promise. And this boy, unnamed, unknown, motherless. Searching, perhaps, for love, for a mother's love.

"Alan, don't you remember your mother at all?"

"No'm, I reckon not. I been with the Mexicans and the Apaches."

"But you speak English. Someone must have taught you. Do you read letters?"

"No'm, I don't think so. I remember talking to people, though, the way I'm talking to you."

"He also speaks Spanish and Apache," Ottmers said.

Nancy moved closer to the fire. She held out her hands to warm them, turned slightly so that more of her dress drew the heat. The boy stood where he had been, watching her. Ottmers twisted around so that his back was to the blaze. Steam rose from his buckskins in a thin mist.

"You didn't just find that boy," Nancy said.

"Well, no, it didn't happen that way exactly," Ottmer said.

"Tell me what happened. I want to know all of it."

"I heard about the boy when I was in Santa Fe. There were some Mexicans trying to sell him. Comancheros, really. They was five of them. I went to see about him. The boy was dressed like an Apache. Comancheros claimed he was part Apache. Their leader was a man called Ojo de Algodón, Cotton-Eye."

"What's a comanchero?" Nancy asked.

"Scoundrels what lives with the Comanches, white men, Mexicans, renegades. They sell the Injuns guns and whiskey and such. Don't belong to no one, really, but the Comanches use 'em to find horses and settlers to make raids on."

"And you dealt with these people?" Nancy asked.

Ottmers turned sheepish-faced, shrugged.

"I could see the boy spoke English and didn't much like bein' with them comancheros, so I asked Cotton-Eye, he had him a cast to one eye, it was milk white, like a spot, what he wanted for the boy. He told me he'd take gold, but I offered him fifty dollars in silver and he took it."

"What were you planning to do with the boy after you bought him?" There was an accusatory edge to Nancy's voice. "Make him work?"

"Well, I never thought much about it. I asked the boy did he want to come with me and live on my little farm and he said he reckoned he would. I didn't buy him to make him no slave. I don't hold with keepin' slaves, although they's some as what does a lively business smugglin' slaves out of N'Orleans, Jim Bowie and his brothers, for instance."

"So what did the boy tell you about himself?"

"Not much," Ottmers said. "He told me he remembered white people gettin' kilt and scalped, and that he went to the mountains with some redskinned people, and they beat him and treated him like a woman."

"What do you mean by that?"

"Likely, I ain't gonna tell you, ma'am, you bein' decent and Christian and all. But, they was downright mean to him, and then them comancheros come and got him and took him to Santa Fe."

"Did they beat him too?"

"Yes'm, they did some."

"Why?"

Ottmers turned away from her so that she could not see the look on his face. "Ma'am, I don't really want to say."

"All of it," Nancy reminded him. "I told you I want to hear all of it."

"Well, when I seen this boy in Santa Fe, he was dressed like a girl. He didn't like it none, so I got him pants and a shirt and had his hair cut like a white man's and told him he didn't have to be a girl no more."

The shock of it registered on Nancy's face. She turned pale as she looked back at the boy, who stood there, impassive as stone, his eyes vacant of meaning, his face a mask. Her mouth opened to say something, but no words came out. Instead, she walked over to the boy and opened his shirt. She recoiled in horror as she saw the scars and burns on his chest. She walked around behind him and held his shirt out so that she could see his back. She cringed when she saw the brutal scars of a whip and the healed-over cuts from knives.

"My God," she said, finally, as she was rebuttoning the boy's shirt, "How could people do such things to children?"

"Ma'am, them Apaches had worse done to them, by the Spaniards and Mexicans. And the whites, too, I reckon. They's a chased and hunted and hated people, and maybe they took some of their own hate out on the boy."

"And the comancheros?"

"They don't much care about people. They stay with the Comanches because they like the smell of blood, the taste of it."

"It's hard to imagine there are people like that in the world."

"Yes'm," Ottmers said, "well, there is a passel of 'em round these parts."

Nancy drew in a deep breath. She walked back to the fire, stood there peering into the flames for several moments. She watched the fire dance, listened to it lick the wood, heard the air pockets crack and snap, sending sparks spewing upward into the air like magic golden fireflies. Neither Ottmers nor the boy said anything while she was ruminating there. They both seemed to be holding their breaths.

"Mr. Ottmers," Nancy said, turning to face the man she was addressing, "I would like to pay you fifty dollars for Alan. If you will help me find my wagon and my possessions, I have money to give you."

Ottmers's mouth fell open. The boy stood stolid as a statue, barely breathing. Nancy turned to him and smiled wanly.

"Well, now, ma'am, are you sure you want to do this? I mean the boy's been through pure hell and he might run off on you. You could be buyin' a pig in a poke."

"I'll take my chances." She turned to the boy. "Alan," she said, "would you like to live with me? It would mean hard work, building a farm, a house to live in . . ."

"Yes'm, I'd rightly be pleased to live with you."

"You can call me Mother if Mr. Ottmers agrees to my proposition."

Ottmers stood up, steam rising from his hot buckskins. He slapped at the warm parts and looked over at Alan.

"Boy, you sure?" Ottmers asked.

Alan nodded.

"Well, I reckon I'm only out fifty dollars. You can pay me when you can, Mrs. Stafford."

"Please, call me Nancy," she said.

"Nancy, then."

"Will you help me find my wagon and goods? And where's my cow?"

"Why, it's just upstream about a mile or so, ma'am. Look at that river, will you? It's a-boilin' and thrashin'. I couldn't get my canoe back in for a couple of days at the soonest. So, I reckon we can help you hunt downstream for your wagon and such."

"Good," Nancy said. "Then it's all settled."

She smiled at Alan and he smiled back. Her heart jumped and the blood drained from her head. She hoped she was doing the right thing, both by herself and by Alan. Maybe this was the way God had wanted it to be. Maybe she was supposed to lose one son only to gain another. When she looked back at Ottmers, he, too, was smiling.

"I guess He does work in mysterious ways, ma'am. I mean Nancy. Don't you think?"

"Yes," she said. "I believe He does."

Then she turned to Alan and looked at him for a long time.

"Alan," she said softly, "you're a boy, not a girl, and you'll be treated as such until you become a man."

"Thank you, Mother," Alan said, his face cast with a serious mien.

Mother, she thought. What a sweet word. She had thought she would never be called that again. The rain stopped suddenly and she could feel the breeze moving the dark clouds to the south. She heard the river roaring and it sounded like God speaking to her, speaking more gently than he had spoken all during this terrible day when she had buried her son.

I have another son, she thought. Then she closed her eyes and began to pray, to give thanks to the Almighty.

Chapter
Ten

Tallman rode to a place where the wide river thinned from a massive sheet of brownish water to a narrow boil in rocky shallows. There, he crossed the Brazos without swimming the dun, Bud following without question. Once across the river, Tallman rode to a grove of cottonwoods that were thick enough for concealment. He dismounted and tied the reins to a scrub oak where there was plenty of grass for his horse to graze on and water in a pool left by the rain.

Bud slid off the back of his horse, groaning with the pain in his leg.

"What you gonna do?" Bud asked.

"From here on, we walk," Tallman said.

"Walk?"

"We have to look over that Comanche camp. I do, at least."

"Ain't that mighty dangerous?"

"Not if we keep quiet. I have an idea."

"Let's hear it."

"If my hunch is right, we may not have to take on the Comanches."

"What in hell would we want to do that for, anyway?"

Tallman sighed. It was time, he thought, to tell Bud why he had been following the Comanches. But first, he had to find out something that had bothered him ever since he found the wounded man at the site of a Kiowa attack on his wagon train.

"Who are you, Bud?" Tallman asked. "What's your full name?"

"I was wonderin' when you'd ask me that. It's no secret. I just didn't think my name was all that important to you."

"It might not be, but I want to know it before we go any further."

"Okay. It's Tom Redford, but those who know me call me Bud."

Tallman gave no indication that he had heard the name before, but he had suspected this was the man Nancy Stafford disliked and wanted nothing to do with. He was beginning to think that she was a good judge of character.

"This isn't your first trip to Texas," Tallman said.

"No. I been here before."

"That's what I thought."

"So?"

"Did you ever ride with Magee?"

Redford's face turned a roseate hue. His neck muscles bulged out so that the veins made taut cords. He seemed to choke on the words that wouldn't come out of his mouth, but recovered enough a few seconds later to speak. "What makes you say that?" he asked.

"I had a hunch."

"Well, no, I never knew Magee," Redford said.

Tallman knew the man was lying. He was about the right age. He carried himself like a military man. But there was something else about Redford that bothered Tallman. He always seemed to be hiding something, like a man on the run.

"You ever been to Nacogdoches?"

"No, never been there," Redford said.

"Well, where have you been?"

Redford swallowed hard, cleared his throat. Tallman could see that the man was making up another lie. He wasn't going to let him off the hook, however. His eyes bored into Redford's like steel lances.

"I come down once just long enough to cross the Red and decide I didn't like it much. I went right back up through the Territories to St. Louis."

"Why did you come back?" Tallman asked.

"Things changed. I heard about Moses Austin bringin' settlers in and I thought the time was ripe."

"Why didn't you come down with Austin?"

"I–I wasn't in St. Louis at the time," Redford said.

Tallman had another hunch about Redford, but he kept it to himself. If he was right, he'd find out the truth about Bud Redford one of these days. A man could only hide so long. Someone, somewhere, would know the man, and Tallman would find out if what he suspected was correct.

"We got to cross that damned river again?" Redford asked as he followed Tallman back to the ford on the Brazos.

"Watch it doesn't take your legs out from under you. You'll likely wind up at San Felipe de Austin."

"Where's that?" Bud asked, with an air of feigned innocence.

"Downriver," Tallman said. He took off his boots, made a sling out of his shirt, put the boots inside, and cradled the sling around his neck. He waded into the river at its widest point, almost the exact place where they had crossed with the horses. He knew the riverbed had a hard bottom there, so he didn't have to worry about quicksand. He didn't look back to see if Redford was following. He was sure the man would be right behind him.

The undercurrent was swift, and Tallman had to watch each step as they crossed the Brazos. The worst of the flooding seemed to have subsided there, but he knew there could be more water coming down over the next few hours. He would worry about getting back across when the time came.

As he reached the opposite bank, Tallman heard Redford puffing behind him. He found a dry spot, sat down and put on his shirt and boots. Redford was a mess. His bandage was wet and bloody, and he had not taken off his boots. Tallman shook his head as he stood up.

"From now on, you be real quiet," he told Redford. "Stay behind me and go where I go, do what I do."

"I'd feel better if this pistol was loaded," Bud said. He had replaced it with a stick in his tourniquet that morning. The pistol was stuck into his belt, a worthless chunk of iron.

"We'll do no shooting just yet," Tallman said.

Bud grumbled some, but soon grew quiet as he followed Tallman up to the plain above the river. Tallman hunkered over and headed south on a parallel course to the place where he believed the Comanche camp to be. Redford did the same.

When the smell of smoke became strongest, Tallman lowered himself and began crawling inland, using grass and bushes for cover. Redford mimicked Tallman's every move. Finally, Tallman began crawling on his belly, stopping every few seconds to lift his head and listen.

He saw the Comanche camp a few moments later. To his surprise, it was not a permanent camp, but more of a gathering place. He saw no Indian women, but there were some boys guarding the horses and a brave or two on watch. In the center of a circle of men, Tallman saw the five comancheros, talking in both sign and speech. He recognized the leader, Cotton-Eye. One of the comancheros was a white man; the others were Mexican, half-breed Yaquis, Apaches, faces mean as those of rabid mongrels.

"You recognize any of those comancheros, Bud?" Tallman whispered the question.

"I never seen any of 'em before," Redford answered.

"Look over yonder, beyond that clump of cactus where the two braves are standing with their lances."

"Yeah?"

"On the ground, sitting."

"Looks like a couple of women."

"Look real close," Tallman said.

Redford was silent for a moment. Then, he let out a long breath.

"I know them two gals," Redford said.

"That's why I'm here."

"How the hell . . ?"

"Comanches hit Jacobs's wagon train yesterday, up river. Stole those two girls. I aim to get 'em back."

"You bit off a lot to chew. There must be two dozen Comanches there, and them five comancheros."

"Watch," Tallman said.

The two men waited, watching the group. They could smell stolen beef cooking and then those in the center rose and began to cut off chunks of meat and ate them as they walked around, talking. The comancheros walked over to where the two captives sat. One Comanche, a man Tallman knew, accompanied them.

"That's the Comanche chief with Cotton-Eye. They call him Big Tree."

"Never heard of him," Redford said.

"Look," Tallman said.

As the two men watched, Cotton-Eye opened a money belt and pulled out several gold coins and some silver dollars. He handed them to Big Tree, who took them and bit each coin. Then the chief gestured to the two Comanche guards. They jerked the captive women to their feet.

"Boy, it sure is them two gals," Redford said. He seemed relieved. "They don't look none too poorly."

"Considering," Tallman said.

"If they's the only two they got . . ."

"It is."

"I don't see how we can help 'em. Do you?"

"Not now," Tallman said. "Just wait. And watch."

One of the comancheros walked over to the two girls. He touched her on the chest in an indecent way. The other comancheros laughed when the girl spat at the man who had fondled her. There was more talk and then two other comancheros grabbed the two girls and led them over to where their horses were standing.

"They're goin' to take them girls," Redford said.

"I was hoping they would."

"You was? They'll be treated bad by them comancheros."

"We have to stop that," Tallman said.

"Five to two," Redford said. "Them ain't good odds."

"No, and we don't want to hurt the girls when we try to take them away from those men."

"How we gonna do that?" Redford asked.

"I don't know," Tallman replied.

As he and Redford watched, the comancheros mounted up. Two of the horses packed double, with the girls riding behind heavily armed men.

"Where do you figger they're takin' them girls?" Redford asked.

"Mexico, most likely."

"How come?"

"They might sell 'em to Apaches when they're through with them," Tallman said, a bitterness to his tone. "Or to Mexicans who buy such chattel."

"It don't seem right."

Tallman said nothing. While they continued watching, the comancheros rode off to the south. They seemed not to be in a hurry. Doves rose up from the plain as they passed, twisting and darting through the air with whistling wings. Tallman made no move to leave.

"How come we're stayin' here?" Redford asked.

"I want to see what the Comanches are going to do before we leave."

"What if they ride toward us?"

"Then we're in big trouble," Tallman said.

The Comanches continued eating the cooked beef,

talking and walking around. Some appeared restless and kept looking to the north. After a time, some of them lay down under their horses, using the animals for shade, and those dozed peacefully.

Tallman started to crawl backwards.

"We're leavin'?"

"The Comanches will be there for a while," Tallman said. "We don't want to let those comancheros get too much distance between us."

Back at the river, the two men crossed as they had before. They mounted their horses and headed south.

Tallman picked up the trail of the comancheros nearly an hour later. The five men and two women were following the course of the Brazos, which wandered southeasterly through gently rolling country dotted with juniper and hardwoods, blanketed over by tall prairie grasses.

Two hours later, the trail led back to the river and there it disappeared as the comancheros rode into the stream. They chose a place where the bluffs rose high and the small canyons were thick with brush and trees. It was a dangerous place to be, Tallman knew, and he grew uneasy as he searched both shores for hoofprints.

"Lost 'em, eh?" Redford said.

"They either know we're following them, or they don't trust those Comanches much."

"So, what now?"

"We get the hell out of here," Tallman said.

He turned the dun, and that saved his life. A split second before that, a rifle cracked and the air sizzled with the sound of a lead ball whizzing past. It smacked into the water and splashed the dun's belly. Redford hunkered low on the bare back of his horse and slapped reins to its flanks, galloped past Tallman, splashing water that filled with rainbows in the glare of the morning sun.

Then, as Tallman spurred the dun, the thicket exploded with a fusillade of rifle fire as four more guns opened up, letting loose the dogs of war and hell on the two trackers caught out in the open.

Chapter Eleven

The boy, now called Alan by both Nancy and Virgil Ottmers, stared at the sleeping woman, trying to remember his own mother. She looked tired, and he studied the lines in her face as if trying to determine what they meant, whether they meant meanness or kindness, but he could not tell. He looked at the closed eyes and tried to dredge up an image of his mother's eyes. Were they brown or blue?

He could only remember warmth and the sound of weeping. When he tried to think of his mother, he heard only faint screams and the harsh guttural grunts of men, and always, the weeping as if from another room. A woman sobbing, and he could not summon up a visage, even one in torment. But he remembered the men, coming and going, riding at night and stopping in small settlements and someone's face in a shroud, a woman's, maybe, and ropes around her, and he always wondered if that was his mother.

He remembered softness and the scent of flowers, the softness of flesh and the softness of a mouth on his cheek, his own mouth on another's cheek or neck and hair tickling his eyes and a voice crooning to him in the dark. He remembered a man, tall and lean, but his face was always so far away he could not recall its features.

He said the word over and over in his mind. "Nancy, Nancy," but it sounded strange to him, and he knew there was no word for her name in Spanish or Apache and that made him wonder where the woman got such an odd name. He wondered where she came from and what her son was like. He did not know many boys his own age. He had seen some, both Mexican and Apache, but he had never spoken to them, and when he heard them talk he never understood what they were saying.

He had been small when the Apaches took him, he knew that, but he had spoken English. He remembered a man reading to him from a book, and he remembered asking questions and the man's answering them, but he could not remember his face, only the low pitch of his voice, a timbrous voice that seemed to boom low in his chest when he read aloud. The woman never read to him, only spoke to him in Spanish, and they were baby-talk words that he barely remembered and felt ashamed of now that he had heard the rough talk of Mexican men. He knew all those words, even if he didn't know exactly what all of them meant, he knew how to use them so that he sounded like those men.

He had kept English as a secret language, a private one, because he thought that he might find his mother and father someday and that the only way they would know that he was their son was if he spoke to them in that language. But he had not heard it spoken until Santa Fe, and when he met Virgil Ottmers, he thought at first that Virgil was his father because he spoke English, but Virgil had told him that he was not his father. And when he had heard Nancy talk, he thought she was his mother but now he didn't think so, because he thought that his own mother did not speak much English. He thought that she must have spoken Apache or Mexican, because he remembered the baby talk and the soft words in Spanish that were like words spoken in a dream, mysterious words from some mysterious source.

Nancy was so beautiful, he thought, so much more beautiful than the Mexican or Apache women he had seen. And she seemed kind, unlike those others who had ordered him around, slapped and kicked him, beaten him sometimes so badly he could not move for days. And, then they would beat him again and call him *peresozo*, lazy. But Nancy had a nice smile and she spoke to him as if he were her own son, called him a boy, not a girl.

He had learned some things from Virgil. With the Apaches, and with the Mexicans, he had never known what kindness was, and, indeed, he did not even know the word. But Virgil had taught him that English word and a lot more, and he had shown him what kindness was. At first, he thought Virgil was weak, maybe like a woman, but he had learned, over the long ride down the river from New Mexico, that Virgil was every inch a man, as much so as any Apache or Mexican he had ever met.

Virgil had told him stories about brave men and heroes, men who were like those in the stories his father used to read to him, and he had told him about cowardice, too, making him see that men who kicked and beat small boys were not brave men, but cowards.

But Nancy, she was different from any woman he had ever known. Virgil had said that she was brave, too, that she had almost shot him. He had never seen a woman with a rifle before, either. And the rifle was something powerful, he knew, something he had dreamed of having one day.

A ray of morning sun, pared thin by the leaves of a tree, slanted across Nancy's face, highlighting her closed eyes. She rubbed the suddenly warmed lids with the fingers of her left hand. She stirred restlessly under the tarp lean-to that covered her lower body.

"She's waking up," Alan said.

Virgil, tending to the morning fire, turned and looked at the sleeping woman. "Yep," he said. "And I haven't even got the coffee started yet."

Nancy opened her eyes slowly and saw the boy standing nearby, staring at her.

"Good morning," she said.

"Good morning," Virgil said. Alan found that he could not speak. He dipped his head shyly, and looked away. Nancy arose from her bed and ran fingers through her tangled hair.

"It's a glorious morning," she said, looking at Alan.

"Yes, 'tis," Virgil said. "Coffee comin' up. Want some?"

"I'd love some," Nancy said. "I'll wash up and be back shortly."

"Can I go with you?" Alan asked.

Nancy hesitated. "No, you'd better stay here, Alan. Some things a woman has to do alone."

Alan blushed. "Oh, yes," he said. "I know."

After she left, Alan walked over to the fire and hunkered down to talk to Ottmers.

"She's pretty," Alan said.

"She's right comely, son."

"I hope she likes me."

"She does. You're a good boy."

"When will she buy me from you?"

"I reckon when we find her wagon and goods. But she's not really buying you, boy. She's just repaying me for what I give them comancheros. You ain't no slave, you know."

"That's what I've been," Alan said.

"Well, you ain't no more, so just don't talk that way around her, hear?"

"Yes sir." Alan got up and started chucking stones into the Brazos. The river had calmed down from the day before and was sweeping by majestically, a slow, steady current carrying bits of driftwood and flotsam from the thunderstorm.

Nancy returned from her ablutions, her face washed, her hair straightened the best she could manage without a comb. She spoke to Virgil while Alan was still down by the river.

"He's pretty dark-skinned, isn't he?" she asked.

"Who? Oh, the boy. Yes. I 'spect he has some Mexican blood in him. Plain to see he's got white blood too."

"Yes. It doesn't matter. I was just wondering who his parents might have been."

"No tellin', Nancy. He doesn't remember."

"I'm pleased with him. He's dark-skinned and handsome and he does remind me a little of my own son."

"He'll make you a fine son," Ottmers said. The coffee began to steam and burble in the pot atop the fire. Virgil got three cups from a canvas bag near the canoe and h.. ..one to Nancy. He called to the boy, who walked up from the river.

"He drinks coffee?" Nancy asked.

"Just like a growed man," Virgil replied.

The three sat down with cups full of steaming coffee. Nancy blew on hers and sipped it as she looked upward at the blue sky.

"You know I came here illegally," Nancy said, sipping her coffee.

"I 'spected as much."

"My husband wanted to come down here with Moses Austin when he got permission. We were sure he was going to get it from the Spanish, so we came down anyway."

"Moses got his land grant, all right," Ottmers said. "But he never lived long enough to see his dream of settlement come true. He had a hard ride back through dangerous country. With the help of his friend, the Baron of Bastrop, Austin drew the favor of General Arredondo, who saw to it that Austin could bring three hundred families down and settle the Brazos valley.

"In January of eighteen and twenty-one, Moses left San Antonio de Béxar and headed for St. Louis. He ran out of food along the way, and then he was robbed. He caught a bad cold and by the time he reached Missouri he was broken in health, near death. Before he died he asked Stephen to carry on, bring the families down."

"I had no idea," Nancy said. "How sad."

"Now, Stephen has his hands full. The Mexicans threw the Spanish out and now the Mexicans want to change all the laws. The Spaniards were smart. They figured with so many leaving the provinces up thisaway that American colonization was the only way to keep the Indians out of lower Mexico. When I was last in San Antonio, the Comanches came and went like they owned the town."

"So I need to see someone about getting a land grant, I suppose," Nancy said.

"Stephen has the authority to give you some land. It's complicated. Take some advice?"

"Yes, I'd be much obliged, Virgil."

"You tell Mr. Austin you're a rancher. Land's cheaper than if you said you was a-farmin', and you can get more of it."

"I'll keep that in mind. How do I find Stephen Austin?"

"Likely in San Antonio de Béxar, or at the first settlement on the Brazos, what they're callin' San Felipe de Austin. But you stake out your land first and then go see Stephen."

"I'll do that. Do you have a grant, Virgil?"

"I surely do. I got what they call a *sitio* or a *legua*, a league, that's four thousand four hunnert and forty-eight acres American."

Nancy whistled out a breath. "That's a lot of land," she said.

"A mite. You got to have a family to do it, though. Me, I hired me an old woman and a girl, passed them off as wife and daughter."

"Would I be able to declare Alan as my son and be considered a family?" she asked.

Ottmers scratched his head. "Don't rightly know, Nancy. I think you got to have a husband, too. A head of the family."

"I see," Nancy said, thoughtfully. "Then I'll just have to see about finding myself a husband, won't I?"

Chapter Twelve

Tallman drove the dun toward the opposite shore, striking hard for a gully that fissured the bank. He knew the comancheros would have to reload their rifles unless they carried loaded spares, so he had some moments before they could shoot again. Redford was already splashing out of the river, his horse trying to gain a foothold on solid ground.

As he reached the gully, another shot rang out and he heard the high-pitched whine of a lead ball sizzle past him. The ball thunked into the wall of the gully a few yards ahead of him, shooting up a puff cloud of dust. The dun shied slightly but kept going, and a few seconds later, Tallman was out of immediate danger. He lost track of Redford, who, he supposed, was still out in the open, unless the wounded man had found another place to conceal himself and his horse.

The dun was breathing hard from the effort, and Tallman brought it to a halt at the top of the gully. He knew he could not be seen from the river at that spot, but he figured the comancheros might come after him. If so, he was in a good place. They could not come up the gully more than two at a time, and more likely in single file. He could hold them off, he figured.

He checked his rifle, making sure the powder in the pan was dry. He also checked his pistol, which would be useful only at very short range. It was Spanish made, .60 caliber, with a large lock, and it could blow a sizable hole in a man at five or six yards.

Tallman waited, listening for sounds of pursuit.

It was very quiet. He no longer heard the sound of Redford's horse, nor any splashings in the river. And still he waited, the silence filling his ears.

None of the comancheros came up the draw. After ten minutes, Tallman heard a sound that arrested his attention. It came from the river, but it was not the heavy splash of hooves hitting the waters. Rather, it was a stealthy splashing that made him think someone was walking his horse through the river, someone not hurrying or else trying to mask his movement.

The odd thing, however, was that the sound was not getting closer to him, but moving away. He listened for the hooves to strike solid ground, but the sound of the river was so loud he could not hear such a noise. His hands started to sweat, and he wiped them on his trousers so that the rifle would not become slippery should he need to draw it to his shoulder.

Tallman waited another fifteen minutes, then he gently urged the dun on to high ground. He turned the horse and rode upriver, well away from where he and Redford had been ambushed. There was a purpose to this, and he took his time, making sure there was at least one bend of the river between him and the spot where the comancheros had lain in hiding for him and his companion to pass by.

Doves flushed at his passing, singles and pairs, up from Mexico for the warm season, and Tallman listened to the peaceful sound of their whistling wings as they glided through the air out of sight like tiny porpoises with wings. Finally, he rode down to the Brazos again and stopped there to check his backtrail and to listen for sounds of pursuit.

He crossed to the other side of the river and let the dun pick its way slowly along the bank, in and out of trees, up small draws and back down again, through clumps of brush, past mesquite trees and yucca going to seed after the spring bloom. The silence followed him like a shapeless cloak, masking his movements, keeping his presence secret and silent upon the land.

He found a set of tracks that he knew well. They told him that Tom Redford had recrossed the river and headed directly for the place where the comancheros had waited in ambush. Tallman did not then jump to any conclusions, since he did not know the whole story, but his suspicions were raised to a high level, and he rode on with a feeling that something had been taken from him, that he had been robbed, not of money or goods, but of trust and a kindness he had shown to another.

He brought the silence of empty places with him as he rode into the thick grove of trees where the comancheros had holed up, and there he found his suspicions confirmed. Redford had indeed joined the renegades and not as a prisoner or hostage, but willingly, and they had ridden off to the south together, six men now and two frail captive women, girls, really, and Redford with a new bandage on his leg, the old one lying on the ground with other objects that set off warning signals in his mind.

This was a place the comancheros had visited before, not a place where they had stopped because it was convenient or handy, but a place they had known, a meeting place they had used before. It was, in fact, a hideout, and it told him a great deal about Cotton-Eye and the men who had fired on him.

Tallman found empty powder kegs, depressions in the earth where bedrolls had carried the weight of sleeping men, a fire ring of scorched stones, ropes in the trees where fresh meat had hung, pipe dottle, a discarded lead mold for making balls, a worn-out powder horn and shot pouch, pieces of leather and string, broken beads, a pair of worn-out buckskin leggings. What was most incriminating, though, was a pile of arrows, breastplates, flint knives, bows, quivers, moccasins, and other such paraphernalia that bore the markings of a Kiowa clan. These were recently thrown away or left behind. The camp stank of blood and human excrement. Tallman found old locks, trigger guards, and broken flints that told him it was an old camp, used for many years by men on the run, men hiding, men bent on murder and other skulduggery.

Tallman gasped for air and left the stenchful place, sickened by what he had found, sickened by Redford's treachery and lying. Something stuck in his mind and he could not dig it out until he had verified it for himself. He no longer had to track the comancheros. He knew where they would go, and the thought of it made his blood boil like syrup in a black kettle.

He rode back across the river then and headed north. Soon he ran across the tracks of six horses. He knew he would be too late to catch them in the act, but he knew where the scurrilous band of men was going. By late afternoon, he came upon the wreckage of the wagon train, the maze of hoof-prints, the evidence that the comancheros had been there. For the second time, he guessed.

Now, he began to read the sign in earnest, for he had to know what happened. He saw the dead, stiffened now, their bodies bloating in the sun, their flesh already scavenged by coyotes and wolves and the flock of buzzards still circling in the sky or flapping about on their feet from corpse to corpse.

A mile away, Tallman found three dead Kiowa braves, their bodies covered hastily with stones. They had been shot and their necks had been broken with hatchets as if to make sure. This discovery told him the whole story, or most of it, and now his jaw set with a determination and intensity that had not been there before.

Well, Tallman thought, that was one thing Redford had not lied about. There had been Kiowa, but they had not attacked the wagon train. These braves who were dead wore no paint on their faces. More likely, they had stopped to trade with the settlers, and the comancheros had taken advantage of the opportunity. It was ironic, in a way, that at least one of the Kiowa had shot an arrow into Redford before he was killed.

As Tallman backtracked to the ruins of the wagon train, the rest of the story became apparent. The comancheros had made a deal with the Comanches, all right, a deal to get the women from them. There were tracks of cattle and horses

that the comancheros had come back to get and deliver to
their friends, the Comanches. He had not seen them in the
storm, but now he could see their fresh tracks, the places
where traces had been cut, the marks of horses and beef on
the hoof, all driven off by the men who had come back to finish their dirty work.

The tracks told a grisly tale of deceit and betrayal. Redford had been a comanchero, probably long before he went
to Missouri and got in with a wagon train. He had broken
away from Jacobs, not over leadership, but to lessen Jacobs's
chances of surviving a Comanche raid. And Redford had led
the other wagon train into a trap, probably signaling to his comanchero friends where they would be and when to strike.
The Kiowas had happened along innocently, not on the war-
path, but just curious Indians bent on trade, or perhaps begging for coffee, sugar, meat, tobacco.

It all became clear as Tallman rode through the scene of
carnage and read the tracks, old and new, and cursed himself
for not seeing it all sooner, for not seeing through Redford
and his lies. Redford must be laughing at him now, now that
he was reunited with his comanchero cohorts and he had the
two captive girls.

The tracks of horses and cattle told Tallman that he had
been right. The comancheros were taking them to the Comanches, who had done their part, a good trade for two white
girls. By tomorrow, the tribe would be gone to other haunts,
gloating over their booty, and the comancheros would—

Suddenly, Tallman knew, without seeing sign, without
tracking further, where the comancheros would go. Or at
least where Redford was bound.

He knew, with certainty, that Redford was going back to
the north, to find Nancy Stafford and add her to his harem. Of

course, that's what he was going to do, Tallman reasoned. Redford knew, after rejoining the comancheros, that Nancy had left the wagon train. The Comanches would have told Cotton-Eye and the others the whole story.

Tallman felt something spoil in his stomach. He should never have left Nancy Stafford alone, despite her insistence that he leave, go on his way. Now she was in dire peril, in true danger from a man she loathed. God only knew what a man like Redford would do with a woman like Nancy if he got his bloody hands on her.

The thought of it made Tallman shudder, and the spoiling in his gut made him almost sick to the point of retching. He gulped in deep drafts of air to clear his head and get rid of the queasiness in his belly.

Somehow, he must find Nancy Stafford and warn her. Even though he had other, more urgent matters to attend to, he could not allow such a woman to fall into the hands of the comancheros. And there was still the matter of the two captive girls. They, too, must be found and delivered from the hands of the treacherous men who now held them prisoner.

Tallman knew it was a big order for a lone man. It might take him days to find her, and by then it might be too late. And as for the two girls, they would have to suffer a while longer. He could not go up against Comanches and comancheros by himself. That would do none of them any good. It would, he was certain, be plain suicide to try and rescue the girls just yet.

First, he must find Nancy Stafford and get her out of harm's way. Then he could plan for the rest of it.

He thought of Redford as he rode off to the north. He wanted to put his hands around the man's neck and squeeze until the breath went out of him. He wanted him to die as Nancy's son had died, as those under Bud's care had died.

The dun sniffed the wind and stepped out as if going on parade, its mane rippling in the breeze as it tossed its head.

Tallman wondered if he would find Nancy in time to warn or save her. The smell of death was still strong in his nostrils, and he had a long way to ride. And it would not be long before the sun set on a day he wished had never happened.

Chapter Thirteen

Nancy's wagon lay against a rock outcropping in the river, badly smashed but some parts still intact. Its wheels were not damaged, but one of the sideboards was partially caved in and the canvas top shredded. For the past two hours, she and Ottmers and Alan had been picking up clothes and dishes, pots and pans that were strewn along the shore for a mile or so.

There was no sign of the ox, and she feared it had been killed. Alan had taken the land route, leading her cow, which Ottmers had left tied high and dry upstream from where he had beached his canoe during the storm. Now Alan led the cow down to the river, where Nancy and Ottmers sat in the canoe, its prow resting on a grassy shore.

"Reckon that cow of yours can pull your wagon?" Ottmers asked.

"I don't know, Virgil," she said. "I need to see if my strongbox is inside so I can pay you for Alan."

"Don't you never mind 'bout that right now, young lady. Let's see if we can get that wagon off the rock and to a place where it'll dry out."

It had been a long day, frightening at times, when she had to paddle furiously through washboard rapids, or past rocks that lurked beneath the river, just enough of them sticking out to make ripply waves that almost hid the danger. Virgil had taught her the basics of paddling and he had told her she was doing well after they traversed a series of short quirky rapids that left her emotionally and physically exhausted.

"I'll swing the canoe around and you step out," Ottmers told her. "Alan, you tie up that cow yonder and come give the lady a hand."

"You mean my mother," Alan said, a stubborn tone to his voice.

"Yes, your mother," Ottmers said, still trying to get used to the idea.

Alan smiled and went to tie up the pregnant cow as Ottmers swung the stern of the canoe around parallel to the shore. Nancy climbed out, not as gingerly as she had several times on the journey when Ottmers had put in to allow her to relieve herself ashore.

The three wrestled with ropes and pries to free the wagon from the river's clutches, an effort that took over two hours and exhausted the three people. When the wagon was on dry land, Nancy climbed up into it and sorted through her things to see what she had left. Surprisingly, she was able to salvage a great deal, including clothes and tools, another rifle, two pistols, axes, hoes, hatchets, cooking utensils, flatware, bowls and plates, not to mention her sewing kit. Her strongbox was intact, buried under blankets and heavy crates. She took out fifty dollars in coin and handed the money to Ottmers.

"You don't have to do this just now," Ottmers said.

"No, I do," she said. "I want no debts between us, nothing but kindness."

"Ma'am, I thank you." Ottmers pocketed the money. "I'll give you a legal paper when I get to home."

"Virgil, you don't have to do that. Besides, we may not see each other again. You live far down the river and I do not yet know where I will settle."

"That's true, but we will surely meet again. You must go to see Don Estévan and obtain a *permiso* for you to settle land here on the Brazos."

"Don Estévan?"

"Stephen Austin. That is what they call him here."

"Then I will pass by your homestead? Your ranch?"

"Yes. But Austin is in Mexico City, last I heard. I don't know when he will return. The politics are vicious here in the upper province. He must learn the Spanish language and speak with all the factions, royalists, republicans, the whole kit and caboodle of cutthroat politicians in the capital."

"You make it sound difficult."

"It might be. Each new governor seems to want to take away what Spain has granted. And each new head of state wants to take away what the Mexicans granted. Austin is tough and shrewd, however. He will see to it that those Americans who settle here are treated well and fairly."

"I see. Well, I will do what I must do. Now, you'd best be getting on home. Alan and I will do nicely on our own."

"Are you sure?"

"Yes, Virgil. Do not worry about us. I will see you by-and-by. First, I must find me a place to build a home for me and my son."

"Good idea. Possession is nine-tenths of the law. Austin is a man who likes to see wild land settled. If he sees that you're serious and have already staked out a ranch or a farm, he'll do his best to make it legal. If you become a Mexican citizen, that will help."

"My husband thought that eventually Texas would be part of the Union."

"I'm afraid he was wrong, Nancy. Texas is a Mexican province now that the revolution has succeeded in taking the country from Spain. Mexico wants settlers, but they also want Texas. Funny thing, though, now that you mention it. I've heard that this feller Tallman has the same idea, but it may not be his idea."

"What do you mean?" she asked.

Virgil scratched his balding head. "Well, now, I heard that Tallman comes from Washington. I mean sent by Washington. Maybe even the president himself."

"I don't understand. Is he a diplomat?"

"More like a spy, I reckon. But he does pop up in Mexico City more often than Austin. So I heard."

"Is he a Mexican citizen?"

"I think so, yes."

"Well, I guess I'll become a Mexican citizen, then. I do want to carry out my husband's dream."

"It won't be too hard, I'm sure. There are a lot of illegals in Texas, up on the Red, for instance, and Austin decries this, but he is a good diplomat and I think he can help you get hold of that dream you and your husband had."

"I hope so," Nancy said.

They were able to hitch the cow to the wagon. Ottmers built a yoke from tree limbs that would serve to hold the cow in harness. Makeshift, but it worked well enough, he told her, as long as she did not go far.

"I expect Alan and I will find a suitable property soon," she said.

"I trust that you will, Nancy. You're a woman with a lot of gumption."

"I hope we see you again, Virgil."

"I'm not hard to find. Down the Brazos a ways, there's a place where the river makes a big bend and a creek comes into it. I call it Walnut Creek, since a neighbor lady name of Marj lives up yonder and makes bowls and such from the trees, harvests the nuts. She passed as my wife when we come down from Missouri. We got us a *sitio* and then split it up. She's married now and has a daughter named Alice."

"I look forward to meeting them one day."

"We hope to be your neighbors," Virgil said. Then he climbed back into the canoe and waved a hand above his head.

She and her newly adopted son said farewell to Ottmers and watched him paddle off downstream. She and the boy took the wagon up on flat ground and continued southward, following the course of the Brazos. The cow rebelled against the yoke and harness, but Nancy did not push her hard and they did not make much progress by day's end.

The long shadows of afternoon drew the forms of trees and tall grasses across the prairie's low and bare spots, an intricate latticework of shade woven throughout living plants. Then these shadows shrank and formed into dark puddles that soaked the land with the sad cloak of darkness.

"We'd best stop for the night," Nancy said, "while there's a bit of light left."

"Yes'm," Alan said, bracing himself as his adopted mother stopped the wagon and set the brake.

"You take the cow's harness off and hobble her so she can graze. Do you know how to do that?"

"Yes'm, I know how to hobble a horse or cow."

"Good," Nancy said. Then she smiled at the boy before she stepped down from the wagon.

"I've noticed you moving your lips all day without saying anything, Alan. Were you praying?"

"No'm, I was saying my name."

"Saying your name?"

He looked sheepish and dropped his head so that he broke eye contact with Nancy.

"I was trying to hear how it sounds in my head," the boy said. "I was saying Alan Stafford over and over."

Nancy smiled. Then she reached out a hand and placed it atop Alan's. "You can say it as much as you want, son," she said. "For that is your new name. One I hope you will carry proudly."

"Yes'm, I will."

Alan leaped from the wagon as Nancy climbed down and attacked the yoke holding the pregnant cow in the traces. Nancy smiled again and grabbed a bucket from the side of the wagon where it was lashed and headed for the river. She was tired, but blessedly so. She had her cow and the wagon and a new son. There was a lightness in her step as she crossed the shadowed sward and found a place that would lead her down to the Brazos.

"Mother," Alan called.

Nancy stopped short, turned around.

"You forgot your rifle."

"Oh? Did I?"

"Yes'm. Mr. Ottmers, he said you always had to carry your rifle in this country. He always did."

Nancy laughed aloud. "You're right, Alan. I should always carry a rifle, and so should you."

"I don't have no rifle."

"I don't have any rifle," she corrected him.

"Yes'm. You have two of them."

"Oh, never mind, Alan. I'll be right back. I'll let you watch out for me while I fetch some water. If I need the rifle, I'll come running."

She did not hear Alan's reply as she continued walking to the river. There, she filled the bucket with water, tasting it several times. It did not taste too salty, but the river was wide there and she thought perhaps the rains had washed the salty water downstream.

When she returned with the bucket full of water, Nancy saw that Alan had done a good job of hobbling the cow and he also had her roped to a wagon wheel. The rope was long enough to give the cow grazing room. Alan was standing near the rifle leaning against the canvas just inside the wagon in back of the seat.

"You did well, Alan," she said. "Hobbling that cow and tying her up."

"Thank you, Mother."

Nancy smiled. She couldn't remember smiling so much. Not with her husband or son. Perhaps she had taken life too seriously when they were alive. Or maybe she had not noticed them as much as she should have. She had harbored many regrets since her husband had been killed. Now she was regretting things she might have done with her son while he was alive, shown him more love, listened to him more, smiled at him more often.

Nancy set the bucket down and walked over and took the rifle down. She handed it to Alan.

"Do you know how to shoot it?" she asked.

"No'm. I never shot no rifle before."

"I never shot a rifle before."

"You haven't?" he asked.

"Alan," she said, smiling indulgently, "you need to learn the correct way of speaking English. You should not use a double negative."

"What's that?"

Nancy laughed. "That's one of the things I'm going to teach you. I was correcting your English. Of course I've shot that rifle before. My father taught me to use one when I was a girl."

"He did?"

"Yes. And I taught my husband."

"Your husband didn't know how to shoot a rifle?" Alan said, laughing.

"Not very well," she said, sighing. It was true. In many ways, Randall had not been prepared to make the journey to Texas, now that she thought about it. He was a nice man, but gentle and naive. He trusted too many people, and he did not particularly like firearms. She decided then and there that Alan was going to grow up to be a man who could defend himself and learn not to trust everyone he met.

"I think I could learn real quick," Alan said. "I seen enough rifles shot."

"Saw," she corrected.

"Huh?"

"Never mind. We'll both have to fetch firewood if I'm to cook supper for us. It's going to be dark soon, and there doesn't seem to be a lot of trees close by."

"Where are you going to build a fire?" Alan asked.

"Why, right here, close to the wagon."

Alan started practicing with the rifle, putting it to his shoulder, closing one eye and aiming down the barrel. He aimed in several different directions as Nancy watched. "You shouldn't build a fire out here," he said, bringing the rifle down, resting the butt on the ground.

"Why not?" she asked.

"Someone can see the fire for a long way. You should always build a night fire that can't be seen unless you're up close."

"Where did you learn that?"

"I . . . I think I learned it from my father," Alan said.

"So you do remember something about your father?"

"I . . . I might. I think he took me out in the wilderness one night."

"My," she said. "That's something. Perhaps in time you'll remember more about him."

But he knew he couldn't. He didn't know for sure whether his father had told him about building a fire. It seemed that he had, but it was also something he had learned from the Apache. They seldom built fires at night and when they did, it was always in some hollow of a hill or near a mountain.

He walked away, thinking about these things, still carrying the rifle. He walked toward the river and knew that he had learned that from the Apaches, too. Rivers were the blood of the earth, and they carried life with them and provided many things, including firewood.

He did not see that Nancy was still standing back by the wagon, studying him, her eyes misty, her chest filled with air that she let out in a long sigh.

Chapter Fourteen

Tallman knew it would be a long and hard search to find Nancy Stafford before the comancheros did. He was forced to cross and recross the treacherous Brazos every few hundred yards to look for wagon tracks, footprints, any sign that would tell him that Nancy had passed by. After a time he realized that she probably had not gotten far in the storm and would still be farther upstream. But he couldn't be sure. He still had to play out the hand he had been dealt.

The comancheros, he knew, would not be traveling fast. They had two women with them, and horses that had been ridden hard for only God knew how long. Unless they changed horses or found more, they would have to take care of the stock they had. And, like Tallman, they had to check the Brazos for tracks. They had no idea where Nancy was, only that she had been with the Jacobs section of the wagon train, and he was sure that Redford and Cotton-Eye knew all about that from the Comanches.

Fret lines etched Tallman's face as the hot Texas sun beat down on him. The wind blew grit against his back until his shirt was layered with a patina of dust. An armadillo scooted out from under the shade of a rock and lumbered off like some ancient battle machine, and swifts roamed the river like debris blowing past him. He thought of Austin and his troubles, knew he had to see him, help him if he could.

Since the Mexicans had won the revolution, everything had changed. When last he'd heard, the government in Mexico City did not want to honor any of the Spanish land grants, which put Stephen Austin in a peculiar position. He was one of the new *empresarios*, empowered by the Spanish government to populate and develop land north of the Rio Grande, and in particular the Brazos River valley. With land selling for two cents an acre, Texas was an attraction for Americans. They would have had to pay at least twenty-five cents an acre on U.S. soil. But the Mexicans, he knew, were still nervous about the United States buying Louisiana and were sure that the government had its eyes on Texas. But Mexicans did not want to live in Texas. The land was harsh, they thought not suitable for raising cattle or growing crops. But all that land had to be populated and protected, so the Spanish had agreed to Moses Austin's proposal to settle the Brazos Valley with Americans who would become both Catholic and Spanish citizens. It seemed the best solution to a thorny problem.

Tallman stopped to rest on a high point overlooking the river. He could see a quarter mile in each direction. He got off the horse and touched the lower part of his back with both hands. "Damn these high Mexican cantles," he said to the dun, who shook off flies and scattered sweat in all directions.

There were few, if any, settlers this high up on the Brazos, Tallman knew. Austin had wanted his people to settle the lower Brazos, had wanted to be near the coast, which Tallman was sure made the Mexicans nervous. The longhorn cattle had drifted from the wild country above the Rio Bravo, the border separating lower from upper Mexico, to the south. The Mexicans down there considered them mainly a nuisance, but killed them for their hides and tallow. Sometimes, a brave family would cook one of the rawboned cattle, but the meat was mostly tough as shoe leather and as hard to swallow as a gritty biscuit. Once in a while, Tallman would see a few strays along the Brazos, but they were skittish and took to the brush like deer.

Tallman rolled a smoke, something he did very seldom, but the tobacco calmed his mind, even on a hot day such as this. He took in the smoke, felt it scratch at his throat and warm his lungs. At times, he liked to say, a smoke was better than breathing fresh mountain air. At others, it was like inhaling wild onions.

Off in the distance to the north, something caught Tallman's eye. It was only a speck in the river as it rounded the bend, nearly a half mile away. Then, as the speck grew closer, he saw that it was a dugout canoe, a small one, paddled by a white man. Tallman watched as the man dipped his paddle deftly into the current, keeping the canoe on a straight course down the middle of the river.

As the canoe drew closer, Tallman took off his hat and waved it in case the man had not seen him. Back came an answering wave, and Tallman saw that the voyager was wearing buckskins. He pointed down to the river and then led the dun down to the shore through a crevice in the land. For a time he could not see the canoe or the paddler, but he had plenty of time to meet him. The river was running slow and the man was not trying to make time, using his paddle only to steer, not to propel.

He was surprised, when he reached the river, to see the canoe hurtling toward him from no more than forty yards away. He stepped away from the dun to show that his hands were empty and waited until the canoeist put the boat into shore.

"Howdy, stranger," the man in the canoe said. "First friendly face I've seen in many a mile."

"Seen any unfriendly ones?"

The man laughed and stood up, then walked in a crouch to the bow. He stepped out of the canoe and pulled it up on the bank far enough so that it would not drift away.

"No, can't say as I have. We just don't see many folks up this way."

"Didn't see a woman, did you?" Tallman asked. "All by herself, pulling a wagon with an ox, a due cow tied to the rear."

"Who'd be askin'?"

"The name is Jon Tallman."

The man's face lost its rigid cast, but he did not smile. He stepped away from the canoe and walked up to Tallman.

"I'm Virgil Ottmers. Heard about you from Don Estévan."

"You the silversmith? Have a spread downriver near the *huecos*?"

"That'd be me,"

"Woman's name is Nancy Stafford."

"I know her," Ottmers said. "Left her upriver 'bout a day's ride back."

"Left her?"

"She wanted it that way," Ottmers said. "I left a boy with her she calls Alan."

"That was her son's name."

"It's a long story," Ottmers said.

Tallman put out his cigarette, dropping it to the ground and grinding it into the soil with his bootheel.

"You got another one of those smokes on you?"

"I do."

"I got some chaw, but my pipe's been empty since I crossed into Texas."

Tallman fished out a small pouch of tobacco, handed it to Ottmers. Virgil turned back to the canoe and rummaged through a rucksack, fished out his pipe. He filled the bowl half-full out of politeness and tamped it down.

"Be generous to yourself," Tallman said.

"I just want a few puffs, thanks."

Tallman tied up the dun and walked over to talk to Ottmers after the voyager's pipe was lit from a burning glass.

"How come you're out to find Nancy?" Ottmers asked.

Tallman told him about Tom Redford, Cotton-Eye, the other comancheros, and the Comanches. All the time he was talking, Ottmers nodded knowingly, as he matched up certain facts that Nancy had related to him.

"So you think Redford was behind the Comanche attack on Jacobs's wagon train?" Ottmers asked.

"Almost certain. I think Redford was with the co-mancheros long before he joined that wagon train. Splitting off from it made Jacobs a ripe target."

"There are bastards in this old world."

"Woods are full of 'em," Tallman said.

"Seems to me you're outmatched."

Tallman worked a clod of dirt with the heel of his boot. He nodded, sighed deeply.

"Nancy wanted to go out on her own," Ottmers said lamely as he finished up his pipe.

"I know. She's one stubborn woman."

"She's here illegally, you know."

"As are many others," Tallman said. "That's not a big problem. You know Stephen. He's very strict and doesn't want drunkards nor profane swearers or idlers. He's already kicked out some families."

"I heard that," Ottmers said.

"Nancy should have no trouble getting Austin to grant her land. It's the Mexicans she has to worry about."

"They don't want us here."

"No," Tallman said. "Austin's in Mexico City right now, fighting to keep his families here."

"I told Nancy what she had to do."

"Good. She's smart. She'll have to go to San Felipe de Austin, though. Maybe to Mexico City."

"You can help her." It was not a question. Ottmers knew that Tallman was no drifter, no idler, and was, in fact, a friend of Austin's. Austin spoke of Tallman often.

"I can, and I will," Tallman said, rising to his feet.

"I'd help you if I could, but I've got to get back. I've been in Santa Fe and, while I have Mexican help, my stock will need lookin' after."

"Don't fret about it, Ottmers. Either one man can do what I have to do or an army can't."

"That boy with her. He's pretty shaky. He's been through a lot."

"He'll go through a lot more, likely." Ottmers had told Tallman the rudiments of the story of how he had found Alan with the comancheros in Santa Fe, and bought him off of Cotton-Eye.

"Austin probably won't let her stay if she doesn't have a husband," Tallman said.

"She says she aims to get one."

"Not much chance of that out here. Even in San Felipe she won't find anyone worth marrying."

"Stephen has a kind heart," Ottmers said.

"But he's all business, too. Best thing that woman can do is hightail it back to Missouri or wherever she hails from. Damned if she has any business out here with no man."

"She's got iron in her, Tallman."

"This country will melt it down to liquid solder."

"She's got spunk left over," Ottmers argued.

Tallman didn't say anything. He was thinking about Redford and his bunch. A lone woman would have little chance against such renegades, spunk or not. It was not worth belaboring with Ottmers. He was a good old soul, but he had his own tending to do, and the day was getting long in the tooth.

"Any idea where Nancy might be by now?" Tallman asked, after a while.

"Well, we're pretty near Mount Nebo, I reckon, so she must be close to Soda Springs or Palo Pinto Creek, my guess. Or maybe up by Red Bluff. Do you know those places?"

"I do," Tallman said.

"That's my best guess. A good day's ride and then some, pert near."

"God," Tallman said, "she couldn't be in a worse place."

Ottmers smiled wanly. "Well, now, I reckon she could."

"I mean that's prime Apache country, and the Comanches make some showing in it, too."

"And Kiowa," Ottmers said.

"I'd best be getting on, then, Ottmers. You watch your back going down. Cotton-Eye and Bud Redford can't be too far behind me."

"Are you sure they're ahind you, son?"

"Hell," Tallman laughed, "I'm not right sure of anything."

"You watch yourself, too, then."

Ottmers pushed off the bank and hopped into his canoe. He waved an airy hand as the current pulled him away and downstream. In a moment he was gone, and Tallman felt the loneliness of that desolate place wash over him as it had in so many other places. Sometimes, he thought, a man who rides alone hasn't got the sense God gave an armadillo.

He didn't know exactly where Mount Nebo was, but he knew it was a Lipan Apache sacred place. He knew where Red Bluff was, and Palo Pinto Creek, and it was a long ride to either place.

A few moments later, Tallman heard shots downriver. Two, three, rifle reports, then a long silence, followed by a single shot that sounded like a period at the end of a bleak sentence. It was dead quiet when he rode away, heading northwest along the Brazos, and he wondered if Ottmers had gotten through, if the last shot had been his.

He hoped that somehow the kindly silversmith had floated past the gauntlet, out of range. Maybe, he thought, that last shot was a futile one by one of the comancheros.

The bitterness rose up in him like something smoking and sulfurous. Ottmers had shown kindness to a captive boy and a lost woman. He didn't deserve to die at the hands of worthless scoundrels. But the world in Texas was a savage place and death did not discriminate between the good and the bad.

"Come on, boy," Tallman said to the dun. "Let's see if you've got any bottom left." And he put the dun into a gallop and the fresh breeze against his face helped him put down the bile that rose in his throat when he thought about Ottmers and those shots that still rang in his ears like thirty pieces of silver.

Chapter Fifteen

Nancy breathed deeply of the clean air as she gazed at the wide countryside. She pulled in on the reins, and the ungainly cow, its belly swollen to the limits, stopped, its sides heaving from labored breathing.

Alan, sitting beside Nancy on the wagon seat, opened his mouth to say something.

"Hush," she said. "Just listen."

A meadowlark trilled and other species of birds answered with melodic phrases, some short, some long. There was a great silence in between the twitters and peeps of small flitting birds. In the distance, Nancy could see the faint outlines of a mountain, and the river curled around the carved contours of bluffs that stood silent and majestic, blushed as though the red dawn had been frozen and sculpted into a monument of creation.

"Breathtaking, isn't it?" Nancy said finally, murmuring, as if speaking only to herself, to her pounding heart.

"Yes'm," Alan mumbled, straining to see what his new mother was looking at.

"Look, there are trees aplenty, growing thick on both sides of the river, and there's mud for chinking, and grass for grazing, and places to walk along the creek. See the creek?"

"Yes'm. Just barely."

"Umm, I know. It's just too much for your young eyes to take in all at once. Let's unhitch the wagon and walk around. I want to explore this place. But it looks perfect."

Alan looked all around, but he made no comment. He climbed down from the wagon and began to unbuckle the harness. He had learned that if they were to move again soon, he should leave the yoke on. He pushed the cow out of the way as he straightened the traces. He had also learned that they tangled easily and it was a chore to sort them out the way they had been before knotting up.

Nancy and Alan began walking over the land, down to the creek, following it to the river, then back up to flat land above the red bluffs. Nancy stopped often to admire the wildflowers, and Alan then stood obediently at her side before she moved on again.

They walked farther southeast and came to another creek, one that was abundant with water. Nancy oohed and aahed over each startling discovery. She tasted the water, cupping her hands and dipping them into the stream.

"Sweet," she said. "Go on, try some."

Alan knelt down and dipped water from the creek, splashed it into his mouth. "Nice," he said.

The two turned around and walked back to the wagon.

"Alan, this is where we'll make our home. It's a perfect place. Do you agree?"

"Seems nice enough."

"But do you like it?"

"Yes. Lonesome, though."

"Why, people will settle here in no time. What we must do is stake out our lands, mark them so that we can obtain ownership from Mr. Stephen Austin. We must draw a map and take measurements."

"I don't know how to do any of that," Alan said.

"I'll teach you. My husband brought all the instruments we'll need. And I have paper and pen. It'll be fun."

"Yes'm."

"You do see how perfect it's going to be here, don't you?"

"I don't know."

Nancy felt some inner resistance in the boy, as if he was quietly challenging her decision. For the first time since she had taken him to her bosom, she wondered if her choice had been right. She looked for signs of sullenness in Alan, but he seemed calm and unperturbed.

"Don't you think you'll like it here?" she asked.

"Yes'm."

"Well, what's wrong, then? You don't sound happy."

"I am happy, ma'am."

"Am I to be ma'am, then?" Despite herself, she heard her voice rise in pitch.

"Yes'm."

"Not mother?"

"Yes, Mother."

"I want to be your mother, Alan, believe me. But I don't know what's bothering you. Can you tell me?"

Alan suddenly became interested in his right foot. He wormed the toe of his boot into the ground and began to make a little furrow in the earth.

"You must tell me what's on your mind, Alan."

Alan looked away, off into the distance. His foot did not stop moving, as if it were some separate part of him that acted of its own will.

"I'm waiting," she said.

Finally, he looked at her. "I thought we would be going to a village, a town, where other boys and girls my own age lived."

"Did Mr. Ottmers tell you that?"

"No'm. Not exactly. He said there was other folks lived where he did."

"Were," Nancy corrected. "Alan, you must have patience. There will be settlers come to live near us. Not right away, perhaps, but some day. And, we will be going to a town, you and I, to register our land claim with Mr. Austin. Can you wait until then?"

Alan stopped wriggling his toe in the dirt and smiled. "Yes'm. Yes, Mother."

"There. That's better. Now, come, we must hurry. There's lots to do before the sun sets and I need your help."

"I'll do whatever you say, Mother."

Nancy smiled warmly. She took his hand, squeezed it gently. Alan rewarded her with a smile of his own.

"First, we must hide our wagon, then wipe out all our tracks."

"Why?"

"We don't want anyone to know we're here until we have a safe place to stay. Do you understand?"

"There is nobody here," he said.

"No, but you don't want to be captured by the Apaches again, do you?"

"No'm, I don't."

"Well, that's why we have to keep our place secret for a while. Until we can protect ourselves."

"I understand," Alan said.

He hitched the cow up to the wagon again. Nancy handed Alan a broom and told him to sweep away all the tracks, to follow behind the wagon while she drove it to a safe place. He nodded, and as she drove off, he began sweeping with the broom as if he'd done it all his life. It was something he had seen the Apaches do with tree limbs and leaves when they wanted to hide where they were going.

Nancy drove the wagon into a thick clump of trees some distance from the river. Then she and Alan walked back along the route they had taken to be sure they had left no tracks. Here and there she filled in the ruts made by the wagon wheels, and on the way back they dropped stones and dirt along the way to hide the marks of the broom.

"You did a good job, Alan," she told him. "I'm proud of you."

Alan looked down at his feet, embarrassed.

"Now, let's make ourselves a camp. We must build no fire that will make smoke."

"I know how to do that," he said.

Nancy smiled.

"We build it under a big tree limb, so the smoke is broken up as it rises."

"Good. You're a very smart boy."

"Yes'm."

Nancy laughed at his ingenuousness. While Alan gathered wood for the fire, Nancy took everything out of the wagon and set it out. She staked the cow in a grassy place and then brought water from the river and set it out for the cow to drink.

That night, they made no fire, but ate cold biscuits Nancy had made that morning, chewed on dried beans from her larder, and drank tea steeped in cold water from the river. The tea tasted salty, but neither of them complained.

"An Apache could find our tracks," Alan told her after they had eaten.

"I know, but we brushed them all away."

"No, I mean, even the sweepings. They could tell."

"Are you sure?"

"I seen 'em do it."

"Saw," she corrected.

"Yes'm. Some Apaches are real good trackers. They can find an ant's trail over rock."

"Are you sure?"

"Yes, Mother. They pride themselves on tracking their enemies. I've heard 'em brag about it."

"Then we must pray the wind comes up or it rains," she said.

"Pray?"

"Don't you know how to pray?"

"No'm, I never heard that word before."

"It's the way we humans ask God for help."

"Oh, God, yes. The Great Spirit."

"Did you have Bible teaching, Alan?"

"I remember someone reading from a book. I think it was called a Bible. I couldn't make no sense of it, though."

"What do you remember?"

"Adam and Eve. A big flood. Noah. I didn't hardly believe any of it."

"Well, it's all true."

"If you say so, Mother."

"Well, I have a Bible and I'll read it to you every night. I'll explain it to you when you don't understand."

"That would be good."

They spent their days working in secret in that secret place. At night Nancy read from the Bible and told Alan what he wanted to know. They completely dismantled the wagon, stacked its lumber neatly, and covered everything they owned with brush.

"Why did we take the wagon apart?" Alan asked her. "Won't we need it when we go to the town to get our land grant?"

"I expect we'll have to find horses to ride. As well as cattle to raise. But, until that time, we'll use the lumber from the wagon for our home."

They began to cut down trees, not all in one place, but at different locations, and they hauled them overland using the straps from the harness, bending their backs and pulling them up and down slopes, and Nancy showed Alan how to trim the bark and notch each log the way her father had done it when she was a girl and her husband had done it after she was married.

"When do we put up our house?" Alan asked one day.

"When we have all the logs cut and the roof beams."

The days passed, with both wind and rain covering their tracks, and Alan told his new mother that the Apaches could no longer find them. She read to him from the Bible and corrected his English, and he tried to remember his real parents every night, but the images kept slipping away and he always wound up seeing only Mexicans and Indians. It seemed his past had been washed out like the tracks they had made in coming to this place where the red bluffs towered over the river and the creeks burbled their ancient songs and gave them sweet water to drink and the cow gave birth to a healthy calf and they had fresh milk to drink at the end of the day.

They dug out a springhouse that was kept cool by the seep of creek water and they stored meat in there, rabbits and deer that they shot. Alan learned to use the rifle and had a keen eye and a steady hand. He was a fine shot, a natural, she told him, and that made him proud.

During that time, Alan showed her the tracks of a horse that had passed by. A few days later, he saw the same tracks again, going downriver, and still later, he saw the tracks of many horses that had passed by and come back again and all of them were shod, so he told her they were not ridden by Indians.

"I wonder who they were," Nancy said to him.

"People, I guess."

"But were they looking for us? Did they mean us harm?"

"I don't know," Alan said, and it was something they both wondered about all the time they were cutting trees and when they were finally putting up the cabin, way back from the river, at a place that was high enough to see a long ways, the path to it hidden by brush and trees. They dug a garden and planted the seeds Nancy had brought in her wagon.

"That is a funny-looking cabin," Alan said, when they had finished building it.

"Have you ever seen anything like it?" she asked.

"Yes'm. I have."

"And what did they call it?"

He smiled and said, "A fort."

"Well, Alan, that's just what it is. A fort. But it's our home, too, and I hope you will be happy here. With me."

"Oh, I will, Mother, I really will. It's a beautiful fort, the prettiest I ever saw."

They built a corral out of the lumber from the wagon and posts they cut from the surrounding timbered places, and they caught fish in the Brazos, and both were tanned from the sun and furtive as any wild animal. Nobody saw where they lived nor came into their world during this time. But one man had noticed the stakes driven into the ground and wondered about them before he rode on, having passed that way twice.

Before he left the second time, he wrote something on a piece of paper and tied it to one of the stakes and covered the note with earth. He hoped someone would read it before another year passed.

The calf born to the cow was a bull calf and Nancy said he would be the start of their dairy.

"What should we name him?" Nancy asked.

"Virgil," he said, without hesitation.

And the bull calf was christened Virgil in memory of Ottmers, who had brought mother and son together many weeks before. They both thought he would be proud to have a young bull named after him.

Finally the day came when they packed food and set off in search of horses. They left feed for the cow and her calf and planned to spend a week away from their fort. Nancy had no idea how they would catch a wild horse, but they carried ropes with them in case they figured out a way they might come close enough to a horse to use them.

But Alan knew, and he was saving that information for a surprise. It was a gift he wanted to give the new mother he had come to love during the past few months more than anything in the world.

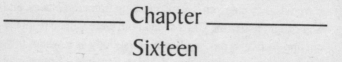

Chapter
Sixteen

Tallman almost missed the stake driven into the ground. If the dun hadn't stumbled over it, he might not have seen it, so it was pure chance that he had ridden over the exact spot. Curious, he had dismounted and looked closely at the stake. It was sheared from a mesquite tree, crudely shaped, no more than a large splinter.

He took a line of sight and rode straight until he found another stake, mentally ticking off the yardage. He smiled to himself as he realized that he had covered a large area. He marked over where the other two stakes would be, figuring a large square that would match up to a rancher's land grant.

He did not try and find the other two stakes right away. From the age of the cut wood, he figured the stakes had been driven in no more than two days before he got to the area. Instead, he rode a large circle, checking the lay of the land, trying to figure where a person might build a log cabin that was not visible unless one rode right up on it. He had already surmised that Nancy and the boy had marked off the section of land. It was just a hunch, but a strong one.

Tallman made camp some distance from the section of land, noting that someone had brushed or swept away all wagon tracks and footprints. Only a practiced eye could have detected the attempt to obliterate the spoor, but he had been a tracker all his life, and while whoever had tried to cover up the markings was pretty good, there were places where the sweeping showed to a trained eye.

Tallman's admiration for Nancy grew stronger over the next few days as he watched the woman and the boy fell trees and skin them out for logs, keeping out of sight and keeping loaded rifles handy wherever they went. He decided not to make his presence known, nor to warn Nancy that Redford was stalking her. She stood a good chance of avoiding discovery if she and the boy continued in their heightened state of awareness.

Tallman made sure his own tracks were obliterated, and when he discovered those made by Nancy and the boy, he dragged brush over those as well. He was impressed that whatever smoke their fires made quickly dissipated before it could be seen from afar.

Tallman stayed, drawing detailed maps of the entire staked area, until the house was built, and he observed its construction with an approving eye. The log house was built like a fort, with a tower and gun ports, and it was well concealed in the trees. He knew that Nancy and the boy she called Alan would be as safe as any frontier family if they kept their wits about them. It was time to leave, for he had matters to attend to and was already late in meeting some of his appointments. He looked in one last time at Nancy and her adopted son, looking especially at the boy who seemed a good, strong companion for Nancy, despite his young age.

Before Tallman left, he wrote a note and tied it to one of the stakes. He carefully covered it with dirt, but hoped Nancy would find it one day before he returned. He rode away with a lighter heart than when he had first come to that place.

Tallman made sure that he left no discernible tracks when he headed south along the Brazos, again crisscrossing it to look for signs of the comancheros. It had not rained since he was at the Stafford place, so he thought he might find tracks. There was still that matter of the two captive girls, and he could not neglect that duty, though he had other concerns on his mind.

One was the weather. For weeks now, ever since the big storm, there had been no rain. The hot desert winds swept across Texas like a fiery rake and he had seen the wildflowers wither and die, the small *huecos* dry up, the Brazos shrink to the size of a creek in some places. If such drought continued, he thought, Austin's first year with the colonies would be bleak indeed. He did not expect Don Estévan to return to San Felipe de Austin until the fall, and he dreaded what his friend might find upon his return.

Tallman found the tracks he was searching for, but it was difficult to put an age to them. They were faint, blown nearly full with dust, and dry as baked corn meal. Still, he followed them across that desolate plain that followed a north-westerly path along the Brazos. At times, they disappeared like smoke only to reappear again in the river bottom, their edges dried and caked as if taken from a kiln.

But he found the remains of old campfires and places where the comancheros had stopped for shade in the sullen heat of the day, and he told himself that he was getting closer to them. They had passed by Nancy's land with no sign of interest and pressed on, oblivious, apparently, to her presence.

Knowing that gave Tallman some small comfort, but as he kept doggedly on the trail of the renegades, he wondered how he could do the captive girls any good if he did come upon them. His tobacco was running very low, but he did not smoke much anyway and he could do without it. Water had not yet become a problem, but it might if the summer furnace continued to blaze.

At night, he made dry camp and lay on his bedroll gazing at the billions of twinkling stars in the sky and listening to the dun munch softly on grass that was sere and slight in nourishment, hoping he would not see the horse's bones poking through his thin summer coat like slats on a wine barrel.

At such times, Tallman wondered how Nancy and the boy were spending their nights in their little fort, and he sometimes regretted that he had not made his presence known, perhaps taken supper with them before riding on. He lay there in the dark with only the silent stars and the bleak bone of a moon above him, feeling more lonesome than he ever had before, but at the same time feeling a part of the vast sky and the endless land spread around him like a sorcerer's carpet.

Tallman rode on, finding faint tracks of horses here and there, and one day, when the afternoon was long and his throat dry as a withered cornhusk, he found something that made his heart beat faster. He was close now, he knew, but his find left him puzzled, too.

The comancheros had gone down to a stretch of the Brazos where the water was deeper and not so briny. They had camped there for three or four days, posting lookouts, feeding on something they had found, like a gift. They had not eaten all of the ox, but they had gotten most of it. Its head was still intact, its eye sockets long since eaten away, its hide dangling in places where the small amount of flesh had been chewed away by rats and mice and coyotes.

Nancy's ox, he knew. He found the place where it had been mired in quicksand, close to the bank where it probably had been able to nibble on grass and drink the salty water long enough to stay alive. Until the comancheros found it and slaughtered it.

There was plenty of sign to read, and Tallman spent two hours putting it all together, picturing everything in his mind. He put the comancheros there for four days, long enough to eat a great deal of ox meat and partake of their evil pleasures. They had salted and packed what was left of the meat and ridden on, but away from the Brazos, heading south now.

He wondered why.

A few moments later, he had an answer to his question. The comancheros had left in a hurry, and not willingly. Tallman found evidence that they had been driven off from that place. There was a number of tracks made from iron horseshoes, showing that an organized party of men had come there and routed the comancheros by force.

Some distance from the main camp, Tallman found more evidence that the comancheros had ridden away fast. There, half-buried under a tree, were the remains of their larder. He found a half sack of cornmeal, some flour, beans, some roots he could not identify, tobacco, coffee beans, and three pounds of salt. He transferred all but the roots to his own saddlebags after tasting the flour, cornmeal, and salt to see if they stung his lips. He would not put it past the comancheros to poison what foodstuffs they left behind. But the foodstuffs tasted all right to him, and he was grateful for the tobacco.

By following the incoming tracks outward, Tallman saw

that the attackers had ridden in formation, indicating that they were probably military. Mexican soldiers, he guessed. He found a number of lead balls that had made furrows in the dirt before they were spent, indicating there had been rifle fire. He also found flecks of blood in the center of the comanchero camp that led him to believe one of the renegades had been wounded.

Evidently, the comancheros had kept their horses saddled in the event they had to leave quickly. Possibly the sentry had given them enough warning that Mexican troops were approaching. The tracks of the fleeing comancheros indicated that they had galloped away at high speed. The soldiers had not lingered at all, evidently, for their tracks showed they had kept up a hot pursuit for some distance.

Tallman followed the soldiers' trail. They all seemed to be heading south toward the Leon River, into flat, tree-flocked country that offered the comancheros some places of concealment in their flight.

Tallman now figured the tracks he was following to be no more than five or six hours old. So the Mexicans must have come upon the comanchero camp early in the morning, around eight o'clock, he supposed. It was now early afternoon, and neither the comancheros nor the soldiers had stopped to eat any food. Likely both hunters and pursued were taking food on the trail, but of that there was no sign.

By late afternoon, Tallman figured he had gained an hour on the soldiers, whose pace now was lagging. He gave the sun another three hours or so to hang in the western sky and by then, the Mexicans would be looking for a place to camp, and the comancheros would probably already be on the Leon River somewhere, forty miles, more or less, from their last camp.

As the sun slid down the blue-sided bowl of the sky, Tallman began to question himself, wondering why he was still pursuing the comancheros when they already had a dozen men tracking them, probably every bit as capable as he. Partly, he decided, it was because he was curious. And he was curious for several reasons. What were the Mexicans doing this far north? From his own experience, he knew the revolutionary government cared little for the Texas province and less about that part of it above the Rio Bravo and the lower Brazos. Still, they did want to protect their property, he knew.

Could such a force sent from below the Rio Bravo be excursionary? Were they sent out to locate unlawful settlers? Or to drive legal immigrants from their lands while Austin was in Mexico City?

Yes, he was damned curious, and to boot, he didn't like to leave loose ends dangling. He wanted to know what was going to happen, and he had to have a look at the kind of Mexican troops who would follow a band, even a small band, of comancheros into what must be unfamiliar territory for the soldiers.

An hour or so later, Tallman came to a place where the Mexicans had stopped to relieve themselves and rest. He figured they had held up for a good fifteen minutes, perhaps longer. They had smoked, they had left cornhusk wrappers and pieces of gristle from beef, small chunks of cooked masa flour that had encased enchiladas, all smeared with a glistening patina of brownish oil. But one set of footprints did not match the others, and that puzzled him.

These prints belonged to a large, heavy man, and the heels were longer, unlike the flat heels of the troopers. He guessed the Mexican soldiers had a white man with them, and that added to the mystery of the force he was following.

He figured they had come at least twenty-five miles south of the Brazos on a more or less straight line. Wherever the comancheros were headed, they were in a hurry to get there and they did not stop, for Tallman found no places where they had rested for more than five minutes. He found those sites and knew the Mexicans must have seen them as well. The women's tracks were quite evident, and if the Mexicans knew anything about tracking they surely knew that the outlaws had two women with them.

The landscape began to fill with shadows that stretched eastward. The plain danced with shimmers of golden light from the intense searing of the sun, and he saw pools of water that bounced and disappeared as he drew closer, like a winter's breath blown against a pane of glass.

The heat was getting to the dun, and Tallman knew he had to get to the Leon before dark or shortly thereafter. Sweat oiled the dun's hide, and lather was building up on the horse's withers like seafoam. Tallman stopped and poured water from his canteen into the horse's mouth, but he knew it was not enough to bring down the animal's temperature. He had just about decided to hole up in the shade and continue tracking after the sun went down when he saw something in the distance, beyond the shimmering mirrors of a half dozen mirages, that seized his attention.

There, on the horizon, stood a pinto pony, a naked Comanche warrior astride its bare back. The warrior held a lance aloft and was making circles in the air with it. Then, as Tallman watched, a line of Comanche riders appeared like smoke out of the trees and joined the lone brave, who then lowered his lance and pointed it due south.

Tallman backed the dun down and held him tight to a spot where he hoped he could not be seen. The dun's color and the dust of his own buckskins would make the two invisible, almost, if they did not move, Tallman knew.

The Comanches were silent as they looked over the tracks, and then they rode around, gesturing wildly to one another. Several of them lifted bows and jerked arrows from their quivers. Tallman strained to see their faces and when the sun was right, he found out what he wanted to know.

The Comanches were painted for war.

Chapter Seventeen

Nancy told Alan about the place where she had seen the wild horses when she was still with the wagon train.

"They were beautiful and so free," she said. "It's a long way to walk, but maybe we'll find some before we get to that spot."

"Where?" Alan asked.

"Near the Brazos. I think they drink from the river. They ran off when we came upon them, but I found their hoof tracks in the mud at the river where my son died."

"We must be quiet," Alan said, "and look hard every day. They'll need water in this heat."

"Yes, it is terribly hot, isn't it?"

They had walked for a day and a half and were now resting in the shade under a tree on the Brazos. They had seen no horse tracks, but plenty signs of other animals, during their trek to the north. Nancy and Alan both recognized the tracks of deer, turkeys, roadrunners, armadillos, small birds, muskrats, mice, rabbits, quail, and other creatures.

During the weeks they had been together, Nancy and Alan had grown close, closer than Nancy would have dreamed possible. In the baking heat of the day she recalled the nights when they were building their fort-house, candles aglow in the unfinished rooms, and talking over supper before they went to bed. Alan was a bright, eager, gifted young man who had never been allowed to use any of his talents. While at first he had seemed backward and shy, once he learned to do a thing, he mastered it, and each task he was asked to perform, he did well. His English was improving, and Nancy had discovered that language was a key to Alan's memory.

The more she spoke to him of proper English, the more he remembered about his parents—not so much his mother, but his father. Alan's memories were vague, though, and whenever she tried to question him more deeply, he skittered away from her like quicksilver in a skillet.

"I remember some things about my mother, I think," Alan said, breaking into the silence of their siesta. "And my father, too, and someone else."

"Someone else?" There was a startled tone in Nancy's voice.

"I think my mother was Mexican. For a long time, I thought she was Apache, but now I think she spoke to me in Spanish when I was a baby. But there was another woman there. I think she was my aunt."

"Your aunt?"

"I think she was my father's sister. She's the one who taught me to speak English."

"I wonder why you're remembering this now?" Nancy asked.

"Last night, when we were talking, and you corrected my English, I remember what the white woman said. She told me that she was teaching me words people spoke. And she said that was different from the words written down in a book or in a letter."

Nancy, who had been resting with her back against a small tree, leaned forward. "Go on," she said. "This might be important."

"She said—I think I called her Auntie Julia—that she wanted me to talk regular so I wouldn't put myself above anyone else."

"What did she mean?"

"I don't know. I can't remember."

"What happened to your Aunt Julia?"

"I . . . I can't . . . I . . . I don't . . . She went away, I think."

"And your mother?"

"I think she was my mother. I think she was with me when I was with the Apaches, but I didn't see her. I mean she was there, but we were not together. They . . . they didn't let me see her no more."

"Any more."

"After I was with the Apaches."

"You poor boy. Maybe it was so horrible you can't remember."

"I remember some," Alan said. "When I go to sleep at night, after we talk or you read to me, I remember some things."

"What else do you remember?"

Alan jerked a sprig of dry grass from the soil and poked it into his mouth. He chewed its juiceless tip as he spoke. "Aunt Julia went away, I think. Just before . . ."

"Just before what?"

"I . . . I don't remember. Just before I was with the Apaches, I think."

"Did they take your mother when they captured you, Alan?"

"I . . . I guess so. It was dark. For a long time it was dark and I don't think I saw my mother. I had an Apache mother after that."

"You poor boy. It must hurt you to think of these things."

"It don't hurt."

"Doesn't hurt."

"No'm, it doesn't."

Nancy did not want to press the boy further to remember unpleasant events in his young life. She was pleased that he had remembered more things about his past, though, especially that he had an aunt. Julia. She wished he could remember his own name and especially his surname.

Nancy wondered if his parents had been killed by Apaches or Spaniards or Mexicans. She might never know, and maybe it was best not to dig up the past. She was somewhat apprehensive now that Alan would remember too much and want to find his real mother. It was a selfish thought, she admitted. She didn't want him to leave her now that she had grown so fond of him. He was now the son she had lost, and she couldn't give that up. Not now, not when they were getting on so well with one another.

"Time to go," she said. "We must find horses or walk all the way back home. And I don't want to leave the homestead for very long."

"No'm," Alan said.

Late in the day, Alan found fresh horse tracks made from unshod ponies. He showed them to Nancy, who became as excited as he. "We'll follow 'em," Alan said. "I've seen the Apaches do that."

"Yes. Maybe Providence is smiling on us at last," she told him.

But as they followed the tracks, Alan became apprehensive. Nancy noticed the change in his demeanor after an hour's tracking.

"What's wrong?" she asked.

"I . . . I don't think these are wild horses," he said.

"Why not?"

"They're too deep. I think they're carrying riders."

Nancy felt a sudden chill in her blood, as if a cloud had passed over the sun. But there wasn't a cloud in sight and she felt the perspiration form on her forehead. Her blouse was soaked and stuck to her back.

"Indians?" she asked.

"Maybe. Maybe Apaches."

"Perhaps we'd better not follow them anymore," she said.

"Just a minute." Alan got down on his knees and crawled around, studying the tracks as he had seen the Apaches do. Nancy stood by, watching him, fanning her burning face with her hand, which did not cool her at all.

"What are you looking for?" she asked, finally.

"Some of the tracks are lighter than others. So maybe they are leading horses without any weight."

"Without riders?"

"Yes."

"But still, we are following wild Indians."

"I think so," Alan admitted. He looked ahead as if trying to see if anyone was ahead of them, shading his eyes with his hand.

Nancy noticed that the boy was trembling. She walked over to him and put an arm over his shoulder. "Are you afraid?" she asked.

"Yes'm."

"Well, if these are not wild horses, we should not follow them."

"It might be plenty dangerous," Alan said.

Nancy breathed deeply, let the breath out in a long sigh. The Brazos snaked northward ahead of them, not as wide as she remembered, and probably not as deep. She turned around to look for another, safer path that would take them upriver.

"Wait, I see something," Alan said. He dropped the hand shading his eyes.

"Where?"

"Over there, in the trees. See it?"

Alan pointed northward to a place where the river took a bend.

"You have good eyes, Alan. I don't see anything."

"By the tree. A piece of red cloth, or something."

Nancy stared hard, but could see nothing.

"We'd better go," she said.

"No, it's . . . it's not moving, but I think I see a face, or a head."

"It could be an Indian waiting to kill us."

"Let me take a look. Wait here. I'll be right back."

Before she could stop him, Alan was trotting away, going toward where he had seen the bit of color. Nancy opened her mouth to call him back, but something told her not to make a sound.

Alan disappeared from view while Nancy stood there, a lump in her throat the size of a hen's egg, throttling her with fear for the boy's safety. She envisioned him being attacked and killed, lying there with an arrow in his chest, breathing his last, or captured and gagged so that he could not cry out for help. She tried to banish these thoughts from her mind, but they grew like mushrooms in a cellar and each passing moment quickened her dread that Alan would be killed at the hands of some savage Indian.

It seemed that hours had gone by, slow crawling hours filled with a nameless terror, before Nancy saw movement where she had last seen Alan. A moment later, she saw him wave, beckoning her to come to him. She let out a pent-up breath and started to run, stumbling over rocks and crashing into brush as she scrambled to reach the boy. Before she got there, Alan was no longer to be seen, and she wondered if she had imagined it all.

"Mother," came a hoarse whisper from the thick foliage of the trees. "Over here."

She still could not see him, but followed the sound of Alan's voice, climbing up the gentle slope to the thicket of trees and brush. Panting for breath, she took the last few steps, the lump in her throat bigger than before and her lungs burning for lack of oxygen.

"Alan?"

"Right here," he said, and she saw his face peering out of the brush. She heard a snort that made her pulse jump, followed by a horse's soft whicker.

"You found . . ." Nancy started to say, and then she

looked down at the tree Alan was standing next to and froze with a sudden wrench of fear. Staring at her with cold dark eyes was a wrinkled old man, a red and yellow bandanna around his neck, long hair down past his shoulders, black paint streaking his face, a scowl on his withered lips.

"Oh, my God," Nancy whispered.

"Mother, this is a man we called Grandfather when I lived with the Apaches."

Nancy's knees turned to rubber and she felt herself going down in a swoon. She opened her mouth to cry out, but what emerged was a mere squeak. Alan leaped toward her and grabbed her before she fell, and she felt the strength in his hands and arms.

"Mother," he said.

"I . . . I'm all right," she said, her voice as faint as a whisper. She felt her legs steady beneath her as Alan held on to her.

"Mother, sit down, please. This man won't harm you. He is old and dying."

"Dying?"

Just then, Nancy heard a horse whicker, and her eyes clouded with puzzlement.

"Over there," Alan said, pointing to a glade where a spotted pony stood hipshot. The pony was hobbled and had a rope around its neck that stretched to a tree some thirty yards away.

"I see it," she said. "Is . . . is this man your friend?"

"I know him," Alan said.

"He's an Apache, isn't he?"

"Yes'm. His name is, well, in Spanish they call him *Anciano*, Old One."

Anciano looked at Nancy, but there was no expression

in his eyes nor on his face. He spoke in a guttural tongue to Alan, who replied in the same language, which was mystifying to Nancy.

Nancy thought the old man looked angry. He moved his hands back and forth and his tone was harsh.

"What's he saying?" she asked.

"He says we must go soon and leave him to die," Alan said.

"Leave him to die?"

"He was left here early yesterday morning by a war party. He wanted to ride with them to this place, a place he saw in a vision. A place where he knows he will die."

"We can't just leave him," Nancy said. "Isn't there something we can do?"

As if understanding her, the old Apache spoke to Alan again. This time there was no mistaking his harsh tone. His voice grated on Nancy's ears like a knife scraping bone.

Alan thought for a moment. "Anciano says the Apache have painted their faces for war," he explained. "They are chasing some Mexican soldiers, and when they have killed them, they will return to see if his spirit has left his body."

"When does he think the warriors will return?" Nancy asked.

Alan looked at the sky, pointed upward. At that moment, Nancy thought, he looked just like an Apache himself. It was if he had shed his young body and grown into something wild and free. There was the look of a hunting hawk in his eyes.

"Before the sun falls from the sky," Alan said, his voice hushed and reverent.

Nancy felt her flesh go cold in the shade of the trees and the fear rose up in her like some unbidden poisonous flower.

"*Vayan pronto,*" Anciano said. Then he closed his eyes

as if saying a prayer, and somehow Nancy knew that he was warning them of danger.

"He says we must hurry and go," Alan said.

"And leave him to die all alone?" Nancy said.

"That is the way of the Apache," Alan said. Then he knelt down and spoke to the old man quietly, so that Nancy could not hear, though she strained to pick up the sound of his voice.

She thought of the old man left to die there, abandoned by his brethren. How cruel, she thought, how inhumane. And then she wondered why an Apache would warn them that they were in danger. Even an old Apache was still an enemy.

"Let's take him with us," she said suddenly to Alan.

Alan looked at her as if she'd gone crazy. He shook his head with vigor.

"If we do that," he said, "then all three of us will die."

Before she could say anything, the old man made a gurgling sound in his throat. His eyes closed tightly shut and he seemed to fold back in on himself. Then, he let out a small puff of breath and shrank back against the tree, looking to her like a withered and wrinkled piece of wood, not human at all.

A moment later, she heard Alan weeping softly to himself.

Chapter Eighteen

The Apaches hadn't seen Tallman. He breathed a short sigh of great relief. Now they were out of sight, over the rise on the horizon, stalking their prey, the Mexican soldiers. And they were stalking, he reasoned, not running up on them hell-bent-for-leather. These Apaches were not a bunch of hotheaded young bucks, but seasoned warriors, their faces painted for battle. He wondered if they were part of a larger bunch, one moving on the rear of the Mexican column, while perhaps others were taking up the flanks.

The Apaches were masters of deception, he knew, and their tactics in the field rivaled that of any American military unit. An Apache could conceal himself behind a blade of grass, could rise up from underfoot without ever being seen until that last terrible moment when the war club descended on a man's crown.

Tallman checked his rifle and pistol, making sure there

was powder in the pans of both weapons. Then he clucked to the dun and moved forward on the backtrail of the Apaches, drifting to the left on a slow line so that he could eventually flank them when he cleared the horizon.

Tallman scanned the ground as he rode, looking for any pony tracks that might indicate a flanking band of Apaches. He saw none, and ticked the dun's flanks to urge him into a faster gait. He dared not push the horse too hard in the fierce heat. The south wind blew at his face with the intensity of a blacksmith's forge fanned by a bellows.

As he cleared the horizon where he had seen the Apaches last, he heard the crack of a rifle. Then it was quiet for several seconds. Before he could take another breath, explosions shook the air like a series of firecrackers popping. The dun shied from the noise, but Tallman reined him back on course. Then he heard the high-pitched yelps and yips of Apaches on the attack.

Moments later Tallman rode over a small rise, and below him on a grassy plain, he saw the Mexican soldiers kneeling down while Apaches crawled toward them on their bellies, bows nocked with bristling arrows. Several yards away, a lone brave held the Apache ponies out of rifle range. Among the soldiers was a man Tallman recognized. Lying flat on his belly, Jacobs had his rifle aimed toward the crawling Apaches. White smoke hung in the air like miniature clouds, and Tallman could smell the acrid stench of burnt black powder.

From his vantage point, Tallman had a clear picture of the battleground. He scanned the surrounding area for signs of other Apaches who might be hiding, waiting to pounce without warning on the island of soldiers. He saw no other Apaches and rode within range of the attackers, pulling his rifle from its sheath. He reined the dun to a stop and put him sideways to the field of action. He counted seven Apaches and picked the one nearest to him as he brought the rifle to his shoulder.

Tallman saw one soldier down, not dead yet, but obviously in pain. Someone had put a stick in his mouth so he couldn't scream. There was also an Apache with a bandanna tied around his arm to stop the bleeding that had already stained his arm crimson.

The nearest Apache turned, as if sensing someone at his back. Tallman brought the front blade sight down on the man, centering it just in front of his arm. He lined up the blade with the rear buckhorn sight, took a breath and held it, then squeezed the trigger. Sparks from the flint sprayed into the pan, igniting the fine powder. There was a tiny puff of air as the sparks flew through the touchhole and ignited the charge in the barrel. The rifle bucked against Tallman's shoulder as orange flame shot out the muzzle through a billowing mushroom of white smoke. The smoke blocked his vision, but he kicked the dun's flanks and guided him to the left with his knees, while he pulled the wiping stick from under the barrel and set it between his teeth.

Tallman heard the thunk of the lead ball as it struck flesh, and when the smoke wafted away, he saw the Apache brave sprawled on the ground, blood pumping from his chest. Four Apaches had turned and were looking in his direction, but he was already pouring black powder down the barrel of his rifle and digging a patch out of his possibles pouch. He removed the wiping stick from his mouth and stuck the patch on his tongue, laved it with saliva as his fingers probed a ball from his pouch.

Before the first Apache arrow was winging its way

toward him, the dun had flanked the warriors and Tallman had the ball and patch seated on the muzzle. He tapped patch and ball down the barrel with the starter's wooden ball, then turned it around and rammed it further down with the dowel on the other side of the ball. Then, he took the wiping stick and seated the ball and patch atop the powder. Finally, he poured fine powder into the pan from the small powder horn and blew away the excess grains before recocking the rifle.

A volley of gunfire raked the plain where the Apache lay and an arrow twanged into the ground a good ten yards from Tallman's position. He grabbed up the reins with one hand and turned the dun to face the Apaches. Then he ducked his head and kicked the horse into a gallop. The Apaches rose and yelled to the horse handler, who leaped upon a pony and rode in their direction, leading the other ponies with a horsehair rope.

Some of the Apaches turned back toward the soldiers and got up on their knees, bending their bows and sighting down the arrow shafts. The soldiers and Jacobs were all reloading their rifles when the arrows were loosed, and they ducked and dodged as the deadly flight winged their way.

Tallman brought his rifle to his shoulder and took aim on the gallop. He picked out the Apache with the broadest back and dropped the sights on him, lined them up, and squeezed the trigger. Through the drifting smoke, he saw the Apache arch his back and reach backward as the ball tore through his flesh and out through the front of his chest, spraying blood and meat all over the dried grasses. The man tumbled forward, and the Apaches got to their feet, drawing fresh arrows from their quivers.

Three of the Mexican soldiers drew pistols as the others

fixed bayonets to their rifles. Jacobs drew a pistol as well. As the Apaches fired their arrows, they ran toward the rifles in a zigzag pattern, pulling more arrows from their quivers on the run. Those Mexicans with pistols fired at their attackers. They fired wildly, in panic, Tallman thought, and missed their targets. Jacobs wisely held off until one of the Apaches came into closer range. He fired, and the Apache he aimed at dropped like a sack of meal, his bow flying through the air with the arrow still attached to the gut string.

Tallman rode up on the last Apache, leveled his loaded rifle at his back, and fired at point-blank range. The brave caught the ball in the small of his back and arched backward in pain, then turned toward Tallman. His belly blossomed with blood and a hole the size of a pie tin. A coil of blue intestine poked out of his abdomen, and his legs flew out from under him.

The Mexicans began to lay down a volley of fire from their rifles. But the Apaches held close to the ground, and the balls passed harmlessly overhead. Tallman wheeled out of range of the arrows and reloaded his rifle on the gallop. The dun took him in a half circle to the rear of the Apaches. Tallman reined in the dun and started to turn him back toward the remaining Apaches.

Two Apaches ran toward the ponies and leaped on their backs. The three remaining warriors rode off as Tallman reloaded his rifle. They disappeared as one of the Mexicans fired one last shot from his pistol. Tallman watched them go, let out a breath, and finished seating the ball in his barrel. He tapped fine powder into the pan, blew the excess powder away until a thin patina of black grains covered the bowl. He closed the frizzen and rode toward the Mexican soldiers.

Jacobs walked out toward Tallman, sliding his pistol back into his belt. The Mexican commander, wearing a captain's uniform, got to his feet and joined Jacobs. The Mexican carried his rifle with the bayonet still affixed.

"Tallman," Jacobs said.

"Didn't expect to see you here, Jacobs."

"Thought I'd hightailed it back to Missouri, did you?"

"I guess I figured wrong. Captain," Tallman said.

"Captain Juan Delgado de Montes y Santiago," the Mexican said. "At your service."

"*Yo tengo mucho gusto en conocerlo,*" Tallman said.

"Ah, you speak the Spanish. Good. It is a pleasure to meet you as well. And you know Jacobs here."

"We have met," Tallman said. "I thought the Comanches had run him out of the country."

Captain Montes laughed. "Jacobs has the story to tell. He told me about you, Tallman. And I have heard of you in Mexico City. From your friend Don Estévan and others."

"And how is Don Estévan?"

"He is well. He is the *gran politico*. Much politics."

"I know."

"I wish you two'd speak English so's a feller could understand," Jacobs said.

As they spoke, the Mexican soldiers began digging a grave for their dead member. Others examined the fallen Apaches and made sure they were really dead.

"The captain tells me you have something to say to me. What of your wagon train?"

"I left it," Jacobs said. Montes walked away and began barking orders in Spanish. Jacobs watched him and continued speaking. "After you left I got to thinkin' about them two gals, and I asked any of the men if'n they didn't want to try and get 'em back from the Comanches."

"None did," Tallman said.

"You got that dead on, Tallman. Bunch of lily-livered jackass cowards. Then, a large force of Mexican troops come up on us and asked if we had immigration papers."

"And you did not," Tallman said.

"None of those with me did, but I showed my papers, signed by Moses Austin hisself, and the commander said I could stay. He escorted the others back up to the Red."

"What about Montes?"

"When I told the Mexican commandant about the two gals, he assigned Montes to help me find 'em."

"Just like that?" Tallman asked.

"Well, no, not rightly. The commandant, he had him some Comanche braves he had took prisoner. Looked to me like he had worked them over pretty good. He said they had give up the gals to a small pack of comancheros. Montes, here, he don't like comancheros none, and he has him two good trackers in his bunch, and we took up after 'em."

"You got lucky, Jacobs."

"How so?"

"You and the soldiers are tracking the right bunch of comancheros. They have the two white women. But they're good, very good, and they know how to lose themselves in Texas."

"You seen 'em?" Jacobs asked.

"I have," Tallman replied. "A friend of yours is one of them. In fact, he's the one who put the Comanches on you in the first place."

"A friend of mine?"

"Redford."

Jacobs swore. "You mean . . ."

"I mean he's a comanchero, and he knew what he was doing all along."

"That sonofabitch."

"No doubt," Tallman said.

"What about them Apaches?" Jacobs asked.

"Lipan. They just wanted some scalps. And horses. They're not with the comancheros."

"Whew," Jacobs said. "I'm sure as hell glad to hear that."

"It's not going to be easy to find Redford."

"Montes has him two good trackers. They can sniff out dog piss a week old."

"Where are the trackers?" Tallman asked. "I'd like to talk to them."

"Up ahead. They wasn't with us when them Apaches jumped us."

"You mean the trackers went off by themselves?"

"Why, sure. They know what they're doin'. What's the matter, Tallman? You worried about somethin'?"

"Jacobs, maybe those Apaches didn't just come up on you by chance." Tallman started to walk over to one of the dead Apaches for a closer look. Jacobs went after him, grabbed his arm.

"What are you tryin' to say, Tallman?"

"I don't know, Jacobs. But I'd say those Mexican trackers are in a heap of trouble."

Jacobs backed away from the look on Tallman's face. It seemed as if he could feel Tallman's eyes piercing his flesh. They were eyes made of hard granite and cold steel. He shivered in the blazing heat as Tallman walked over to a dead Apache and knelt down to look at the fallen brave.

Chapter
Nineteen

Nancy stood silent for a moment, awed by the spectacle of death, stunned by the dreamlike unreality of seeing a man alive one minute, dead and gone the next. Alan stood with her for a moment, respecting her need for silence.

"Should . . . should we bury him?" she asked.

"No. His people will want to know. They will be back."

"It seems so cruel to leave an old man all alone to die like this."

"That is the Apache way," Alan said.

"I hate to just leave him like this. It . . . it seems so disrespectful."

"We must go," Alan said. "Anciano left us a good pony, and that will help us find more to take back to our ranch."

"Oh, I couldn't do that. It would be like stealing. His

friends left him the horse so he could ride home if he got better."

"No, that is not why the Apaches left the pony here," Alan said.

"Why else?"

"The pony was for food. If Anciano had hunger, he would kill the horse and eat it."

Nancy shuddered.

"Really?" she asked.

"Yes. Come, I will get the pony and we will ride away from here. It would not be good if the Apaches found us here. They would make us slaves."

"Yes, yes, of course you're right, Alan. You know them, don't you?"

"Yes'm."

Alan caught up the pony, rigged reins from the horsehair rope, biting through the strands with his teeth as Nancy watched, deftly weaving all the broken strands back together again.

"Horse don't need no bit," he said. "He's knee broke, but this'll give me a better handhold."

"Where did you learn about horses?" Nancy asked. "From the Apache?"

"No'm, I reckon my pa done learnt me."

"My father taught me," she corrected.

"Mine, too," he said. He patted the horse's back behind him. "Can you get up here?" he asked.

"I . . . I don't think so."

"I'll put him on a slope, so's it'll be easier."

The pony responded to Alan's legs and knees, carrying the boy to the top of a slope where it was directed. Nancy walked over. Alan gave her his hand. She took it and swung her leg over the horse's rump. Alan took the sack of food from her and put it between his legs.

Together, they rode off upriver away from that place of death, Alan eyeing the ground for horse tracks, Nancy holding on to his waist with both hands, jouncing atop the horse despite trying to match its rhythm with her own. Soon, her rump began to ache and pain coursed through her dangling legs.

"I think we're both too heavy for this small pony," she said. "Perhaps it would be best if I walked."

"He can carry a deer what weighs more than you do," Alan said.

"I'm hurting, Alan."

"You'll get used to it, ma'am."

"Mother."

"Mother," he said.

"Do you remember your father teaching you about horses?" she asked.

"Some. I know he put me on a horse when I was pretty small."

"You must remember what he looks like," she said.

"Yes'm. He was a cow pony, brown as a nut with a close-cropped mane, bobbed tail."

"No, I mean your father."

"Oh. Well, I don't remember much. His face is all blurred, shadow-like. I 'member he had a deep voice and he didn't talk much. Mainly showed me what to do. I was scared of him."

"The horse?"

"No, my father."

"Why?"

"I don't rightly know. I guess 'cause he was big and I

was so little. He seemed to know everything and I didn't
know nothin'. I mean when I made a mistake he showed me
what I done wrong and I felt bad."

"Sounds to me as if you had a good father."

"Yes'm. I was still scared of him."

"Did your mother love him?"

"Aw, I don't know about that. I was too little."

"Well, did you see them embrace? Your mother and father? Did you see them kissing?"

"No'm, I reckon not. Not that I remember, anyways."

"I wish you would remember more than you do," she
said, a vein of exasperation in her voice.

"Yes'm, I keep tryin', but I only see my ma and pa as
shadows. No faces. I remember one thing, though."

"What's that?" Nancy asked, eagerness in her voice.

"I called him Pa and called her Mama."

"Not Mother?"

"No'm. I called her Mama."

"That's interesting," she said.

They rode for an hour until Nancy begged him to stop
and let her get down and stretch her legs. She walked around,
pondering the meager information she had gleaned from
Alan, trying to piece together a picture of his lost and forgotten parents, but she could come up with no more than a
deeper mystery. Still, his parents must have been kind to him
and loved him, and they had evidently taught him a great
deal. He spoke well, if in an unschooled manner, and his father must have known something about horses. Alan had apparently learned a lot from his mother and father, as well as
from the Apaches and Mexicans. She wished she knew more
about him, though.

"Ready to go on?" he said. "I think we're coming close

to a place where I saw horse tracks when I was comin' down-river with Mr. Ottmers."

"I . . . I don't recognize this part of the river," she said.

"It's a heap farther up than where Mr. Ottmers found you."

"It is? Then, it must not be far from where—" She could not finish the sentence. An image of her own son, her own Alan, burst like a flash of light in her mind. She wondered if she could bear to see her son's grave now that she had found Alan, and how it would affect him if she broke down and cried.

It all seemed so long ago, her husband's death and her son's, yet only a few weeks had passed, not even a year or even nearly a year and yet Alan, the new Alan, had given her a sense of fulfillment, a sense that a new time had been given to her, a new life that enclosed only the two of them and shut out all sadnesses and losses, all pasts, both his and hers.

Alan was walking around, leading the pony, and she had almost forgotten about him. When she lifted her head she saw that the boy was looking at the ground with an intensity that was almost palpable.

"Alan, what do you see?" she asked.

"Old horse tracks. Unshod tracks. Maybe this is the bunch whose tracks we both saw."

"How old?" she asked.

"Two, three days. Less than a week."

Nancy felt a flutter of excitement in her chest. They were running low on food. She had planned to be gone no more than a week, and had put a little extra in the sack, never-theless, she was conscious of time flitting by.

"Can you track them?"

"Yes'm, I can."

"Do you want me to wait here?"

"No, we'll go together. Sun's so hot, the tracks have dried up, but I can see the scuff of their feet on the ground. They won't drift far from the river in this heat. You rested up?"

"Yes," she said, lying just a little bit. "I'm ready."

"You know, I just remembered something my father told me."

"What was that?"

"He told me that if a man breaks a horse, he's the horse's master. But he said no man can be another man's master."

"I wonder why he told you such a thing," Nancy said after a moment. "It's almost as if he foresaw that you would be kidnapped and made a slave."

"Yes'm, I thought about that a lot when I was with the Apaches. It didn't make no difference, though."

"What do you mean?"

"The Apaches," he said, "never heard what my father said."

Nancy and Alan rode off at a slow pace. Alan followed the dim horse tracks upriver. These wound in and out of brush, followed a game trail, rose up on to flat prairie, over grazing land, back down to the river, then to dust wallows.

"Are the tracks any fresher?" Nancy asked, after an hour or so.

"No'm, they 'pear about the same."

"Maybe we're wasting our time."

"I don't think so. We'll ride a while longer, see if we can't catch up to 'em."

"Whatever you say, son."

She could almost feel Alan smile, though she could not see his face. The ride grew more comfortable for her, although her bottom was sore and her legs chafed a bit from rubbing against the pony's flanks. The pony did not seem to tire, and Alan seemed to be in perfect control of him. Occasionally Alan spoke to the horse in either Apache or Spanish, Nancy didn't know which, and his voice seemed very soothing to her. She closed her eyes and began to doze. She was glad that Alan had put the ropes in the same sack as their food and cooking utensils. She didn't have to worry about that. And he was carrying the heavy rifle, which they had taken turns carrying when they were both afoot. She considered herself very lucky to have such a smart son.

Late in the afternoon, Alan reined the pony to a sudden halt. Nancy bumped up against her son's back, which jarred her out of her drowsy state.

"What is it?" she asked.

"I saw a horse."

"Where?"

"Up ahead. Just a quick look, his legs and part of his body. But definitely a horse."

Nancy leaned to her left and peered from behind Alan's back. The land dipped ahead into a shallow draw choked with trees and brush.

"I don't see anything," she said.

"Shush. He's in there. Maybe more than one." Alan spoke in a soft whisper.

Nancy kept silent, but she continued to look down into the shallow draw, hoping to see the horse Alan said he had seen. The heat from the sun created shimmers on the land around the draw and she wondered if Alan's eyes had been playing tricks on him.

"He's holding tight in there," Alan said. "I can see him now."

Nancy strained to see anything resembling a horse, but she saw nothing.

"I'm going to get off," Alan said. "You hold the pony and wait here."

Alan slid off the pony's back, then helped Nancy to dismount. He set the rifle down, retrieved one of the ropes from the sack. He handed her the reins, then began to stalk toward the grove of trees, hunching over. Nancy thought he looked like an Indian in white man's dress. She had sewn him clothing—pants, shirt, underwear—from bolts of cloth she had brought with her. Alan disappeared into the trees, making no sound that she could hear.

Several moments passed and Nancy thought she could hear thrashing in the brush, the snap of sapling limbs, the rustle of leaves. Her eyes ached with the effort of trying to see what was happening. The pony began to fidget, pulling on the rope, trying to back away from her. She tugged with both hands to bring the animal back under control. Then she heard what sounded like a crashing sound and a shout.

"I got one," Alan yelled.

More thrashing in the noisy brush.

"Whoa, whoa," Alan cried out.

"Be careful," Nancy said, trying to make her voice loud, but her throat was constricted with concern and the words came out in squeaks.

The brush seemed to break open and she saw the head of a horse emerge, followed by its chest and the rest of its body. There was a rope around its neck. At the end of the rope, Alan was holding on for dear life. But the big horse was too much for him. Alan went down, crashing to the ground heavily, and Nancy felt something squeeze her heart.

"Whoa," Alan screamed and the horse dragged him out

of the brush and over rough ground. Still, he held on as Nancy watched in horror.

"What can I do?" she screeched.

Alan was too busy to reply. The horse was bucking to throw the rope and twisting as it stood on its hind legs. The horse seemed to dance as it arched its back and galloped first one way, then another.

"Let him loose," Nancy begged, but Alan held on to the rope with both hands, even though she was sure he would be killed.

The horse disappeared over a rise and Nancy's hand flew to her mouth as if to stifle the scream that lodged in her throat.

She still heard the sound of Alan's body being dragged, and as she wondered what she could do to help, the horse appeared again, galloping straight toward her. When the big animal saw her, it veered back toward the brush.

Alan tried to get to his feet, managed to gain partial footing before the horse jerked him down to the ground again. Nancy heard a resounding crack as the horse smashed into the small brush and disappeared.

Alan bounced along like a rag doll, too small for the horse's thundering energy. The boy tried to brace himself to avoid being smashed against a large tree. Nancy saw Alan crash against it, heard the sound of his body thudding into the wood, saw the rope fly up into the air like a dead snake. Then, the scene grew quiet, and Nancy stood for a long moment, trapped by a rising fear that choked off her voice. Alan lay very still, and she no longer heard the horse moving in the brush. It was as if time itself had stopped and all things in motion had come to a sudden jarring halt.

"Alan," she whispered, fighting off tears. "Don't die, please. Please don't die."

She pulled on the rope and started walking toward where Alan lay.

As she drew closer, she saw the blood covering his face. In her heart she knew he wasn't breathing.

The tears came flooding from her eyes as she approached the fallen boy.

She knew that Alan, like her real son, was dead and that once again she was all alone.

Chapter Twenty

Tallman grabbed the dead Apache by the hair and lifted his head, looking hard at his paint. Jacobs walked up and stood over him.

"Apache, right?"

"Lipan," Tallman said.

"Like you said."

"Look at his nose," Tallman said, pointing a finger at the dead man's nostrils.

"It's got a scar on it."

"It's been cut clean through. Then sewed up. See the little wrinkles at the edge?" Tallman twisted the head back and forth so that Jacobs could see the scars.

"So? Somebody doctored him."

"This man," Tallman said, "figures to be close to thirty years old. He was a prisoner of the Comanches. They cut his nose, probably to teach him a lesson. He got away, had some medicine man sew him back up."

"What are you gettin' at?" Jacobs asked.

"Maybe this bunch was friendly with the comancheros."

"Apaches and Comanches? They're sworn enemies."

"True," Tallman said, "but what if the comancheros took this Comanche slave and set him free? He would owe them something, wouldn't he?"

"Maybe."

"Maybe this Apache, and the rest of them, were trying to help the comancheros. Maybe to repay a favor."

Jacobs whistled. "I see what you mean. Do you think——"

"I think these Apaches wanted to slow you down so those trackers could walk right into a trap. Let's go talk to Captain Montes."

Jacobs grunted.

Tallman let the head of the dead Apache fall back to the ground. He stood up, dusted himself off. His jaw set in a grim cast, he started walking toward Montes, Jacobs following alongside.

"Do you take scalps?" Montes asked.

Tallman shook his head. "No."

Montes smiled. "That is too bad. It might teach these savages a good lesson."

"I don't think the Apaches need any lessons," Tallman said. "It was the white man who taught them to cut off hair."

"I do not believe that."

"I expect the Spaniards taught them a hell of a lot more than that."

Montes stiffened. "I have Spanish blood in me."

"I was talking about Cortez."

"Even so. I hope you are not trying to offend me, sir."

"No. I think these Apaches were renegades. They are Lipan, but that one over there was once a Comanche prisoner."

"You are sure?"

"I am pretty sure."

"So, what are you trying to tell me, Tallman?"

"I think the comancheros are lying in ambush just ahead. The Apaches wanted to slow you down."

"You seem to know a lot about the Apaches and the comancheros," Montes said, a note of suspicion and a hint of accusation in his voice.

"I have had dealings with both."

"Are you a Mexican citizen?" Montes asked.

"I was a Spanish citizen before, and I am a Mexican citizen now."

"You own land here?"

"On the Brazos, yes."

"We are checking everyone's papers," Montes said, an officious tone to his voice.

"You may check mine when you come to my ranch."

"Be sure that we will, sir. Now, we must bury our dead and say our prayers, then continue in pursuit of the comancheros."

"I would like to ride with the captain if he would find me worthy," Tallman said, oiling his words with perfect Spanish diction.

"I would be grateful for your company, sir."

"I would make that burial quick if I were the captain. Comancheros don't mind cutting throats in the dark."

Montes paled as if Tallman had struck him with a dueling glove. "Sir, I have two scouts tracking the comancheros. They will be back soon and we will know where the enemy is." He clicked his heels together and barked orders at his men.

Tallman walked to one side and reached for his tobacco. He offered some to Jacobs.

"Let me get my pipe out of my saddlebags," Jacobs said. A moment later he was back, but he had tobacco of his own.

"Case you're runnin' short," he said, offering the pouch to Tallman.

"Thanks, I was."

The two men lit their tobacco with a burning glass and smoked as they watched the Mexicans digging a grave for their fallen comrade. The ground was dry and hard as far as they dug, and they didn't dig deep.

"Where you figger them comancheros is laid up?" Jacobs asked, drawing on his pipe.

"They ought to be at the Leon by now.' '

"River yonder?"

"Yes," Tallman said. "A lot of places to hide between here and there and all along that river."

"You been there?"

"I've been there. Tell me, Jacobs, why did you decide to come after those two girls held captive?"

"I got to thinkin' 'bout Redford and the fight we had over the wagon route. I thought he acted mighty peculiar and it got to eatin' at my innards."

"You thought Redford might be behind the Comanche attack?"

"I was pretty damned sure he was when me and the others in my train got to talkin'. Redford acted mighty peculiar from the beginning, when we started out from St. Louis. I got to thinkin' that he bulled his way into comin' along and none of us really knew much about him."

"Did you suspect he'd been in Texas before?"

"He never said no word about it, but me and the others

noticed he seemed pretty comfortable once we crossed the Red. Almost like he was a-comin' back home."

"He was, I think," Tallman said.

"I don't think Montes trusts you," Jacobs said, looking toward the Mexican captain.

"I wonder why he's this far north in the first place."

"He told me he was with a larger force that was seeking out illegals, comancheros, Comanches, and others threatening Mexico's sovereignty."

"He's likely a revolutionary. They think anyone on Mexican soil is an enemy."

"You may be right, Tallman. Montes seemed pretty bent on catching them comancheros and gettin' the girls out of their clutches."

Tallman said nothing. No need to put bad thoughts in Jacobs's head. Montes might be the best of men, but he was operating in a wilderness, and the laws that applied in Mexico City were often forgotten this far north of the Rio Bravo.

The men finished digging with their bayonets and tin cups. Montes ordered the body put into the shallow grave. Tallman and Jacobs stood in reverent silence as the grave was covered with dirt and stones. Then Montes said a few words of prayer, blessed himself, and ordered the men to get their horses. Some of the soldiers made the sign of the cross as they walked to their mounts.

"Check your rifles and pistols," Montes said, "then mount your horses."

Tallman and Jacobs climbed atop their mounts, waited for the captain to give further orders. When all the soldiers were ready, the captain looked them over, then spoke in rapid Spanish.

"What's he sayin'?" Jacobs asked.

"He is talking to a corporal named Bendigo, telling him to lead out. He is telling the others to form a skirmish line fifty meters apart."

As Tallman explained, the soldiers lined up on Bendigo. The corporal lifted his hand and gave the signal to move out. The captain stayed behind the line of mounted troops, watching both flanks as his head turned from side to side.

The calvary had not moved more than thirty yards before the corporal raised his hand again and reined his horse to a halt. A moment later, a rider came out of the trees ahead, his horse moving at a slow walk. Behind him emerged another man, swaying in the saddle, leaning forward, both hands gripping his saddle horn.

"Looks like trouble," Jacobs said.

Tallman said nothing. He rode up to fall in at the captain's side.

Montes looked at Tallman, his eyebrows raised.

"Those are your scouts?" Tallman asked.

"Yes" the captain said tightly.

The first soldier rode through the halted ranks and stopped before his captain. There was blood on the side of his shirt from a flesh wound. Tallman saw the rip in the soldier's shirt. The trooper had the high cheekbones of an Indian, the sanguine hue to his cheeks. He had small, close-set dark eyes, a flat nose, thick lips.

"Report," the captain said, in Spanish.

"Captain, the comancheros have turned back toward the Brazos. They have the two gringo girls with them. One of them had an eye like the white of an egg. They surprised us and there was shooting. Martínez is badly wounded."

"And you, have you been shot?" the captain asked.

"It is only a little thing, my captain."

"How do you know they have turned back and are going to the Brazos?"

"We were following when we lost sight of them. They had gotten water from the Leon and were riding to the northeast."

"How is it that you did not know they were waiting in ambush for you, Santiago?"

"Only one man ambushed us, my captain. He was not on his horse and we did not expect him to be waiting for us."

"Stupid," Montes spat. "Very stupid."

"Yes, my captain."

Martínez, the other scout, rode up, slumped over forward in the saddle. As he stopped, his eyes rolled to the backs of their sockets. He slid sideways and fell from the saddle. Not a single man moved to help him.

Tallman stepped out of the saddle and walked to the fallen soldier. He knelt down, checked for a pulse, and found that the scout was still alive but had lost a considerable amount of blood. There was a hole in the man's left arm, and he appeared to be bleeding from his abdomen.

Tallman pressed a spot on the wounded man's arm, and the bleeding stopped. He ripped a portion of the soldier's torn sleeve and made a tourniquet. He found a stick and tightened it.

"Thanks," the man said in Spanish.

"You have the luck," Tallman said in the same tongue.

Tallman felt the man's abdomen. He was surprised to see a slash there, as one made by a knife.

"You are cut," Tallman said.

"The comanchero, he tortured me."

"Why?" Tallman asked.

"He asked me about the white woman on the Brazos."

A warning sounded in Tallman's brain.

"What white woman?" Tallman asked.

"The one who has built the fort. The one with the young boy."

"You saw her?"

"We have seen her, yes."

Tallman turned and looked up at Montes, whose face was impassive.

"This man will live," Tallman said. "He was shot and then tortured."

Montes turned to the other scout. "Is this true?" he asked.

Santiago nodded.

"You did not tell me this," Montes said.

"There was no time."

"I will want to hear your full report," Montes ordered. He gazed down at the wounded man with a wilting look of utter disdain. Then the captain glared at Santiago and spat to one side, as if daring the tracker to tell even one small lie. "You let yourself be captured by those filth, those savages?"

"Yes, my captain, that is what passed."

"What kind of a soldier are you?"

"An obedient one, sir."

Montes spat at the ground again, more as a demonstration of his disgust than from a need to expectorate. Then, he growled an epithet of contempt for his subordinate that was nearly untranslatable. Santiago did not blink. Instead, he stared at Captain Montes with eyes that blazed with pride and defiance. Montes turned his head to look at Tallman, who was still kneeling next to Martínez.

"This miserable example of a man is a traitor," he said, nodding toward the fallen scout. "He has provided us with no useful information."

Tallman stood up, looked at Montes directly with flashing eyes. "On the contrary, Captain," he said, "Martínez gave us a great deal of information. And I'm sure he'll give us a great deal more. If you will be patient, I'd like to ask him a few more questions. May I, sir?"

Montes thought for a moment, then nodded curtly.

Tallman nodded in exchange and knelt back down to talk to the scout. He spoke loud enough for Montes and Jacobs to hear him, and he spoke in Spanish.

"I want to know what the comanchero asked you and what you told him, Martínez. Can you tell me?"

"Yes. He wanted to know if we had seen the white woman who lives on the Brazos, the one with the young boy."

"And what did you tell him?"

"I told him we saw no such woman."

"And then he tortured you?"

"Yes. He put the knife in me then."

"And what did he say about the white woman with the boy?"

"He said that he would give me gold if I told him where the woman was."

"But you told him nothing," Tallman said.

"I told him nothing."

Martínez's eyes glazed over with a rush of pain that shook his body. Tallman stood up, wiped the dirt from his hands on his buckskin trousers.

"Of what use is this information?" Montes asked.

"It means Redford and the other comancheros are hunting for the woman and the boy," Tallman said. "It means they are headed back to the Brazos. It means I must go after them and stop them."

"You know where the white woman is?" Montes asked.

"Yes, I know."

"Does she have papers?"

"She is a personal friend of Don Estévan. He has her papers in order."

"I do not believe you," Montes said.

Tallman shrugged and looked the captain straight in the eye. "If it comes to that, then I must tell you that the woman is my wife and the boy my son and they are here under my papers."

"*Bueno,*" the captain said sharply, "we will ride with you to see this white woman and the boy you say are your wife and son. If I find you are lying, she will be driven from Texas and you will return in irons to Mexico City with me."

"You, Captain Montes," Tallman said, "are a bastard."

"If I am a bastard, sir, then you are the son of a whore."

"We may both be right," Tallman said, looking at Jacobs, who had remained silent. "It is a wise man who knows his own father."

Chapter
Twenty-One

With fumbling fingers, Nancy tied the pony's rope to a bush near where Alan lay. She sobbed softly, a heavy weight in her heart.

"Oh, Alan," she cried, "why did you have to die?" Tears blinded her as she turned to where his body lay in a heap at the foot of a large oak. She stiffened as she saw the blood covering his face. Streaks of it streamed down from his forehead and onto his cheeks, girding his neck in a crimson scarf.

She knelt down, her hands still shaking, and touched his chin. She felt the sticky blood on her fingers and reached in her pocket for a kerchief to wipe the blood from his face. She was sure that he wasn't breathing, and her own heart seemed to stop beating as she brought out the kerchief and began to dab at his face.

The horse in the brush made a sound. Nancy's heart seemed to jump. She wanted to kill the animal. A mindless rage rose up in her as she began to wipe Alan's face gently, tenderly. The horse whickered and she wondered absently why it had not run away. The Apache pony pawed at the ground with its right forehoof.

"Oh, Alan, poor Alan," Nancy breathed.

Then the boy's eyelashes fluttered and she saw his chest heave.

"Alan?"

He did not respond, and Nancy felt her heart sink. She thought she might faint if Alan were to die. She gently slapped his cheeks and blew air on his face. "Alan, please, Alan, wake up," she crooned. "Please, please, my son, don't leave me."

Alan's eyelids moved slightly, as if he was trying to open them.

Nancy's heart fluttered, then she shook his body, desperately trying to bring him back to life. She prayed silently for God to breathe life into Alan.

Alan moaned, and his eyelids opened slowly. He stared up at her blankly for a long moment, and Nancy's voice caught in her throat.

"Mother," he rasped. "Mother?"

"Yes, Alan, yes, I'm here. Please wake up. Oh, please."

He coughed, and his eyelids batted twice but then stayed open. He breathed so loudly she could hear him inhaling, then letting the air out slowly. She drew him close to her, crushing him against her breasts. She rocked him as if he were a baby and caressed his hair with her hand, murmured in his ear.

"I-I'm all right," Alan said finally, and she held him away from her as if to reassure herself that she was not imagining any of it.

"You poor boy, you gave me a fright."

"I hit my head," he said, touching a finger gingerly to

the back of his hair. He winced when he touched the knot that was growing there. "Ouch."

Nancy laughed out of relief. She helped him to his feet.

"Are you strong enough to stand?" she asked.

"Yes, I just got the breath knocked out of me is all."

Then they both heard the pony snort in the brush. Alan's eyes lit with excitement. "He's still there. I knotted the rope, hoping it would hang him up."

"Wait," she said, when he started to run into the brush. "You-you're not strong enough yet."

"I'm all right, really. Just got a little headache is all. I'll be right back."

She watched him go, her hand touching her throat in fear that he would never return, and she heard him crashing through the brush like a wild animal.

It was quiet for a moment, then she heard more noises and Alan's voice speaking in a tongue she didn't understand. After several seconds, the noises grew closer and Alan emerged from the brush, leading the horse on the rope. The horse seemed willing enough to follow Alan.

"You got him," Nancy said.

Alan grinned. "He's a beauty, isn't he? I should say she, she's a mare. Good clean lines, good legs, strong chest." He rubbed the horse's chest, leaned against her muzzle.

"Is she wild?"

"A little. She'll tame down. What do you want to name her?"

"You name her, Alan."

Alan thought for a moment. "Let's call her Linda. That's a Spanish word. It means beautiful."

"Linda is a fine name. Can you ride her?"

"I don't know. I'll try after she gets used to me. Can you

get the pony and we'll walk them together for a ways. That might tame Linda down."

"We don't have a name for the Apache pony," Nancy said.

"We'll call him Pinto. That means paint in Spanish."

"I guess that's a good enough name," Nancy said, smiling wide for the first time that frightful day. She felt her heart swell with love for her adopted son, as she caught up Pinto and led him over to Alan and Linda.

"Should we head back home?" Alan asked.

"Yes, Alan, let's go home," Nancy said. "We have two horses when before we had none. I'm feeling very rich at the moment."

"It's a good start," Alan said, grinning. "Someday, we'll have many horses."

"We will," she promised.

The two began walking down toward the Brazos, each leading one of the horses. Alan stopped often to let Linda graze, and he patted her neck and spoke to her in English and Spanish. He rubbed her nose and between her ears, kneaded her chest.

"I've been looking at her hide," Alan said after they had been walking for more than an hour.

"What?" Nancy said.

"Linda's hide. I've been looking at it. She's been rode before."

"Ridden," Nancy corrected.

"Well, anyway, she has marks on her side where a blanket rubbed. I don't think she had a saddle on her. I don't see any cinch marks, but she's been rode before."

Nancy did not correct him this time, just smacked her lips and blew air through them.

"Do you want to try and ride her?" Nancy asked.

"We could make a lot better time if we were both riding."

Nancy looked at the pony for a minute. "I'm not sure I could ride Pinto by myself."

"Sure you could," Alan said, smiling. "I'll bet you're a good rider."

Nancy wiped sweat from her forehead and smiled wanly. Alan began to fashion a halter at one end of the rope tied to Linda. He cut a length free and made the knots that created bands across the muzzle and in front of and behind the horse's ears. He then made a loop underneath to hold the reins and secured that neatly. When he was finished, he slipped the halter over Linda's head and made reins from the remainder of the rope.

"Are you ready to ride?" he asked Nancy.

"Will you help me up?"

"Just lead Pinto to the hill there and mount from the high side."

Nancy did what Alan suggested and crawled on top of Pinto. She smiled, a look of triumph on her face. A moment later, Alan climbed aboard Linda, and she held fast for him. He patted her neck and spoke comfortingly to her. Then he pulled on one rein and the horse turned to the south.

"We're off," Alan said, and Nancy followed him on Pinto. She was soaked with sweat and her legs chafed as they rubbed against the pony's side, but she was happy to be moving. Even a little breeze was some relief from the intense heat.

The beating sun was a tortuous, merciless beast breathing fire upon the land, sucking out all the moisture from the earth and its beings. Lizards sought the shade of rocks and tree boughs, and the armadillo curled up in muddy wallows

near the river, while the roadrunners did not stir from grassy
patches of shadow in search of snakes that refused to move
from their lairs.

Nancy and Alan were soaked with sweat, and the horses'
hides glistened in the bright sunlight until it seemed they had
swum the river and only recently emerged. They stopped
often to let the horses drink and rest. Still the heat boiled
down upon them, the air hot as a blast furnace, the wind
nonexistent. Nothing stirred upon the land except the two riders whose lips turned parched as the earth upon which they
trod, whose eyes ached from staring at the dancing mirrors of
mirages, whose blood thickened to aspic and left their brains
gasping for reason and searching for images of cool climes,
the deep blue waters of memory's ocean.

Nancy felt that she was going to faint and fall from
Pinto's back. She opened her mouth to call out to Alan, but all
that came out was a horrid rasp that startled her as if she had
heard her own death rattle. Alan rode ahead, slumped over
Linda, his shirt sodden with sweat, his hat drooping over
sightless eyes.

"Alan," she said huskily, and her voice did not carry
above the dull thud of hoofbeats. "Alan, we've got to stop;
we've got to find shade."

This time, her voice, louder than before, reached Alan's
ears, and he turned to look at her with vacant, red-rimmed
eyes. He pulled on the reins and Linda stopped, her neck
bowed, her head drooping like some sorrowful denizen of a
broiling hell.

"What?"

"I . . . I can't go on. Alan, we've got to find shade. Got to
rest."

Alan turned the horse and rode back to her. He lifted her

canteen, weighed it in his hand. "You've hardly drunk any water," he said, his voice as hoarse as hers.

"I've been rationing it."

"Rationing?"

"Saving it. Look at the river here. It's hardly a trickle."

"You must drink it," he said.

She took out the cork stopper from the wooden canteen and held the pouring spout to her lips. She drank a tiny swallow.

"You must drink all of it," he said.

"Then it will be gone."

"The water will be inside you," he said. "Where you are dry. The Apache fills his body with water when he crosses the desert, when the heat is like this. He says that the white man dies because he keeps the water in his canteen."

"I'm not an Apache," she said weakly.

"And you will die if you do not drink like one." There was a sharp edge to his voice that she had never heard before. He grabbed her canteen and put it to her lips. "Drink," he said. "Drink until you choke on it."

"You're cruel, Alan. The water's hot. It doesn't taste good."

He poured the water down her throat until she gagged. She spluttered and fought for breath while Alan held the canteen at the ready until her choking spell had passed. Then he put the canteen to her lips once again and poured the warm water into her mouth. This time Alan let the water trickle into Nancy's mouth, and she was able to swallow it more easily. When the canteen was dry, he stoppered it and let it hang from her shoulder.

"I'm sick," she said. "My stomach hurts."

"You'll get over that."

"What about your canteen?" she asked.

"It's empty."

"What are we going to do for water?"

"I've been looking for a creek or a spring. We can, if we have to, drink from the Brazos."

"But it's so salty along here. We'll die."

Alan looked at her with pity in his eyes.

"We'll drink it if we have to," he said grimly. "We won't die."

"How's your head, Alan?"

"It hurts. I've got a lump on it the size of an apple."

"You poor boy."

"We have to keep moving," he said.

She looked around, but there was not a tree in sight. It was as if the earth had suddenly gone barren. There was brush along the river, small trees, but none that would give them any fair amount of shade. To her the land looked desolate for as far as she could see.

"I remember there being trees all along the river," she said.

"We just hit a stretch where none have grown. It's open to the wind here and nothing grows big."

"It's a horrible place."

"The sun will be down soon, and we'll find shade before then, I'm sure."

"What about water?"

"We'll find water, too," he said. "Good, sweet, cool water."

She thought of an oasis in shade, a place of deep bubbling springs and fresh cool breezes, and her stomach quieted and she no longer felt so giddy. The images vanished quickly as Alan turned his horse and started to ride away.

"Come on," he said. "We have to keep going."

"Yes," she breathed, "we must. We must keep going."

The pinto moved at the prodding of her heels, following Linda dumbly as a pack animal, its ears twitching at the flies that swarmed over its head. There were streaks of blood in the pony's sweat, little crimson rivers that striped its shoulders, and she winced at the sight. If she was suffering so, she thought, the horses must be suffering just as badly, or even worse.

They rode on into the hottest part of the afternoon, stopping to let the horses test the river water. Neither Linda nor Pinto drank from the brackish waters, but they snorted water through their nostrils and snuffled water through their teeth and squirted it back into the river undrunk and even more foul.

The sun began to sink in the sky, and it seemed to Nancy that its lone eye was staring directly at her, reaching out with its flames to scorch her to a crisp. She could see its anger shimmer and lash out through the heavens like some avenging god, and she wondered if she would ever see shade again or drink water that was not laden with salt.

Alan, just ahead, was a blur as sweat drenched and stung her eyes until they burned with the acid tang of raw lye. But she was not so thirsty as before, when Alan had made her drink all the water, and she was not so light-headed. She could almost feel the moisture in her muscles and sinews, the healing waters that now were giving her life. She knew she surely would have fainted had the boy not forced her to drink.

How long, she wondered, until the sun went down? It seemed to hang endlessly in the sky, not moving at all, just holding steady in one spot, burning like an open furnace, as if to destroy all life in its fiery path.

Of what use were the horses if they were dead? she thought. She should never have suggested that they go in search of stock when a drought was on the land. They could not go on much longer. She felt weak, but not hungry, and unless they found some water, they would both dry up inside like gourds and fall senseless to the ground to leave their bones with those already dotting the empty, treeless countryside, bones that were like grave markers, bones of animals bigger and stronger than they, bleached from the pitiless, heartless blaze of the sun.

They reached a stretch of the Brazos where there was no water flowing whatsoever. It was a place Nancy remembered from before. Ottmers had floated down it on his dugout canoe. But now it was as if the river had never been here. Rocks and sand and dried roots jutting from the bank made Nancy lick her dry lips. Pinto whickered at the sight, and Linda bleated pathetically as she sniffed the dry sandy wash where once a river had flowed.

Alan climbed down from Linda and knelt in the sand. He dug underneath it, scooping with his hand. He held up the soil and it trickled dry through his fingers.

"I feel very weak, Alan," Nancy said. "I must have water."

Alan stood up and looked downstream. For as far as he could see, the river was dry. Either it had changed course or it had gone underground. How far underground, he did not know. He shaded his eyes and peered at the sun. It was still above the horizon, pulsating with flames and hurling heat down on them in nauseating waves.

"Where is the water?" Nancy asked.

"Gone underground," Alan said, "Maybe the river changed course."

Nancy's shoulders sagged. "No, it didn't change course," she said, the despair evident in her voice. "It just vanished."

Alan held a hand up to the western horizon. He clamped fingers together and placed them between the sun and the earth. Four of his fingers fit in the space.

"What are you doing?" she asked.

"Measuring how long the sun will stay in the sky. Each finger means fifteen minutes."

"You put up four fingers."

"Another hour," he said.

Nancy crumpled. Her insides ached, her mouth was dry, her throat parched so that she was sure it would bleed if she tried to speak. She slumped and felt the life drain from her. She could feel the heat smothering her. Her lungs began to burn, and a dizziness assailed her.

Alan started to walk toward her just as she toppled from the back of the pinto. His legs were wobbly, but he managed to run the last few feet and catch her before she fell to the ground. Her weight forced him to his knees, but he held her so that she was not hurt.

He looked down at her wan face, her cracked, dry lips, her face like chalk and heard her shallow breathing.

"Mother," he croaked.

But Nancy did not answer.

Chapter
Twenty-Two

Montes ordered his troops to check their canteens. He shook his, which was empty. Corporal Bendigo examined each man's water supply and gave his report to his captain.

There is less than two liters among us," Bendigo said.

"Then we must fill our canteens before returning to the Brazos," Captain Montes said.

"But where?" Bendigo asked.

"We must go to the Leon."

"That is a ride of two hours at least," the corporal said.

Two men worked on Martínez, cleaning his wounds, applying salve and bandages to the knife cut. The hot, still air reeked of medicants and blood. Then the two helped Martínez to his feet and pushed him onto his horse. He held on to the saddle horn, gritting his teeth.

Montes ordered his remaining scout to lead his troops

toward the Leon River at a slow, stately pace, both horses and men showing the effects of too much sun and not enough water. Tallman lagged behind slightly, but he was aware that Montes was watching him. He gestured with his head for Jacobs to slow down and join him.

When Jacobs fell in step, Tallman leaned over and whispered to him, "Does Montes speak English?"

"Some. Why?"

"I need to head back to the Brazos. I don't want him stopping me. Are you game to come with me?"

Jacobs nodded.

"How's your canteen?" Tallman asked.

"Almost empty. What about you?"

"I've plenty of water to take me past sundown."

"Enough to share with me?" Jacobs asked.

Tallman just nodded, for Montes was looking their way.

"What are you whispering about?" Montes asked Tallman.

"About how hot it is," Tallman lied. "Like a furnace, *como un horno calido*."

"It is more hot than hell," Montes said and turned away.

"How are you going to give this bunch the slip?" Jacobs whispered after a few moments had gone by.

"Give him another forty-five minutes or so, when he's closer to the Leon. He won't give chase with most of his canteens empty."

"He'll track you, sure as hell."

"He'll track sand and sage and hot air through an empty sky," Tallman said.

The two men fell silent and rode slightly to Montes's rear. The scout was well ahead. There had been no sign of him for almost a half hour. The sun hammered at them on the open plain, the only shade thrown by bushes too small for a man to crawl under. The cavalry horses all dropped their heads, plodding along like beasts condemned to the slaughterhouse.

The gaps between the riders grew wider until the men lost their formation and were strung out along a line a quarter of a mile long. Tallman gradually fell farther behind, Jacobs following his lead, until both men were out of earshot of Montes.

"Let him disappear over the horizon," Tallman said, "then we'll turn our horses toward the Brazos."

"It's a long ride in this ungodly heat."

"We won't push it. Your horse looks sound. The dun hasn't pissed in half a day. He knows how to keep his water."

"I don't know, Tallman. That sun ain't goin' to let up none."

"I don't want Montes tagging along. I've got to find Nancy and see that she's safe."

"From the comancheros?"

"And from Montes. I don't trust that bastard as far as I can throw a thousand pound of brick."

"You think he would harm Mrs. Stafford?"

"I think he would put her in irons as soon as look at her," Tallman said, then turned his horse as the rump of Montes's horse dropped from view.

Jacobs reined his horse into a tight turn, and the two headed for the Brazos, the sun now hanging off their left quarter. Sweat had soaked through Tallman's buckskins, and Jacob's cloth shirt and cotton trousers were sodden as washrags.

Jacobs kept looking over his shoulder for the next grueling five miles, but never saw any Mexican soldiers coming in pursuit of them. Finally, he stopped looking when he noticed that Tallman never looked backward at all.

"Do you think he'll send soldiers after us?" Jacobs asked.

"No, he won't split his forces. There are still Apaches out there who damned sure know what he's doing. He'll want every man in case he's attacked again."

"I hope you're right. But we could run into the same bunch of Apaches ourselves."

"We could at that," Tallman said, and unstrapped one of his wooden canteens. He reined his horse to a stop and passed the canteen to Jacobs. "Drink all you want. It may be the last."

"And then what?" Jacobs asked, taking the canteen.

Tallman shrugged. "God will provide." Then he started examining the ground, walking around bent over. He picked up a pebble and put it in his pocket. A few minutes later he picked up another of approximately the same size. He put that one in his pocket as well.

Jacobs said nothing. He drank the warm water and made a grimace. "It burns all the way down," he said. "I don't feel much wetter inside than I did before."

"At least your muscles won't bunch up on you. Hell of a thing to die of thirst."

"How would you know?"

"I saw a man too far gone from the heat once," Tallman said. "Up on the *Jornada del Muerto*, the Journey of Death. I tried to pour water in his mouth, but he couldn't even open it. His lips were purple and cracked, his skin almost as black as the ace of spades."

"You couldn't save him?"

"I pried his mouth open. Poured water down his throat and he strangled on it. Couldn't even swallow it. I had to turn him upside down and pour it all back out."

"Jesus," Jacobs swore.

"His muscles were rigid as barrel staves, his belly swollen like a pregnant sow's. He couldn't talk, couldn't walk, and couldn't reason. His eyes begged me to put him out of his misery."

"And did you do that?"

"No, I gave him some shade under my horse and wet my bandanna and put it on his lips, hoping he would suck some water into his gullet."

"Did that help? Did he get some water in him?"

"No," Tallman said. "But he finally got his voice back."

"He spoke to you?"

"He did."

"What did he say?" Jacobs asked.

"He said, 'Shoot me.' "

Tallman lifted the dun's head and poured some water into its mouth. Then he walked over to Jacobs's horse and did the same. The dun didn't drink as much as the other horse. Tallman shook the canteen. It was empty.

"How much water you got in that other canteen?" Jacobs asked.

"Enough," Tallman lied.

Jacobs snorted. "What about that thirsty man? What did you do after he asked you to shoot him?"

"I told him to make his peace with his God."

"And you just watched him die?" Jacobs asked.

"He closed his eyes and breathed one last breath."

"As if he wanted to die."

"He wanted out of the sun," Tallman said.

"What did you do then?"

"The man's horse was already dead, bloating in the sun.

I walked over and checked the saddle and saddlebags. The man had four canteens with him."

"All empty?"

"No. One was almost empty. The other three were almost full. Some of the water had evaporated in the heat, but there was plenty of water."

"Why didn't he drink it and save himself?"

"He did drink it. Like most men in the desert, he was conserving it. He must have lost track of time and forgotten to drink, forgotten how much water he had left."

"You're saying he was addled by the heat," Jacobs said.

"That happens. Without water, a man can get confused and lost. I looked at the tracks of his horse, and the man had been riding in circles for most of a day, I figured."

Jacobs scratched the back of his head. "It don't seem possible. The man could have lived. He was just dumb."

"No, he wasn't dumb, Jacobs. He just didn't drink enough water. I figured the heat to be a hundred and twenty degrees that day. Such heat can cook a man's brain pretty quick."

"You're making me thirsty, Tallman."

"It's not that hot, Jacobs. And not long until sundown."

Jacobs frowned in disbelief. Then, Tallman reached into his pocket and pulled out the two pebbles he had picked up earlier. "Here, put this in your mouth, Jacobs," he said, "and tuck it inside your cheek."

"A stone?"

"It'll stave off the thirst for a time."

Tallman popped the other pebble into his own mouth. Jacobs stared at Tallman as if the man had lost his senses, but he put the pebble into his mouth. After a moment, he smiled.

"I think it works," Jacobs said.

"Just make believe it's hard sweet candy," Tallman said, "loaded with juice."

"It still tastes like rock."

The two men rode on, with Tallman leading Jacobs on a southeasterly path toward the Brazos. The sun fell away to their backs so that they were no longer squinting one eye.

Tallman felt cool in the buckskins. His sweat formed a cushion between his skin and the heat, cooling him as he rode. Jacobs kept wiping sweat from his forehead and pulling his shirt away from his chest to let air cool him off some.

"What was that story you told Montes about Nancy being your wife?"

"Just a story," Tallman said.

"Montes would want proof."

"Where did Montes come from? What are his orders? Do you know?"

"He is quartered at Béxar. The way I heard it, the Mexican government doesn't want anything to do with the settlers on the Brazos or the Colorado. But Montes works for Colonel Lujan, who takes his orders from the district governor."

"That would be Trespalacios," Tallman said.

"I believe I heard that name passed about."

"Why was Lujan sent out to survey the Brazos, I wonder," Tallman said.

"Montes told me they were hunting the Karankawas who murdered a lot of Austin's settlers. The governor, Trespalacios, you say, ordered Lujan to protect the settlers."

"Then Captain Montes is overstepping his authority. He's not supposed to check the settlers' papers."

"Montes seems bound to make a name for himself," Jacobs said.

"The Mexican policy has been to leave the settlers alone," Tallman said, "and Austin has complete authority. Looks to me like Montes might not like Americans in Mexico."

"Montes wants to take Injun scalps back to Béxar. He don't care much what tribe they belong to."

"And you want him to go after those Comanches that hit your wagon train."

"I'm thinkin' about them gals, Lorena Belton and Sara Jane Wells. It's a damned shame."

"But the Comanches don't have those girls anymore, Jacobs. Comancheros do."

"I reckon that's so."

Tallman headed the dun in a more northerly direction, taking a direct route to the Brazos, a course that did not take them close to any shade trees, although some were visible at various points of the compass.

"You seem to know where you're goin'," Jacobs observed.

"Could be," Tallman said. "Look ahead, just over the horizon."

Jacobs squinted his eyes and stared hard at the blue cloudless sky ahead. After a moment, he grew excited.

"Is that what I think it is?" Jacobs asked. "Dust. Or smoke?"

"It's dust."

"Not much. It's pretty faint."

"It's just hanging there, Jacobs. No wind. I've been watching it for about ten or fifteen minutes now."

"What do you make of it?"

"Could be the comancheros. Or what was left of those Apaches."

"Which do you figger?"

"Comancheros, probably."

"Lord. And we're right on their track."

Tallman said nothing. The dust slowly filtered back to earth and no more appeared. But Tallman held to the line he had marked in his mind, and a half hour later, he pointed to the ground.

"What?" Jacobs asked.

"Horse tracks."

"Be damned. Sure enough."

"An hour old, at least."

Tallman stopped the dun and climbed out of the saddle. Jacobs reined in his horse and stepped down as well. Tallman hunched over and studied the tracks. He worried the pebble around in his mouth as he walked several paces to make sure.

Jacobs leaned against his horse on the shady side, seeking some shelter from the blistering blaze of the sun. He sucked on the rock in his mouth, and the rock was dry as bone. He pushed it to the other side of his mouth with his tongue and tried to salivate, but he was too dry to produce any moisture. His mouth felt full of dust and his throat was raw from dehydration.

"I'll take a swig from that other canteen you got there, Tallman," Jacobs rasped.

Tallman stood up, looked at the former wagon master.

"You'll have to wait a while longer to wet your whistle, Jacobs."

"Why? I can't hardly get no breath down my throat as it is. I'm plumb dried out."

"Suck on that pebble I gave you."

"I've sucked it down to a nub and it don't give me no taste of water."

"It'll be tough. You just have to bear up."

"Ain't you got no water left in that canteen?" There was a dangerous edge to Jacobs's voice.

Tallman walked to his horse and slipped the other canteen from his saddle horn. He shook it and there was no sound. He pulled the cork and held the canteen upside down.

"Damn you. You lied to me."

"It got you this far, didn't it?"

"What in hell's that supposed to mean?" Jacobs demanded.

"If I'd told you there was no more water, you'd have fretted about it all this time and worry would have dried out your innards quicker than the sun."

"Who do you think you are, God?"

Tallman smiled wanly. "No. I just know what heat can do to a man. You bear up a while longer, Jacobs, or you won't make it to the well."

"Well? What well?"

"The well these comancheros are heading for. It's an old Apache well. Not many people know about it."

"Well, why in hell didn't you say so? How far is it?"

"About ten miles."

"Ten miles? Jesus God Almighty, I doubt if my horse can make it."

"He'll make it, and so will you, if you grit your teeth and keep your mind off how thirsty you are."

"Where is this well anyways?" Jacobs asked.

"See those tracks? Those are the comancheros, all right. And they're headed straight for that well."

Jacobs's face drained of color. He looked for a moment as if he might break into tears. His lips trembled when he spoke next. "What if they're waiting for us there?"

"They just might be. My guess is they'll not need much

water if they filled up their canteens and goatskins at the Leon. And they'll push on to the Brazos, which is probably where they're headed."

"I hope to hell I can last another ten miles."

"You can last twenty if you want to," Tallman said and recorked his canteen and climbed into his saddle. He rode off, not looking back. After a moment, Jacobs spit out the pebble in his mouth and pulled himself up into his saddle. He did not try to catch up to Tallman, but now he wished he had not spit out the pebble. His mouth was drier than ever, and his vision was beginning to blur. He recognized that as the first sign of a thirst so powerful, he could well die if he did not get water into his stomach soon.

Jacobs fell farther and farther behind, but he could still see Tallman's back up ahead. The man sat straight and tall in the saddle as if he had not a care in the world.

"Bastard," Jacobs muttered, and then began to wonder if Tallman had been sneaking water from that canteen all along and that was why it was now dry. He kicked his horse in the flanks, but the animal did not respond.

Ten miles, he thought. It might as well be a hundred. He was going to die like that man Tallman had told him about, the one on the *Jornado del Muerto*.

Jacobs slumped in the saddle, strangling on the dust that seemed to fill his throat from somewhere inside him. When he looked up, after a while, Tallman was nowhere in sight. The sun beat at his back, drawing the sweat from his body until there was none left and he felt as if he were burning in hell.

Chapter
Twenty-Three

Nancy moaned as if she was in pain, but her eyes remained closed. Alan knelt down beside her and leaned down to listen to her breathing. For a moment he thought she might have died, for her breaths were so short and shallow he could barely detect them.

"Mother," he said softly, but Nancy remained unconscious.

He lay his rifle down close by, then hobbled the horses before returning to Nancy's side. He picked her up in his arms, surprised at her lightness, and carried her toward a small bush that offered some shade. The sun was just barely above the horizon, but he knew he had to cool her down quickly.

Alan searched the dry riverbed downstream for fifty yards, and around a bend he found a small pool of water surrounded by wet sand. Above the bend, a stand of trees grew along a fissure that provided runoff from the plain. He tasted

the water and it was sweet; no salt. Satisfied, he returned to
the spot where Nancy lay aswoon, picked her up, and carried
her to the waterhole.

He lay her in the water with her head on high dry
ground. Then he returned for their rifles and the horses. He
untied their hobbles and led them to the trees, tied them up,
and put the hobbles back on. The horses nickered when they
smelled the water, and he soothed them with soft words. He
had much to do.

The place he had chosen was shielded from the falling
sun, and he knew it would be dark soon. He went down to the
pool and propped Nancy up against the bank. She had not regained consciousness. She looked so peaceful, he thought,
but her skin was so pale it seemed almost transparent.

When she seemed settled, he went back to the pool of
water and cupped his hands. He splashed water on Nancy's
face and on her chest to cool her down. He filled a canteen
and brought it to her, uncorked. He put the lip of the spout up
against her lips and pried them open with his fingers. He gently poured a small amount of water into her mouth, waited to
see if she strangled.

When she did not, he carried the canteen up to the horses
and watered Linda first, lifting her head up and pouring water
onto her teeth until she opened her mouth. Then he did the same
with Pinto until the canteen was empty.

Shadows began to stretch across the riverbed, and the air
began to lose its heat gradually. He could no longer see the sun
in the sky and knew it would sink beyond the western horizon
in a few moments, bringing with it a blessed coolness to the
scorched land.

Alan refilled both canteens and took one to Nancy.

Again he poured water into her mouth, a small amount, feeling gratified when she licked her lips. Her eyelashes fluttered, and he gave her more water.

"Mother," he whispered. "Mother, wake up. You must drink."

Nancy stirred, shivered slightly, and opened her eyes. For a moment, she stared blankly past Alan's face, then her eyes came into focus on him. She opened her mouth, and Alan held the canteen up to her cracked, parched lips. "Drink it slow," he said.

"Slowly," she said huskily, a faint smile on her ravaged lips.

"Slowly," Alan said, smiling at her.

Nancy drank the warm water, swallowing with difficulty. She wanted more, but Alan took the canteen away, shaking his head.

"That's enough for now," he said. "You will get sick if you drink too much right away."

"I . . . I'm so thirsty, so dry," she said, her voice sounding tired and weak.

"I know. The sun is going down and it will be cooler soon. I'll give you more water in a few minutes. Just sit there and rest."

"You're such a good boy," she said, and leaned back, closed her eyes.

Alan dug out the edge of the pool, and more water bubbled up from underneath the riverbed, widening the pool. Then he filled the canteen Nancy had been drinking from and stoppered it. He lay it next to the other one by her side, touched her hand briefly, then rose and walked up the bank to fetch the horses.

He brought Pinto and Linda down to the pool and let them drink more water, but took them away from the hole before they foundered. He gave them each more rope so they could graze; the sun went down, and he could feel the sudden coolness in the air. He carried their sack of food and cooking utensils down to the river and set them near the water.

Nancy opened her eyes as he sat down beside her and lifted a canteen to her lips. She drank eagerly, a little more than a cupful, before Alan took the canteen away.

"More," she said.

"In a little while, Mother. Feel any better?"

"Some. I'm just so thirsty."

"You can drink more after you get used to what you already drunk."

"Drank," she corrected.

"Yes," he said, smiling.

She reached out and patted his cheek. "You saved my life," she said. "I dreamed I was dead."

"That was not a good dream," he said, suddenly sobering.

"I don't know if it was a dream, maybe just a notion. It seems unreal now, but I thought I was laid out next to my husband and my son and was going to be put into the ground with them."

"Don't think those things no more," he said.

"Any more."

"Any more," he repeated.

"You'll learn to speak correct English yet," she said.

"Yes'm."

The shadows thickened and it was quiet for a while, the only sound the snuffling noises of the horses feeding on dry grass, the *whick* of grass roots being torn from the earth and mashed up in their mouths.

"Are you hungry?" Alan asked Nancy.

"No. My stomach is all knotted up."

"You can have more water now."

"Good," she said, and this time she held the canteen to her lips by herself and drank until Alan motioned for her to stop. She handed the canteen to him and he drank a cupful.

"Is this the first drink you've had since we got here?" she asked.

"Yes'm. I wasn't all that thirsty."

"You are a remarkable boy," she said.

"Yes'm," he said, grinning.

"Maybe you should eat," she said.

"I'm not very hungry either. I'll wait until you want to eat."

"I'm so tired. I don't seem to have any energy."

"You'll get back your strength before morning. I'll lay out our blankets and we'll get some rest."

"That would be nice," she said, her voice weak and lazy, as if the thought of sleeping had mesmerized her.

Nancy dozed as Alan made up the bedrolls on soft ground. Crickets and frogs chittered and croaked as dusk came on swiftly, and soon the sky was dark as black velvet and stars blinked into view like tiny lamps, glistening lanterns hanging from invisible wires.

Alan let Nancy sleep. He did not light a fire, but checked their rifles, moved the horses up by the trees where they could be easily caught up and still have plenty of night graze. There was still no wind and the darkness was close, fetid, warm and balmy. He sat above the river, where he could see a long way in several directions, and listened to the nightjars purl their monotonous and repetitive songs, watched the bats prowl the air on silent wings. Somewhere in the distance, he heard the soft trill of a screech owl, and, later, the coyotes called out in chilling ribbons of notes rising into the upper register of the voice range and he thought the sound was the most beautiful he had ever heard, like women singing or children crying out at play.

For some reason, Alan was not sleepy. His senses seemed keyed up as he listened to the night sounds. He could even hear Nancy breathing and was glad that she was resting after an exhausting, skin-blistering day. He was worried about her. He could not remember such a drought in his lifetime, although he remembered summers with the Apaches when it was very hot. But they always knew where to find the natural rock bowls where water collected. The Apaches called them *tinajes*. They knew where the hidden springs were, and places where there was shade and cool breezes.

He plucked a blade of dry grass and chewed on the bitter root, lost in thought. He should be tired, but his muscles were singing with energy; he felt alive and vibrant with the rhythm of the night, calm in the solitude of a sky full of stars and no moon up yet, but his eyes were keen enough to see the shapes of rocks and bushes and trees and the horses grazing. Often, with the Apaches, he had sat up with the other boys watching after the herd of horses and cattle, and at such times he had felt free and happy.

He tried to think back to the time when he was a small boy and still with his mother and father, tried to hear their talk, tried to remember what they said, what they called each other, and he closed his eyes and felt transported back to those times when he was just learning to walk and play.

He saw himself as if he were another person, and he could smell the scent of the new adobe bricks some men were making by the side of a stream, Mexicans who let him play in the mud and straw, and he watched them and tried to make little bricks without the wooden forms and he heard the Mexican men laugh and joke with each other and speak about him and his mother. And, in that state, he remembered what they called his mother, that they said she was beautiful and kind, and her name rose into his memory like some buried flower that suddenly blossoms unseen in the darkness of night.

And, in the distance, Alan heard voices, human voices, deep and harsh, and his blood seemed to freeze in his veins. His eyes popped open as a ball of fear formed in his stomach. He could not tell how far away the voices were, but he sensed the danger and he hopped to his feet and scrambled down the bank to the place where Nancy sat, now deep asleep.

Alan put his hand over her mouth and whispered into her ear. "Wake up, wake up," he said, and in the light of starshine saw her eyelids fly open.

"Whump?" she mumbled, her mouth covered by his hand.

"Someone's comin'," he said. "We have to get away. Don't make a sound. I'll get the horses."

Nancy nodded, and he took his hand away. Then he ran as quietly as he could to the horses, slipped their hobbles and untied their ropes from the trees. He led them down to the water pool and Nancy was standing there, waiting for him.

He helped her onto Pinto's back and handed her the sack of utensils and food and her rifle. Then he picked up his own rifle and climbed onto Linda's back. He motioned for Nancy to follow him and headed south down the dry riverbed, the canteens hanging from his neck on either side.

Later, he beckoned for Nancy to ride up alongside him.

"What did you see?" she asked.

"I heard voices. Men talking."

"Who?"

"I don't know. They spoke Mexican, I think. Too far away to tell."

"What do you think, Alan?"

"I think they were comancheros."

"Why do you think that?"

"Just the way they talked. Not like Mexican ranchers or herders, but rough talk, with a lot of bad words."

"You have seen comancheros before?"

"Yes, they are very bad men. Mr. Ottmers bought me from comancheros."

"That's right. I had forgotten. Are they still after us?"

"I don't know, " Alan said, "but they will be when they come to that pool of water."

"How do you know this?"

"They were riding down the riverbed, right toward us. Their voices sounded hollow, as if they were between the high banks of the Brazos."

"You are a smart boy," she said.

"We must keep going. We will not hear them talk again. They will not make noise after they find out where we were." Alan did not tell his mother that he had also heard women screaming, screaming in English. He did not want to worry her any more than she already was. But the women's screams lingered in his memory, and he could only imagine what the comancheros had been doing to them. He would tell Nancy about them when she was more prepared. Now was not the time, he knew.

Nancy looked at the boy who had become her son, and

her heart swelled with pride. He was so wise for one so young, she thought.

Alan rode ahead of her, waving for her to follow him. He did not tell her why, but she stayed obediently behind him. The pinto splayed up sand and gravel from the dry riverbed as Alan galloped off. He disappeared from view, and she felt suddenly alone. She looked over her shoulder to see if anyone was following them, but she could not see anything that would cause her alarm.

She wondered, for a brief moment, if Alan had abandoned her, and dismissed the thought as silly, beneath her. But the apprehension built up inside her as she tried to peer through the darkness and see where Alan had gone.

Nancy's horse began to get frisky, picked up its gait as if something was chasing it. At first, Nancy tried to hold it back, but there was no bit in its mouth and she had to give the pinto its head.

The riverbed wound through low and high banks, and the moon rose, shedding a soft light on the landscape. Nancy held on to Pinto's mane so that she would not fall off. She wondered if anyone could hear the clatter the horse made as it dug up rocks and pebbles, even though it was unshod.

When Nancy rounded a bend, Alan was waiting for her, clearly illumined by the dusky light of the moon. He had held up because ahead of him lay a stretch of river water that had surfaced.

"Water," Nancy said.

"Yes, and trees."

She looked and saw the trees lining both banks, but she didn't recognize it as a stretch she had passed, even though she knew she must have come by here in daylight.

"What now?" she asked.

"We'll ride close to the shore to lose our tracks, then I think we ought to ride up on the plain some distance from the Brazos."

"Why?"

"We need to step up the pace of our horses. We don't want the comancheros to catch up with us."

"No, we don't," she said. "Do you know where we are?"

"Yes." Alan pointed the sky. "I've been guiding on the North Star. I figure we're about twenty miles from home."

"Twenty miles," she sighed. "That's not so far, I guess."

"We could walk it in five hours. With the horses, we ought to reach home in four or less."

"Still a long way," she said.

"The horses can't be pushed too hard."

"What time is it?" she asked.

"Near midnight, I reckon."

"So we might be home before dawn, when it'll still be cool."

"Maybe," Alan said, and clucked to his horse. "Follow exactly where I go," he called back to Nancy. "There may be quicksand."

They rode through the water for a quarter of a mile, then Alan guided Linda up a small fissure made by flash flooding, and they reached the plain on the east side of the Brazos.

Alan slowed Linda's pace, and Nancy was able to catch up to him. She rode along in silence for a while, then asked him for a drink of water. He slipped one of the canteens from around his neck and uncorked it. Then he handed it to her and pulled Linda to a halt. Nancy reined in Pinto and drank deeply from the canteen.

"Feeling better?" Alan asked.

"Some. I'm not so tired." she drank again. The water was warm, but she knew she needed it to replace water she had lost through perspiration.

"I think I remembered my mother's name," Alan said.

"You did?"

"Yes. While you were asleep, I thought back to when I was a little boy. I remembered the Mexicans making the adobe bricks and me playing in the mud trying to be like them. They spoke of my mother."

"What was her name?" Nancy asked.

"Esperanza, I think."

"What a beautiful name. What does it mean?"

"It means hope, in Spanish."

"Hope," Nancy breathed. She handed the canteen back to Alan. He drank a sip or two, then put the stopper back in and slung it around his neck.

"I think my father called her something else. A nickname, maybe."

"Do you remember your father's name?"

Alan did not reply at once, but seemed to be mulling something over in his mind. Nancy looked at him apprehensively, hoping he might remember his father's name.

"The Mexicans did not talk about him much. I think they respected him, or maybe were afraid of him. All I can remember them saying about my father was *hombron*. But that doesn't mean much to me."

"What does the word mean in English?" Nancy asked.

"Big man. Much man. Something like that."

"I wish you could remember your father's real name, Alan."

"So do I," he said, then motioned for them to go on. He

clapped his heels into the mare's flanks and the horse bounded ahead. Nancy strapped her horse with the trailing rope and urged him into a trot to catch up.

They could hear no sounds behind them and none ahead. They rode on and let the night swallow them up on their journey home.

Chapter Twenty-Four

Tallman stood next to the well, his facial features drawn tight as a death mask, a faint frown on his brow. The ground was littered with horse tracks, piss holes, moccasin scuffs, burnt tobacco, and the air was filled with the scent of human and equine excrement.

Jacobs rode up, bent over the saddle like a mounted mendicant, to find Tallman standing by his horse, a handful of dirt in his hand, slowly slipping through his fingers. Tallman did not look at Jacobs, but only at the well, or what was left of it.

"Is this the Apache well?" Jacobs asked, his voice a gravelly croak, barely a whisper.

"It was," Tallman said. He opened his hand and poured the rest of the dirt on top of the well.

"Not much of one, is it?" Jacobs asked.

"The bastards filled it in," Tallman said.

"What?"

"Take a look," Tallman said, turning his back on the well, looking Jacobs straight in the eye.

Jacobs lifted himself from the saddle and groaned as he let himself down to the ground. He walked over to the well, wrinkling his nose up at the smell. He looked at it and dropped to his knees before it as if he was at some lurid shrine.

"It's full of dirt and rocks," Jacobs said. "I don't see no water."

"The comancheros filled it in," Tallman said softly. "Deliberately."

"Those dirty bastards. How could any human do such a goddamned thing?"

"Comancheros fight to the death," Tallman said. "And they use anything they can get their hands on."

"But to fill in a well . . . in this country . . . in this godawful heat. It ain't human. It ain't right."

Tallman ran the toe of his boot through the dust. He looked back at the sun and gauged how long it would remain in the sky. He wobbled the pebble in his mouth to the opposite side and Jacobs could hear the stone click against Tallman's teeth.

"You sonofabitch, Tallman. You'd said we'd find water."

"I said we'd find a well. There it is."

"But . . . can we dig it out?"

Tallman looked at Jacobs with eyes that seemed close to being filled with pity. "You can bet they spent time kicking rocks and dirt down that hole, time we don't have. The Apaches would kill them for that, but the comancheros are long gone from here."

"You're saying we won't get any water out of this well, Tallman?"

"First they let their horses foul it with dung, then they squatted over it themselves to foul it worse before they dragged blankets over it with their horses," Tallman said, "until the water wouldn't rise. Then, they chunked wood and rocks and more dirt down it to close it off. It would take a week to dig it all out. You can bet on that."

"Shit. That ain't fair."

Tallman didn't laugh. There was nothing funny about it. "Comancheros don't fight fair," he said. "Best find you another pebble and stick it in your mouth. We won't find water until we get to the Brazos."

"How far do we have to ride?"

"All night, likely. And no guarantee there'll be water in the bed when we get there."

"What in hell are you sayin', Tallman? A dry river?"

"I've seen it dry up in places. Go underground. This is one hell of a drought, Jacobs. I just hope the horses can hold out until we can get to the Brazos."

"The horses? What about us?"

"We can go another day without water, I'm thinking," Tallman said.

Jacobs's neck swelled with rage until the veins stood out like blue cords and blood flushed his face a scarlet hue that pulsed like the sun. He spluttered for curse words that eluded him in his anger so that he wound up growling garbled words at Tallman.

"Getting mad won't help none," Tallman said.

"You're seven kinds of sonofabitch, Tallman. Lyin' to a man dyin' of thirst, leadin' him across desert through a blazin'' hell."

"Quit your bellyachin', Jacobs, and let's get moving or we'll leave our bones by this well."

"You bastard," Jacobs grumped as Tallman mounted the dun and slapped the trailing ends of his reins against the horse's rump. Jacobs had no choice but to follow Tallman eastward toward the Brazos, the rage in him building like a fire in a furnace.

Tallman listened to the epithets hurled at his back by Jacobs and kept his composure until the wagon master's ire began to subside. The sun was still at their backs and no shade visible as far as they could see. Tallman slowed so Jacobs could catch up to him.

"Settle down, Jacobs," Tallman said, "so I don't have to kill you."

"You're already killin' me, Tallman."

"I had a thought to shoot you back there just to shut you up."

"I wouldn't put it past you," Jacobs said.

"I could live another two days on what's in your guts and another day or two on what's in your horse's belly."

Jacobs appeared to be aghast as he listened to Tallman berate him. He started to swing his rifle up, but Tallman reached out and grabbed his wrist. "I'd shoot you before you got that piece cocked," he said.

"I believe you," Jacobs said, as he looked into Tallman's unfathomable eyes.

The two men were silent for a time, each harboring his own thoughts. Then Jacobs coughed and reached into his possibles bag. He pulled out a piece of flint and stuck it in his mouth.

"Don't cut yourself on it," Tallman said. "I've sucked on flint myself a time or two."

Jacobs looked at Tallman as if he had never seen him before. He worried the square of flint in his mouth until he began to salivate.

"Who in hell are you, Tallman? I mean, who are you, really?"

"What do you mean?"

"I told Montes about you. He knew your name."

"I've never seen Montes before," Tallman said.

"Montes knows you by reputation. You're no scout, like you told me when we first met. That's not all you are."

"I reckon no man's just one thing."

"Montes thinks you're a damned spy."

"A spy? For whom?"

"For the U.S. government."

"Why would the U.S. government need a spy in this part of the country?" Tallman asked.

"I don't rightly know, but Montes said you weren't to be trusted."

"With the Mexicans, appearances are everything. They see what they want to see and they show what they want to show."

"I don't get your meanin'," Jacobs said.

"Austin told me once that the way to understand the Mexicans was to listen to their proverbs, their sayings. He said there was one in particular that helped him to stay out of trouble with the Mexicans."

"And what was that?"

"The Mexicans have a saying: *'Dios castiga el escándalo más que el crimen.'* "

"Which means?"

"God punishes the scandal more than the crime," Tallman said. "Dignity is everything to a Mexican. If you don't get caught, you won't be punished."

"So, you are a spy," Jacobs said.

"No, Jacobs. As you can see there's nothing to spy on

out here. I'm just an American trying to put down roots in a good land."

"Montes said you were down here before Austin. He said he had heard of you in Mexico City and in Béxar."

"Mexicans also love gossip," Tallman said.

"He said you were in thick with the Spaniards, that you married one of their women and she ran off with another man."

Tallman said nothing for several seconds as they rode through the cauldron of the Texas plain. The dun's head was starting to droop, and each step seemed slower than the last.

Jacobs said no more as the horses plodded on into the gathering sunset, as if he was fighting his own internal battles and too absorbed in them to notice that Tallman on the dun was stretching the distance between them.

It was only when the sun had set and Jacobs's horse whinnied that the man came out of his sun-razed stupor and saw that Tallman had disappeared from view. But ahead of him stood a small line of cottonwoods wrapped in a scrim of shadow, and small willows drooping in the twilight.

Jacobs's horse whickered again and broke into a trot. In moments, the horse reached the bank and scrambled down it. The horse plunged into a pool of water around a bend where trees shaded the river. Tallman's dun was already drinking, and Tallman himself was filling the canteens downstream.

Jacobs gave a whoop and leaped from the saddle. He threw himself into the water and drank, slurping water into his mouth in frantic gulps. He looked out of the corner of his eye at Tallman, who was hunkered over the water, watching water burble into both canteens.

"Don't drink too much, Jacobs." Tallman stood up and corked the canteens. "You'll get sick."

Jacobs wiped his mouth with his sleeve and tried to see Tallman's eyes through the murk of dusk. He could not read the expression on Tallman's face.

"You lied to me again, Tallman."

"Probably."

"You told me we wouldn't get to the river until mornin'. This is the Brazos, ain't it?"

"It is."

"Seems to me it weren't no more'n eight or ten miles from that well."

"Closer to twelve, I'd reckon."

"So, did you lie, or didn't you know how close the river was?"

"I lied," Tallman said, wading to shore.

"Why?"

"You were pretty stove up from the heat, Jacobs. I figured if you had to reach down and get some muscle to get you through the hottest part of the day, you'd have to get mad at me and that would keep you going."

"Pretty smart, aren't you?"

"No. I just know it was damned hard to go that last twelve miles. Men have died of thirst at less distance from water. They give up too soon."

"Damn you, Tallman. Why do you always have to be right?"

"I don't, Jacobs. I was hurting for water just as much as you. I wasn't sure I could make it."

"What do you mean?"

"I figured if I had you to worry about I'd quit thinking about myself."

"Well, I'll be damned," Jacobs said.

"Fill your canteen, Jacobs. We've some riding to do."

"Why can't we just stay here and rest the night?"

"Look at those tracks yonder. You'll see why."

"Hell, I can't hardly see my hand in front of my face. What tracks?"

Tallman stood on the shore and pointed all around him. Jacobs walked over and hunched down to look.

"They's a passel of 'em," Jacobs said.

"I figured them out before you got here."

"And what do they mean?"

"Comancheros passed by here, not too long ago. Before that, two more horses stopped. Horses not known to me. Unshod."

"Is that all?"

"No, I found tracks of the two girls, and another belonging to a woman or girl. And, still another, to a young boy wearing shoes."

"And, what do you figger?"

"I figure the woman and boy stopped here first. She lay down there under that tree on the bank, and then the two of them mounted up and rode south. Later, the comancheros came by and read the same sign. They didn't linger, but got right on the track of those two."

"Nancy and her boy?"

"Not her boy. But a boy she got from a man named Virgil Ottmers. He told me about it."

"Who is this boy?"

"I don't know. But the comancheros sure as hell do."

"How do you figger that?"

"Ottmers told me he bought the boy in Santa Fe off some comancheros, who got him from either some Mexicans or Apaches."

"I'll be damned," Jacobs said.

"Mount up, Jacobs," Tallman told him. "Check your powder and don't drink too much water."

"Anything else, Tallman?" Jacobs asked sarcastically.

"Yes. It's going to be hard tracking, and you make as little noise as possible. When I stop, you stop. When I wave you back, go back."

"How close are we to these comancheros?"

"We're so damned close, I can smell them," Tallman said.

Chapter
Twenty-Five

Sometime during the night, Nancy remembered watching Alan cross the river, but it seemed as if she were still asleep, still dreaming. She did not have to rein the pinto to turn; the pony followed Linda down the steep bank and through a large pool of water that glistened in the moonlight like a lighted mirror. She saw the reflection of Alan and Linda in the water, and that, too, seemed as if it were part of her dream, and then they were climbing another steep bank and Alan turned and stopped Linda to wait for her, and when she rode up, he took the ropes from her hands and held them so that she had to hold on to Pinto's mane to keep from falling off.

She fell back asleep with the pony's motion rocking her gently, and every time she started to fall, her eyes would open for a moment and she would straighten up and see Alan's back just ahead of her and then her eyes would close again and she was deep in a rocking slumber under a night strewn with stars and a high moon soft as any light she'd ever seen and so blessedly cool she never wanted to awaken.

The dream drew her deep down into it and she felt as if she were in a canoe, riding on the cool flat water down a canyon filled with moonlight and the sweet smell of lilacs blooming in the shade of night. But there were long arms along the shore reaching out for her with grasping hands and she tore away from them and saw her husband crying out for her before he faded into darkness, and then there were two Alans, her own and the one she had adopted, and they called to her in a language she could not understand and then sank from sight as the canoe started riding the river uphill, the grade getting steeper all the time until she felt herself falling backwards and more hands trying to grab her dress and pull her into the water.

Nancy awoke with a start and did not know where she was. She felt around her lap for the rope reins and then remembered that Alan was leading her through the darkness and when she looked up, he was still ahead of her, Linda climbing a gentle slope where there were trees growing. She heard whippoorwills calling like lost souls from somewhere off to her left and then they went silent as they drew near.

The sleep hadn't helped, Nancy thought. She was still very tired, and the dream had seemed so real. She touched her dress to see if it was torn, if hands had really plucked at her and tried to pull her into the deep of night and drown her.

"Alan," she called, and Alan turned around. She could barely see him in the dim light of the moon and stars, but she saw the bleach of his face and knew that he was looking at her.

"What is it, Mother?" he asked.

"Where are we?"

"Close to home," he said.

Nancy breathed a sigh of relief, and they rode on until the sky began to pale and the stars wink out one by one, turning invisible as the light in the east began to glow and spread across the horizon. Then there was only the ghost of the moon far away on the southern reaches of the heavens, and the whippoorwills grew silent as the dawn took hold, and the light in the east turned red and streamed across the sky like a fiery stain from hell's own cauldrons.

The livid sky began to turn a periwinkle blue as the conflagration in the east began to subside behind a thin bank of clouds stretched from north to south in a roll of gray batting tinged golden underneath. Nancy's eyes widened in awe at the spectacular dawning of another day that she knew would be brutally hot, mercilessly savage. Still, she could not deny the dawn its beauty, a reminder that each day was part of some divine plan.

Alan rode back toward the river again, and when it came into sight, he stopped his horse and turned to Nancy, pulling on the rope reins to draw her close to him.

"Are you awake enough to handle Pinto from now on?" he asked.

"Why, yes, I'm awake, Alan."

He handed her the rope reins. She took them, a puzzled look on her face.

"Is there something wrong?" she asked.

"I don't know. Just a feeling, is all."

"What kind of feeling?"

"It feels like something's crawling up my back. An itch in my mind that I can't scratch."

He kept looking back toward the route they had taken to

this place and there was a nervousness about him that she had not seen before. His actions made her feel apprehensive.

"You said we were close to home. I don't recognize anything around here."

"See that stretch of river down there?" he asked, pointing.

"Yes. It's almost dry, though."

"That's why you don't recognize where you are," Alan said. "We're less than ten miles from the house, closer to five."

"Then we should hurry," she said, "if those comancheros are still behind us. Do you think they are?"

"Yes, and I think one of them is right behind us. The others are further back, following his trail. And ours."

"What makes you think that, Alan?"

"Every so often, I've heard something that didn't sound right, way back there. Like a clicking of stones hitting together, a dry branch breaking. Sound travels farther at night, and these were very faint, but I know I heard them."

"They could have been made by wild animals," she said, not wanting to think the worst.

"Even so, something disturbed them."

"Alan, you're scaring me."

"I don't mean to, but we're going so slow, they're going to catch up to us. And we can't go much faster without killing the horses. They're plumb tuckered."

Nancy looked down at Pinto. His head was drooping. He looked tired, looked as if he were asleep on his feet. Linda, too, was not moving, and her eyes were closed, her head hovering close to the ground.

"I don't know if I can go another mile," Nancy said, suddenly weary beyond words. Yet when she thought for a moment about giving up, she seemed to touch something deep inside her, some wellspring of inner strength that she had not known she possessed. She drew herself up straight and spoke soothing words to Pinto.

Alan looked at her in surprise, his eyes wide and filled with wonder.

"We'll go on, Alan," she said. "We'll do what we must do."

"Yes, I think we should. I have an idea that might help us."

"You do?"

"It might give us a little more time," he said.

"What is it you want to do?" she asked.

"Come," he said. "Follow me."

Nancy took the rope reins in hand and followed Alan as he rode down to the river once again. They followed a wide shore left by the receding waters as the land began to light up with the rise of the morning sun.

Soon, they came to a clump of cottonwoods, small willows, and other trees lining the bank. There, Alan pulled Linda to a stop and dismounted. He carried the sack of cooking utensils and food to a place within the trees and began unpacking it. Nancy watched in fascination before she found a place to dismount. She held tightly to the rope reins in fear that Pinto might run away.

Alan worked swiftly, with confidence. He laid out the two tin cups, a ladle with a hole in the handle, two spoons, and a knife. Then he began to untwist a length of rope that was left over from the one he had used to catch Linda and make her bridle and reins. When he had several strands of thin rope, he tied them together and threaded them through the handles of the cups and the ladle, and he cut smaller pieces of rope, which he used to tie around the spoons and knife.

Nancy watched with rapt attention as Alan strung the whole contraption up through the trees, setting the smaller strands in place by tying the ladle and spoons near the cups, and, for good measure, the knife on the opposite side where it could strike the bottom of a cup.

When he was finished, he straightened the spliced rope strands and brought the end to a place some distance from where the utensils hung in the trees. Then, he gathered up the bundle and placed it beneath the place where the cups and ladle, knife and spoons dangled.

"Mother," he called in a sharp whisper, "get back on Pinto."

Nancy, despite her weariness, climbed back on Pinto and rode over to where Alan waited for her, his rifle in hand. He reached out and touched the stock of the rifle she carried.

"Let me have that, too," he said.

"What are you going to do?" she asked.

"You'll see. I want you to take Linda with you and ride beyond this place around the next bend. Wait for me there. Don't move from that spot and stay quiet."

"Alan, I-I'm afraid. Afraid you'll get hurt."

"I'm going to wait here and make noise. If a comanchero comes close enough, I'll shoot him. I hope I don't miss."

"What you're planning to do is very dangerous, Alan."

"If I trick them, I'll still have a chance to get away. You'll see me running up. Be ready to ride away fast once I get back on Linda."

"Maybe I should stay here and shoot the other rifle," she said.

"No. It will be easy for me to hide. They'll be looking for two people on horses."

Reluctantly, she gave him her rifle. Then she rode over to Linda and picked up her trailing rope reins. Alan shooed her away and she rode downstream. She looked back and saw Alan walking to the bank and behind a small mound where he lay down, holding the end of the spliced thin rope in his hands.

Alan waved at her, and she rounded the bend and reined to a halt, waiting there, her hands trembling, her heart racing fast. She resisted the urge to go back and stay with Alan. In a moment, she began to pray.

Alan laid the two rifles out beside him and checked the pans for dry powder, worked the triggers to make sure they would fire. Then he cocked both rifles and began to pull gently on the strand of spliced rope.

The knife and spoons began to strike the dangling utensils, making it sound as if someone was setting them out to cook. He stopped almost immediately and listened. After a few minutes, he made the utensils rattle again. Then, again, he waited.

The sun rose higher in the sky and brightened the land. Alan could feel the heat begin to build and he began to sweat in the breezeless air along the river. He developed itches, but he ignored them. Instead, he stared upriver and scanned the banks. Occasionally, he looked up toward the plain on both sides and back downriver.

The longer he waited, the more Alan questioned the wisdom of setting such a trap for the wily comancheros. He had lived with the ones who had taken him to Santa Fe for a time, and he knew they were treacherous and smart. He had seen them do things that surprised him. He knew them to be merciless and cruel, and he knew, without a doubt, that they would kill him if they got the least chance.

Again, Alan tugged on the strand of rope and made the

cups jingle in the cottonwood tree. It was then that he heard a sound that chilled his blood, made the hackles on the back of his neck bristle and tingle.

Upstream, he heard the sound of hoofbeats that suddenly stopped, leaving a gaping silence that shattered his ears. He reached out a hand and touched the nearest rifle, grasped it loosely, ready to bring it to his shoulder.

Then, with his other hand, Alan jiggled the spoons, cups, ladle, and knife again. They made a soft clanking sound before they stopped moving.

Alan saw the comanchero sneak around the bend. To his surprise, the man was on foot, but leading his horse. He hoped the renegade would see the sack and think it was someone sleeping. Still the comanchero came on, slowly, making no noise, carrying a rifle in one hand.

Carefully, Alan lifted the rifle and brought it close to him. He let the rope strand fall from his other hand. The comanchero came closer, and Alan strained to see his face beneath the brim of his hat. There was something familiar about the man.

The comanchero stepped behind his horse and disappeared from view for a moment or two. Alan slid the rifle beneath him and brought the butt to his shoulder.

Then the comanchero reappeared, pushing his horse in front of him as he held on to its tail. Alan knew he was using the horse for cover as he approached the cottonwoods.

Alan got ready to aim the rifle as the comanchero stepped away from the plodding horse for a moment. That was when Alan got a good look at the man's face. He sucked in a breath as he recognized him as one of those who had taken him to Santa Fe and sold him to Virgil Ottmers.

The comanchero was a Mexican, half Yaqui, half Spanish,

named Pedro Quintero. His friends, the other comancheros, called him Pato, or Duck, because of the way he waddled when he walked. That was what had seemed so familiar to Alan, that waddling walk.

As Alan watched, Pato raised his rifle to his shoulder and took aim on the sack of food and cooking utensils. Alan heard the sound of the rifle cocking as Pato settled the butt of the weapon into the small of his shoulder.

Alan held his breath and brought his rifle up. He set the front blade sight on Pato's chest, dead center, and lined it up with the rear buckhorn of the flintlock.

The comanchero squeezed the trigger of his rifle, and the crack jarred Alan's ears. A billowing cloud of smoke followed the orange flash of flame and puffed out from the muzzle. Alan heard the lead ball hit the sack and strike metal.

Through the smoke, Alan could still see Pato's chest. He made sure the sights were still aligned and squeezed the trigger, both eyes open. The rifle bucked against his shoulder and the explosion roared in his ears.

For a moment, Alan could not see Pato, but he heard the thunk of the ball as it struck flesh and cracked bone. Then he heard a soft sound as Pato grunted and threw up his arms. His rifle fell to the sandy shore with a hard thud.

As the smoke cleared, Alan saw Pato clutching his chest, staggering around in a circle, blood gushing from the wound that had ripped through his breastbone. Pato made terrible gasping sounds, and blood bubbled out of his mouth and soaked his shirt with a crimson stain.

Alan began to tremble with buck fever. He had never shot a man before, although he had seen comancheros and Apaches kill men without any qualms. But Alan found it difficult to breathe, and he could not control the shakes that gripped him.

He wondered why Pato did not fall down but continued to weave in a circle, blood pouring from a wound that had to be fatal. Transfixed, Alan watched the comanchero try to breathe through the blood clogging his windpipe. Pato pulled on his torn shirt and lifted his gaze to the sky in his struggle for oxygen.

Alan knew he had to pick up the other rifle and run away, but he could not move. His body felt leaden and his throat constricted in horror for having mortally wounded another human being. Finally, Pato fell to his knees, then pitched forward onto his face.

Pato twitched a couple of times, and one leg kicked out in the final spasms of death. Then the comanchero was still. The horse ambled over and sniffed at the dead man.

Alan gulped in a deep breath and struggled to his feet. He picked up Nancy's rifle and slung his own over his shoulder. Then he turned and began to run downriver, the image of the dying comanchero still vivid in his mind.

How long, he wondered, would it take the others to catch up to him and shoot him as he ran? He could almost feel them riding him down, but he heard no sounds of pursuit. He ran, fear-driven, faster than he had ever run before, and finally rounded the bend.

There, Nancy waited on Pinto, and when he saw her, he nearly fell to the ground in gratitude. He was out of breath, but he managed to speak to her as he ran.

"Go, go," he panted. "I'll get on Linda."

"What happened?" Nancy said, in a state of bewilderment.

"We must go," Alan gasped, stumbling toward her. He

handed her his unloaded rifle, grabbed the rope reins from her and climbed atop Linda.

"Are you hurt?" Nancy asked.

"No. Please, we must go. We've got to get out of here."

Stubbornly, Nancy did not move. "Not until you tell me what that shooting was about," she said.

"God, I killed a man, Mother. A comanchero."

Nancy's face fell as if she had been stricken.

"And the rest of them are going to be coming after us," Alan said, twisting Linda around to head south.

He rode up to Nancy and reached down and slapped the rump of Pinto. Pinto jumped and followed Alan as he rode off.

The two horses galloped down the wide shore, then gradually slowed as their tired muscles gave out.

Alan pulled Linda to a halt and waited for Nancy to catch up.

"Alan, Pinto's all worn out. He can't ride this fast."

"I know. We have to let them rest, and they need water."

"But what about the other comancheros? Where are they?"

Alan looked back upstream, cupped a hand to his ear.

"I doubt if we have more than ten or fifteen minutes before they catch up to us. Better give me my rifle so I can reload it. Yours is still loaded."

"Alan, I don't think I could shoot a man," she said. "Even if it meant saving my life."

"I didn't think I could either, Mother."

The look that passed between them was laden with sorrow and deep knowledge that neither wanted to have. And in that same all-knowing look there was an understanding, too, that they might be silently saying good-bye to each other, to life itself.

Chapter
Twenty-Six

Tallman abandoned the course of the Brazos and set out on a straight line that would iron out all the twists and turns of the river and put him and Jacobs at a point where he thought they might intercept the comancheros.

He knew the horses were suffering from the day's heat and that it would not cool down until past nine o'clock that night, so he did not hurry the dun. The horse showed its courage and faith by keeping a steady gait across a land still warm from the burning sun.

Jacobs plodded on behind Tallman, his horse following blindly in the dun's steps like any herd animal, its feet sore from the baked soil, the hard scorching rocks.

The two men might have been ghosts, they were so silent, and the horses dead except for their footfalls, their moving legs, rhythmic, slow, stiff, their tails switching at flies that had not gone to sleep with the dying of the sun.

The moon rose and silvered the riders and their mounts, heightening their ghostly appearance as they traveled across a landscape parched and sere from the drought that gripped the land. Tallman listened to the crunch of dormant grasshoppers under foot, few of them taking flight to avoid death under the iron hooves of the horses.

Tallman knew he was far enough away from the river that they could not be heard by the comancheros, but at the same time, he was riding blind and deaf through the night; he could not see nor hear them either. But he was chopping miles from their route downriver; he used the stars to guide him and the faint outlines of trees that surfaced from time to time off to his left, like dark beacons marking the river's path.

Gradually, the earth began to cool, and Tallman finally halted and set down to let the dun drink. He whispered to Jacobs to give his horse water and to drink some himself. The two men drank after the horses had slaked their thirst, and Jacobs reached for his tobacco. But Tallman grabbed his arm and shook his head.

"I need a smoke," Jacobs whispered.

"Save it," Tallman said.

"They ain't a comanchero what can see us."

"They can smell the smoke, if nothing else."

"Where do you figger they are, Tallman?"

"I think we're going to get ahead of them sometime around dawn, maybe sooner."

"Maybe they've holed up and we're already ahead of them."

"I reckon they're pushing on," Tallman said. He thought of Redford and the other comancheros. Redford wanted Nancy, and he was not a man to give up. No, he would be riding, and the others would go along with him. They had plenty of water and they could track like Apaches at night.

"We'll go on," Tallman said, after a few moments. "Horses will stiffen up if we stay still too long."

"They can't get no stiffer than I am," Jacobs said.

Tallman climbed aboard the dun without further conversation, and Jacobs mounted up right behind him. The two men drifted across the plain like pilgrims on an ancient quest, their bodies turned pewter by the soft light of the moon. In the distance, coyotes laced the night with melodic streamers of chromatic voices ranging up and down the scale, an eerie sound that carried far across the desert land and then brought in a silence that seemed sad and eternal.

And the moon rose higher and shed light in all directions as far as the eye could see. A jackrabbit jumped up a few yards ahead of the dun, and the horse took no notice as the rabbit bounded away and turned invisible when it stopped next to a bush.

The coyotes stopped singing well before midnight. A light breeze sprang up and then died just as suddenly, leaving what was left of its passing in a stifling hush that made horses and men draw in air as if to prove it still existed and had not been taken away by the slight enigmatic breeze.

Tallman marked the miles in his mind, ticking them off and imagining the Brazos, with its twists and meanders, snaking through the valley above and below the bed it had carved over the centuries as it headed for the far ocean.

He patted the dun on the neck, speaking to it so softly Jacobs could not hear his voice. "You'll get watered soon, boy. You just keep on going a while longer."

The while turned into hours, and Tallman began drifting

the dun toward the Brazos as the moon sailed toward the south so slowly its speed could not be marked by the casual eye. But Tallman knew that morning was not far off. And he felt the miles in his bones, the distance in every sinew and muscle. His eyes were so heavy he had to fight with himself to keep them open, but he knew he dared not sleep, not even doze, or he would lose track of his mission and time itself.

He knew Jacobs was asleep; he could hear his lazy snores, but he also knew the wagon master's horse was following the dun and would not halt for fear of being abandoned in a desolate and lonesome place.

The sky began to lighten when Tallman saw a small band of silver shimmering in the fading moonlight. The dun whickered softly at the scent of water, and Jacobs stopped snoring as he awoke with a jolt.

"Tallman," Jacobs called, after he had cleared his throat, "where in hell are we?"

"River's yonder," Tallman said in a loud whisper.

Then, he halted the dun so Jacobs could catch up to him. Jacobs stopped his horse next to the dun and waited for what Tallman had to say.

"Stars are fading out," Jacobs said. "Be daylight soon. And hot."

Tallman said nothing. He looked at the eastern horizon as it paled and could almost feel the heat building even before the sun appeared. Venus was still fairly bright in the sky and he could see Mars, too, winking a faded red glimmer across countless miles of space. The rest of the stars had gotten so dim he could no longer see them.

"Listen," Tallman said, his voice so low, Jacobs had to strain to hear him.

The two men listened. At first, Jacobs shook his head to

indicate he could hear nothing. Then, as he looked at Tallman, his eyes widened and he began nodding.

Faint footfalls, indicating some large animal sounded from the direction of the river, each landing with a dull thud, as if the animal was walking on dry sand.

Tallman held a finger to his lips. Jacobs nodded again.

The two men waited, listening. Then another sound intruded, and Tallman's head snapped around to face the source of the sound. He pointed downstream as he looked at Jacobs. Jacobs touched the butt of his rifle stock. Tallman held up a hand to stay him from drawing the weapon from its boot.

"What is it?" Jacobs whispered.

"I don't know," Tallman admitted. The sound of footfalls stopped as if the creature—or man, perhaps—was listening to the alien sound as well.

The sound, Tallman knew, was not natural. It was a faint tinking, a clanking, as if something metal was being struck or banging against something metal.

Tink, tink, then a silence.

Tallman patted the dun's neck and turned it southward toward the metallic sounds. Jacobs followed. Then, abruptly, Tallman reined up, and Jacobs followed suit. The two men strained to hear the sounds coming from the river.

As they rode closer, the clanking sound started up again. Then Tallman heard a low grunt from another direction, then the scrape of a hoof on sand. He motioned for Jacobs to be quiet and stopped his horse so that he was motionless and could hear sounds emanating from both directions.

The clanking stopped, then, a few moments later, started up again. Puzzled, Tallman cupped a hand to his ear and turned his head in the direction north of the tinking sound.

Tallman dared not ride to the bank and look down into

the riverbed, even though he was curious about what was going on down there. Instead, he waited, listening, trying to sort out the sounds he heard, trying to form an image of what or who was making the noise. Perhaps they had stumbled on the comanchero camp and they were making breakfast. But he smelled no smoke and the sounds were too uniform, too similar each time they sounded.

More waiting, and more sounds of a horse or animal moving, but another sound with that, as if a man was walking alongside the hoofed animal. Then more clatter from downriver.

There was a long silence, then the sound of a rifle cocking. Tallman tensed, let his hand drift to the butt of his own rifle. He looked all around, but no one was up on the plain. All the noises came from the riverbed.

A moment later, a loud explosion, the crack of a rifle, shattered the silence. Tallman drew his rifle from his sheath. He looked back at Jacobs, who was slipping his own rifle from its scabbard.

Then there was another shot, from downstream. He heard a man groan, and the sound was close, upstream. Seconds later, he heard more noise, then the pounding of hoofbeats, which quickly faded. The sound had traveled downstream, away from where he and Jacobs sat their horses.

Tallman waited until the silence told him nothing more was moving down at the river. He tapped his heels into the dun's flanks and turned it to head toward a place where they could descend to the bed. He kept his rifle across his knees, one finger inside the trigger guard, another on the hammer.

Jacobs followed, rifle laid at an angle across the pommel of his saddle. The sun cleared the eastern horizon, and both men had to duck their heads to catch the shade from their hatbrims.

"Watch yourself, Tallman," Jacobs murmured.

Tallman nodded and descended through a slight ravine. He saw the body of the comanchero lying a few yards away, his horse standing hipshot five or six yards off to one side, its head drooping. Tallman looked both ways before he rode up to the body. Seeing nothing out of the ordinary, he swung out of the saddle, rifle in hand.

Tallman prodded the comanchero with the muzzle of his rifle. The man didn't move. He did not seem to be breathing. Kneeling down, Tallman stayed well behind the man in case he was playing possum, but still the comanchero showed no signs of life.

Jacobs rode up a few seconds later and started to dismount. Tallman turned and stared up at him. "Stay on your horse, Jacobs," he said. "Keep your eyes peeled. You shoot anything to the north that moves."

"Whatever you say, Tallman."

Jon Tallman turned the body of the comanchero over. He saw the chest wound. The ball had not exited, was still in the man's body, probably lodged against the hard bone of his spine. The blood was no longer pumping, but it stained the man's shirt and chest. Flies started to blacken the bloody stain.

"He dead?" Jacobs asked.

"Dead as yesterday."

"Comanchero?"

Tallman stood up. "Yes."

"Ever seen him before?"

"His name is Quintero," Tallman said. "They called him Pato."

Jacobs licked dry lips. He looked at the dead man and blinked his eyes nervously. "Wonder where the rest of 'em are."

"They'll be along, I reckon. Come on, follow me. We don't want to be caught here when they do ride up."

Tallman looked downstream, saw something glint in the sun. Then he saw the light fabric of a flour sack nestled against the bank. He walked toward it, leading the dun. Jacobs plodded along behind him, more nervous than before.

The sack was torn, a black hole in it from a rifle ball. Tallman picked up the sack, looked inside. There were cooking utensils, foodstuffs that he did not take the time to examine. But he slid the sack under the thongs holding his bedroll secure behind the cantle, and looked up at the tree just beyond.

He walked over and noticed the string tied to the cups, spoons, and knife. He picked up the string, untied it from the utensils, and took them down. He spent a few seconds putting those in the sack, repacking it so it would not make noise. He looked at the maze of tracks, nodded in satisfaction, then climbed back aboard the dun.

"What's all that stuff doing there?" Jacobs asked as they rode south, following the clearly visible tracks along the wide bank.

Tallman rode the dun to the water, let it drink before he answered. Jacobs had no choice but to let his thirsty horse dip its head and put its muzzle into the river.

"Nancy and the boy were here," Tallman said. "One or the other shot Pato. Didn't have enough powder in the rifle. But the ball did its work on Pato. I figure one or the other set up that rig to make noise and waited in ambush while the other rode on ahead. After Pato was killed, the one who stayed behind ran off to catch up to the other one."

"You can tell all that from the tracks?"

"Pretty much," Tallman said. "If the boy set up the ambush, he was pretty good at it. Pato was not easy to fool. If Nancy did it, then she's as smart as I took her for."

"She's not dumb," Jacobs said.

"Their tracks disappear in the water, so one or the other knows enough to try and throw the other comancheros off their trail."

"What about this Pato? How come he was all by himself?" Jacobs asked.

Tallman thought about that for a moment. He turned to Jacobs as he pulled on the reins to take the dun's mouth from the water.

"I reckon he was scouting ahead of the bunch," Tallman said, digging his heels into the dun's flanks. "The other comancheros must be far enough behind not to have heard the shots."

"But not too far away, I guess."

"No, not too far away. They'll read enough of the sign to know we're here and they'll make plans to get us all, if they can."

Jacobs slapped his horse with the tips of his reins, and the horse took one last slurp of water and shook its head before moving on in the dun's wake.

"What about Nancy and the boy?" Jacobs asked when he had caught up with Tallman. "Would they be far ahead of us?"

"No, but we could get shot if we come up on them without them knowing who we are."

"So what are you going to do?"

"I'll decide when I pick up the tracks again."

Tallman bit his lower lip lightly, squinted his eyes against the glare of the rising sun. Grasshoppers took flight as the dun cleared the water and took to the sandy bottom that had been revealed by the low water. Some landed on Tallman's clothes and on his saddle. A couple rode behind the cantle, and the dun shook off one that had gotten tangled in his mane.

"How you gonna let Nancy know it's us?" Jacobs asked.

"I'm not worried about that so much," Tallman said.

"What are you worried about, Tallman?"

"I'm thinking of Redford and the other comancheros."

"What about them?"

"Maybe Pato wasn't an advance scout at all."

"Huh?"

"Maybe Redford did what we did last night."

"I don't get you, Tallman."

Tallman scanned the dry ground for tracks that would show him Nancy and the boy had ridden out of the water and made tracks on either side of the trickle that the Brazos had become in the heat.

"Redford may have ridden on ahead to wait for Nancy and that boy. Pato would have just been left behind to make sure they wouldn't escape any trap set for them."

"Hell, we could all be riding into big trouble if Redford did that."

"That's the big question, isn't it?"

"Nancy and that boy are in a heap of trouble if Redford's up ahead waitin' for them." Jacobs pulled the brim of his hat down on the left side, but it did not keep the burning sun off his face. He squinted until his eyes were nothing but molelike slits.

"Redford could have taken to the high ground and gotten ahead of us all, I'm thinking," Tallman said. "If so, we're all in the pickle barrel."

Tallman pointed to the edge of the water. Even Jacobs

could not miss the tracks that emerged: two unshod horses had left prints in the wet sand that had already dried under the blazing heat.

"That Nancy and the boy?"

"Those are their tracks," Tallman replied.

"Well, we'd better catch up to 'em."

"They're not more than twenty minutes ahead," Tallman said.

"My horse doesn't have much git in him."

"No, we can't push it. We just have to hope we catch up to them before the comancheros do."

Tallman clapped heels to the dun's flanks, but the horse didn't change its gait. It was just past dawn, but he figured the temperature was already above eighty degrees, and by noon it would be over a hundred.

He wondered if Nancy and the boy could go on much longer. The good thing, he thought, was that they were not far from where they had settled. Less than half a day's ride, perhaps.

It was then that the dun balked and came to a halt, its ears twisting in half circles to pick up the faint sound less than a mile ahead of them.

Tallman's blood pounded in his temples.

"What was that?" Jacobs asked.

Tallman didn't answer, but he knew damned well what it was.

The sound he heard was a woman's scream.

Chapter
Twenty-Seven

Alan guided Linda out of the shallow river, turned to see if Nancy was following. She had dropped back about thirty or forty yards, but she saw where he was going and waved. He kept going, however.

When Nancy finally caught up to him, he turned to look at her. She smiled wanly, her eyes nearly closed to ward off the rays of the sun.

"Do you recognize where we are?" Alan asked.

Nancy looked around, shading her eyes with her hand. She shook her head.

"We're about eight miles or so from home."

"Home," she sighed. "I sometimes wondered if we'd ever see it again."

"We should be there in under two hours, I think."

"Alan, you're a treasure," she said.

"Thanks. Ready to go?"

Nancy nodded.

Alan started to head Linda up to the flat, where the going would be easier. Just as he turned his horse, they both heard the scream. A woman's scream.

Alan's heart jumped. He turned to look at Nancy. Her face was pale and she had her mouth open wide. Both horses had their ears perked. Alan turned Linda back toward the river, alarm seizing his body in a viselike grip.

"What on earth was that?" Nancy gasped.

"A woman screaming."

They both sat their horses, stunned, listening as if to see if their ears had heard right. There was a long silence and both began to shake their heads.

"That couldn't be what it was," Nancy said.

"Maybe I was wrong," Alan said.

Still, they waited, and just when they both thought it was safe to leave, they heard a second scream, louder than the first.

"It is a woman," Nancy said.

"Yes'm."

"Where?"

"Up ahead," Alan said.

"Someone's in trouble. We must go to her."

"No," Alan said, his voice quaking.

"Why, Alan, how could you stand to see another human being suffer?"

"It's a trick," Alan said.

"That scream was real."

"I know," Alan said. "Just wait, please."

"We can't wait. It sounds as if that woman's being tortured."

"Comancheros," Alan said, shuddering visibly.

Nancy rode over to him. "Why, Alan, you're trembling all over. What's wrong?"

"I . . . I . . . nothing, I mean, we can't go to help."

"But we must."

"No," Alan said in a loud, firm voice that took Nancy by surprise. She started to protest when they heard the woman again. This time she was screaming a name.

"Nanceeeeeeeeee!"

Nancy stiffened to hear her own name being called. She looked at Alan, her face mirroring the horror she felt inside.

"That . . . that's Lorena," she gasped. "Lorena Belton. She was captured by the Comanches. We must go to her."

Nancy started to turn her horse, but Alan shot out an arm and put his hand on her wrist. He gripped it tightly as he shook his head.

"You're hurting me, Alan. Let me go."

"I . . . I can't. Don't you see? They want us to come after your friend. It's a trick."

Just then they both heard the soft sound of hoofbeats behind them. Hoofbeats and the clatter of rocks and the swish of sliding dirt. They both turned to see two men riding down the bank toward them, both holding rifles in their hands.

Alan brought up his rifle defensively as he released his grip on Nancy's wrist. He started to bring it to his shoulder as the man on the dun rode up to him.

"No, don't," Nancy pleaded. "Alan, don't shoot."

Tallman reached out as he rode up and knocked Alan's rifle barrel to one side. Alan grabbed the stock with his free hand and started to swing it toward Tallman.

Jacobs rode up, then, and got in between Alan and Tallman. "Settle down, boy," he said. "We ain't goin' to hurt you none."

Alan looked at Nancy in bewilderment. She, almost as puzzled as he, blinked her eyes and found her voice.

"These are friends, Alan."

"Huh?"

"That's Mr. Jacobs and Mr. Tallman."

Tallman looked at the boy and nodded. Alan relaxed and let the rifle down into his lap. He stared at Tallman in confusion. He tried to speak, but could only splutter something unintelligible.

"Take it easy, son," Jacobs said. "We're friends."

"Nancy," Tallman said. "Looks like we caught up to you just in time."

"Mr. Jacobs," Nancy said, "I just heard Lorena Belton call my name."

"We heard," Jacobs said.

"You'll likely hear it again," Tallman said, a somber tone to his voice.

"I told her we can't help her friend," Alan said, suddenly finding his voice. "It's a danged trick."

"Alan," Tallman said. "Is that your name?"

"Yes, sir."

"Well, Alan's right, Nancy. Let us handle this."

"But Lorena's hurt. We must go and help her."

They all stopped talking as Lorena screamed again.

"Nancy, help meeeeeee!"

Nancy shuddered again. Her eyes opened wide in a display of her torment. She looked as if she was going to bolt away on her horse at any second.

"They know you're here, Nancy," Tallman said. "They want you and the boy to come after Lorena. It's an old comanchero trick."

"That is Lorena's voice," Nancy said stubbornly.

"I know it is," Jacobs said. "But you've got to listen to Tallman here. I think he knows what he's talkin' about."

Tallman said nothing. He was looking at Alan with a piercing gaze. Alan's face was pale, and it was plain to see he was fighting a battle within himself.

"Spit it out, boy," Tallman said. "You got something to say."

"I think I know them comancheros," Alan said. "They brung me to Santa Fe and sold me to Mr. Ottmers."

"That one back there. Pato. You killed him?" Tallman asked.

"I done it."

"Did it," Nancy corrected.

"I shot him," Alan said. "It was Pato all right."

"Do you know Redford?" Tallman asked.

Alan shook his head. "Pato, he rode with some other bad men."

"Know their names?" Tallman asked.

Alan nodded. "Alicante was one; they called him Flaco. Another was Federico Lucero, they called him Gusano. And, ah, the meanest one, Alberto Figueroa. They called him Lobo."

"There's one other," Tallman said.

Alan nodded, his eyes flaring wide from fright.

"Paco Sanchez," Tallman said.

"They called him El Diablo," Alan said. "How come you know them?"

"I run across them before," Tallman said. "I never knew about Redford, but I knew there was one other in that bunch who was never seen much."

"Redford is one of those comancheros?" Nancy asked. "Are you sure?"

"I'm sure," Tallman said.

Lorena screamed again. "Nancy, please help me. Hurry. Nanceeeeeee!"

Nancy covered her ears with her hands, her face contorted to a frozen mask of agony. "I can't stand it any more," she said. "They're torturing that poor woman."

"Mother . . ." Alan started to say.

"That's how they want you to feel, Nancy," Tallman said.

"I don't care. We can't just stay here and let Lorena go through that. We must do something, Mr. Tallman."

"She's right, Tallman," Jacobs said. "It's inhuman to let this go on. If you don't want to stop it, I will."

Tallman looked at Alan, who returned the look. Nancy saw the exchange, and her surprise was reflected in her face. She took her hands away from her ears and glared at Tallman.

"The boy knows," Tallman said. "Don't you, son?"

Alan nodded.

"What do you mean?" Nancy asked. "Alan, what is Mr. Tallman talking about?"

"The comancheros want us to ride after them. They're waiting for us." Alan seemed to squirm inside his skin. It was plain to see that he was uncomfortable, that he did not want to talk about what the comancheros were doing and planned to do.

"Chances are," Tallman said, "that your friend Lorena isn't being tortured at all."

"That's bull—" Jacobs said.

"I don't believe you," Nancy said. "How can you be so heartless?"

"Nancy," Tallman said, "if I were to put a gun to that boy's head and tell you to scream, what would you do?"

"I'd scream."

"Likely, that's what Redford is doing. He has two women prisoners, and he's using one against the other. He's not going to hurt one of them without a damned good reason."

"But you don't know that, Mr. Tallman."

"No, but Alan there does. Don't you, son?"

"I've seen 'em do it different ways," Alan said.

"What do you mean, 'different ways'?" Nancy asked.

"Once, they wanted to draw a man out of hiding when I was with them," Alan said. "They had his brother with them. They made the brother scream and flushed the other'n out and caught him too."

"How did they do that?" Nancy asked, an undertone of panic in her voice.

"They tied the man they had to a tree and started shooting at him. They made the bark fly on that tree. The man was tied so his brother could see him. And every time them comancheros shot a ball into the tree, the tied-up brother screamed bloody murder."

"How awful," Nancy said.

"Yes'm," Alan said.

Tallman looked at the boy closely as he spoke, watching his facial expressions, his hands, the way he used them, and the way he said the words when he spoke.

"So, what are you going to do, Mr. Tallman," Nancy asked. "Just let this terrible thing go on?"

"No'm," Tallman said. "Jacobs and I are going to try and flank the comancheros, if he's willing, and get those two women away from them."

Jacobs cleared his throat.

Tallman shifted his gaze to Jacobs.

"Mr. Jacobs, are you going to help him?" Nancy asked.

"I reckon so. I just don't know what in hell we're dealin' with here is all."

Alan looked straight into Tallman's eyes. "I want to go with you," he said.

Nancy did not hesitate. "No," she said. "It's too dangerous. You're just a boy."

"He's pretty haired-over for a boy," Tallman said. "He shot Pato, didn't he?"

"He's still a boy," Nancy said. "I won't have him risking his life unnecessarily."

"You'd better stay here, son," Tallman said. "Jacobs. You ready?"

"I guess I'm as ready as I'll ever be," Jacobs replied.

"We'll leave the horses here. You take the left flank. I'll take the right."

Jacobs dismounted, tied his horse to a root coiling from the bank of the river. Tallman rode his horse downstream a ways and swung out of the saddle. He looped the dun's reins around a young willow, checked his rifle and pistol.

"We'll all go," Nancy said suddenly.

"What?" Tallman eyed her as if she had gone crazy.

"Alan and I can shoot. You're both going up against five men."

"I thought you were worried about the boy," Tallman said.

"He wants to go. He can go with me."

Tallman walked over to Alan, looked up at him. "Do you think you can take care of Nancy and yourself?" he asked.

Alan nodded.

"You and your mother stay behind us at least fifty yards. If you see us duck, you duck. And, if you shoot, be careful you don't hit one of the women."

Nancy slid off the pinto's back and walked over to Tallman.

"Just get those women back safe," she said. "Alan and I will do what we have to do."

Alan, smiling, jumped off of Linda's back and stood there, rifle in hand. Tallman took it from him, checked the powder in the pan, handed it back. He looked at Nancy's rifle, too, and found it was primed.

"Let's go," Tallman said.

Lorena screamed again, begging Nancy to come to her.

"Call out to her, Nancy," Tallman said. "Tell her you're coming."

Nancy took a deep breath and shouted: "Lorena, I'm coming. I'm coming to you."

Tallman turned on his heel and ran to the right bank of the river. Jacobs clung to the left bank as he picked his way over rocks and debris left by the shrinking river.

Lorena screamed back. "Hurry, Nancy. Help me!"

Tallman turned and waved Nancy to silence. Then he began to creep along the shoreline, the river thin between him and Jacobs, the heat oppressive in the airless river bottom.

As they rounded a bend, Tallman motioned for Jacobs to hold up, indicating that he would go ahead. Nancy and Alan, a few feet behind Tallman, stopped when they saw Tallman stop and motion to Jacobs.

Tallman crept around the bend, holding to cover, bent over to make as small a silhouette as possible. Soon, he disappeared from sight of the others and stopped to look downstream for any sign of the comancheros. From the sound of Lorena's screams, he figured they were about four hundred yards away, perhaps less. They had covered less than a hundred yards from the place where they had left their horses.

Tallman listened for any sound ahead of him. He scanned both sides of the river and saw nothing that alarmed him. But he had no illusions about the ability of the comancheros to conceal themselves. They were experts at fighting, at ambush. He was sure that they had thought about this for a long time and had picked a good place to make their stand, to wait for Nancy and the boy to walk into their trap.

Very slowly, Tallman picked his way along the bank, stopping frequently behind cover, careful to avoid making any noise. Soon, he knew, at least one of the comancheros would have to take a look, to see if Nancy really was coming.

Perhaps, he thought, they'd be expecting her and the boy just to ride up like innocents. But it was obvious to him that Redford and the others were taking no chances. The next few moments, Tallman knew, were crucial. Either he'd spot one of the comancheros, or they would see him and start shooting.

Tallman took another six steps through thin brush, pushing past saplings and sliding over rocks, before he stopped again for another look downstream. At the edge of an outcropping of bluff, he saw the slightest movement, something flickering in and out of sight.

At first, Tallman could not make out what it was. He took another two steps to get a better look. When he brought his head up and pried away a bunch of leaves at the end of a dry bush, he saw more flickering, something dark and waving, and something else beyond, a darker patch.

Then, Lorena screamed her appeal to Nancy once again, high and shrill. This time, her voice was more piercing, more frantic, and that's when the flickering object moved and he heard a soft whinny from beyond the outcropping. The scream sent a chill up Tallman's spine.

Tallman slid another half foot over sand and rock, took a position in a small niche in the bank of the river. The flickering was a horse's tail; he could see it plainly now, and the whole of the horse's rump. And something else.

"Damn," Tallman said, under his breath, and moved still closer, four feet, five feet, six.

There was a cottonwood growing next to the left bank of the river, and the horse stood beneath it. A man stood at the horse's head, holding on to its bridle and reins. Atop the horse, which was stripped of its saddle, the strap marks still showing in its hide, sat a young woman, her hands tied behind her back.

Tallman sucked in a breath and held it until it burned his lungs. Then he let his breath out slowly when he was sure of what else he saw. The woman had a rope around her neck, a hangman's noose, and the rope was draped over a cottonwood limb, knotted tight at the bough.

He failed to see the barrel of a rifle inching through the leaves of the cottonwood tree, edging through the foliage like the nose of a deadly snake. He stared at the woman and knew that she had not been the one who had been screaming. If the man holding the horse's bridle ever turned loose, the horse would run right out from under the woman and leave her dangling by the neck, suffocating as the noose tightened around her neck.

Chapter Twenty-Eight

The young woman had on a filthy dress, and her hair was tied back with a leather thong. Tallman could not see her face. He recognized the man at the head of the horse as one of the comancheros; he couldn't be sure which one. But it was not Redford.

He knew he had to look beyond, find where the others were, where the other woman was being held. He slid along the small bluff through more brush and was about to take another step when the hairs on the back of his neck stood on end.

A rifle cracked, and Tallman saw the puff of smoke, the bright orange flame from its muzzle. Instinctively, Tallman ducked and he heard the ball sizzle just above his head, thunking into the bank. Chunks of rock and dust stung the side of his face, and he threw himself flat on the ground, his head behind a rock large enough to conceal him.

The shot had come from high in the cottonwood tree. Tallman knew that much. He knew it would take several seconds for the shooter to reload. But, he also knew that by now there were other guns trained on him. As if to punctuate his thoughts, another shot cracked the air with its explosive force and he heard the lead ball strike the rock in front of his head and felt the sparks sting his forehead as they fell.

The ball caromed off the rock in a shrieking whine and ricocheted off the bluff across the river. Tallman knew he was in a bad spot, with most of his body exposed and at least one rifleman zeroed in on his position. If he raised his head, he'd take a ball between the eyes. If he moved forward, he would expose more of himself. He was pinned down. He could not even get off an answering shot. And once he shot his rifle, they'd be on him like a swarm of hornets before he could reload or draw his pistol for a final shot.

Tallman moved his head slightly to see to one side. He was rewarded with still another rifle round that spanged off the rock by his head. He moved his head again to see if there was any other concealment nearby and, again, someone fired a ball at him. It furrowed the sand next to his leg, and he knew then that he had to move or die.

Out of the corner of his eye, while glancing to his left, Tallman saw movement. He twisted his head slightly to see what it was. His heart soared to see Jacobs picking his way along the left bank of the Brazos. His path kept him shielded behind the outcropping. As long as he stayed hunched over, the man in the tree was not likely to see him.

Jacobs looked over at Tallman. Tallman dared not move to warn him, but hoped that the wagon master had been able to assess the situation. Jacobs wasn't going to be of much help unless he exposed himself. As long as he stayed behind the outcropping, he'd be safe, but he would find no targets unless he stepped around it and found one of the comancheros out in the open.

Tallman kicked his right leg quickly, drawing another rifle shot that spanged off the top of the rock and spun off in a grating *paooong* overhead. Then he scooted backwards, away from the shielding rock, and rolled to his right. Another shot spunked a ball into the dust where he had lain and left a doodlebug crater the size of a baby's fist.

A split second after the second shot, Tallman backed away another three or four yards, and this time, nobody shot at him. He slid his legs around so that they faced the opposite bank and braced himself against a thin sliver of shoreline. But in this position, he could bring his rifle to bear on the man sitting in the cottonwood tree. It was a long, difficult shot, but it might buy him some time.

Jacobs looked over towards Tallman and nodded, as if he understood the situation. Tallman hoped that Jacobs now knew where at least two of the riflemen were. But there was no way to warn him that one of the women was ready to be hanged whenever the comancheros were threatened.

Despite his misgivings, Tallman waved to Jacobs, urging him to hold his position. Jacobs shook his head as if he didn't understand. Tallman gestured again with his hand, motioning for Jacobs not to move. He needed time to think. If either he or Jacobs charged the comancheros, they'd kick that horse out from under Sara and she would be a cottonwood blossom.

Jacobs slid down until he was seated. He wore a look of disgust on his face and shook his head as if in disbelief.

Tallman brought his rifle up to his shoulder, which exposed his upper torso to the comanchero in the tree. He tried to get a bead on the man, but could not see him clearly through the leaves.

"Tallman, don't do it," shouted a voice from beyond the outcropping of limestone. Tallman thought the voice came from the tree. He recognized the voice.

"Redford?"

"Where's the Stafford woman?" Redford shouted.

"She's not feeling well," Tallman lied.

"Better give her up, or Sara Wells will get her damned neck broke."

"Can't do that, Redford," Tallman said. But he brought the rifle down to show his good intentions.

"I'm not goin' to pussyfoot with you, Tallman. Either you bring Nancy Stafford up here, or I'll put a whip to that horse you see under Sara Wells."

"Give me a minute to go and get Mrs. Stafford," Tallman said.

"You move your ass quick, Tallman. I'm about out of patience."

Tallman turned around and crawled away from his spot. He didn't trust Redford not to shoot him if he stood up. He had no intention of giving up Nancy, but had another idea that might work if Redford would wait him out long enough.

As it turned out, the decision was taken out of Tallman's hands. As he got out of range of the man in the tree, he heard hoofbeats coming from the north. He stopped stock-still and brought his rifle up to his shoulder.

A horse came galloping around the bend, and on foot, Nancy was running after it, rifle in hand. Tallman strained to see the rider, but could not see if the horse was mounted or not. As the animal drew closer, Tallman recognized it as a horse he had seen before.

Pato's horse.

Tallman let his rifle down as the horse sped toward him. Then he saw Alan hugging its side, holding on to the saddle horn with one hand, his rifle with the other.

Out of the corner of his eye, he saw Jacobs stand up, bring his rifle up to fire. Tallman waved at Jacobs not to shoot, and Jacobs slowly let the rifle fall from his shoulder.

Then Tallman waved for Alan to stop, but it was plain to see that he was going to ride right on by. In an instant, Tallman knew what he had to do.

As the horse passed by him, Tallman was already running toward the place of ambush, trying to keep the horse between him and the comanchero perched high in the tree.

"Come on, Jacobs," Tallman yelled and Jacobs got the idea and started running along the bank. Behind him, Tallman heard Nancy's footfalls as she ran toward them.

Two shots boomed close together and Tallman saw dirt spout up in front of him. He also saw the man in the tree expose himself as he fired. Stopping quickly, Tallman brought his rifle up, cocking it on the fly, took quick aim and squeezed off a shot. He saw the man reach out to break his fall, then come tumbling down through the branches just as Alan reached the place where Sara sat atop the horse with a noose around her neck.

Tallman started running, pulling his powder horn up to his mouth, pulling the stopper out with his teeth. He poured powder down the barrel on the run, then dug in his possibles pouch for patch and ball. He started the ball down the barrel, jerked the wiping stick out from under the stock, and rammed the ball home atop the powder.

He saw Alan rise up a little and lay his rifle across Pato's saddle. Then he saw the rifle sprout flame and smoke, but he didn't know if Alan had hit anyone.

Jacobs reached the outcropping and slipped around it, disappearing from sight. Tallman lifted his smaller powder horn and dusted the pan of his flintlock, running faster than before.

He heard another shot but heard no one cry out. Then there was another shot, and as Tallman cleared the outcropping, he saw Alan turn Pato's horse and charge toward the cottonwood. As he passed the outcropping, he saw a comanchero running out from the bank, aiming at Alan, who slid almost under the belly of Pato's horse, Apache-style, to conceal himself.

Tallman stopped, took aim on the comanchero's back, held his breath as he cocked the rifle. When the blade sight dropped on the target, Tallman squeezed off the shot, and the rifle bucked against his shoulder. He knew he must have overloaded it when he poured the powder in, since the pain in his shoulder nearly drove him to his knees.

Beyond the billowing smoke, Tallman saw the comanchero fall forward, his rifle ejected from his hands at the moment he pulled the trigger. The explosion twisted the rifle through the air like a flung baton until it fell to earth like a smoking Roman candle.

Tallman saw Jacobs reach the horse that Sara sat on, but someone swung a rifle butt at him, striking him in the head. Jacobs went down as the horse danced, jiggling Sara atop its back but not running out from under her.

Alan swung Pato's horse toward Jacobs as Tallman

raced up in time to see Redford release his hold on the bridle of Sara's horse. Several yards away, Lorena stood, tied to the base of the cottonwood tree, a dead man at her feet.

"Tallman, you sonofabitch," Redford yelled and smashed the horse under Sara with his fist to send it on its way.

Tallman threw down his rifle and drew his pistol. As the horse started to bolt out from under the hapless captive woman, Alan rode up, sliding into the saddle of Pato's horse. He reached out and grabbed Sara by the waist as her horse bucked and shot toward Redford, who tried to step out of the way.

It all happened so fast, Tallman barely knew what he was doing. He saw the horse's shoulder graze Redford, who was drawing a knife from its sheath as Alan's horse came to a halt.

Then Redford leaped toward Alan, brandishing the knife in his hand. He slashed as Alan turned the horse, the blade barely missing his leg.

Jacobs struggled to rise, holding one hand to his bleeding head.

Tallman aimed his pistol at Redford, fired, and the shot went wild. He threw it down and drew his own knife as he charged toward Redford who was, once again, trying to unseat Alan from Pato's horse.

"Hold on to her, Alan," Tallman shouted as he closed with Redford. Redford whirled to meet his attacker, and Alan spun Pato's horse in a circle to get away from Redford and his knife.

Lorena screamed as Redford lunged toward Tallman. Tallman sidestepped the arcing blade and slashed at Redford's arm, the knife ripping the man's shirt and grazing his flesh as he passed.

Recovering quickly, Redford turned back toward Tallman as Alan looked down on the two men, gripping Sara
tightly so that she would not fall from his lap.

Nancy ran up, out of breath, and raced towards Lorena.

"Look out," Jacobs yelled at Nancy.

Redford turned away from Tallman and ran to intercept
Nancy. He reached out for her, his hand brushing against her
waist, but she spun away and slammed him in the belly with
the stock of her rifle, knocking the wind from his lungs.

"Damn you," Redford spat, and slashed at her with his
knife. The blade tip caught the sleeve of her dress and sheared
it open from shoulder to elbow.

Then Redford turned to see Tallman charging down on
him, and he braced himself for the impact. Tallman barreled
into Redford at full speed, and the two went down, both grab-
bing for each other's wrists.

The two men rolled over and over, each struggling for
an advantage against the other. Nancy dropped her rifle and
ran to untie Lorena as Alan worked to loosen the hangman's
knot snugged up tight against Sara's neck.

Redford brought his legs up and kicked out, knocking
Tallman away and to one side. Tallman rolled out of the way
just in time as Redford slammed the knife down toward Tallman's belly. Scrabbling to his feet, Redford came after Tallman, who spun around and kicked out with one leg, catching
Redford in the shin.

Redford crashed down on his side and jerked his knife
from the ground where it was buried, bringing it up as Tallman crabbed over to him to deal the death blow with his own
blade.

Redford swiped his knife out in front of him and cut a

gash in Tallman's wrist. Tallman kept driving in and down and smashed Redford's mouth with his left hand. Blood squirted from Redford's crushed lips, and he shook his head in pain.

Then Tallman drove his knife into Redford's side, twisting it into the flesh as blood gushed over his hand. Redford groaned in agony as the wide blade sank in and tore through meat and veins and sinew. He stabbed at Tallman with his own knife, but there was no energy in his feeble thrusts.

"You bastard, Tallman," Redford gasped.

Tallman wrested the knife from Redford's hand and tossed it away. He looked into the dying man's eyes with a steely stare.

"You haven't got long, Redford," Tallman said.

"Finish it, then."

"No, you won't go easy. You'll just leak out blood until you haven't enough left to make soup."

"It was a good fight, *Hombròn*, eh?"

Alan slipped the noose from around Sara's neck and she collapsed into his arms, breathing heavily. He heard what Redford called Tallman and looked down at him.

Tallman stood up, wiped the blade of his knife on his trousers and slipped it back into its sheath. Tallman felt Alan's eyes on him and looked at the boy.

"Sorry you had to see that, son."

"I-it's all right," Alan said, as if in a stupor.

Nancy finished untying Lorena, and the two women embraced. Tallman helped Sara down from Alan's lap and held on to her. She was shaking like a willow in a windstorm.

"Are you all right, ma'am?" Tallman asked.

"I'm beholden to you, sir, and that brave young man

there." Sara pointed to Alan, who seemed dazed by all that had happened.

"Nancy?"

"We're just fine, Mr. Tallman."

Tallman walked over and helped Jacobs to his feet. Jacobs shook off his arm once he was standing. He rubbed his head with a hand already bloody from touching the place where the rifle had smashed his skull.

"Did we get 'em all, Tallman?"

"I think so. Feel like checking them out?"

"Sure. What about that Redford? You ought to finish him."

"He won't last long."

"I'd like to shoot his damned head off. All the trouble he's caused me and a lot of other people."

"That would be the kindest thing to do," Tallman said.

Jacobs went to examine the fallen comancheros. Tallman walked over to Alan, who still sat atop Pato's horse, his face chalky, his lower lip quivering.

"Are you all right, son?" Tallman asked, looking up at Alan.

"Sir, I . . . I don't know. I feel funny."

Tallman looked at Alan's face with narrowed eyes. Then he spoke to him so low no one else could hear.

"Como te llamas, chamaco?"

Without thinking, Alan replied, *"Me llamo Rafaél."*

"No," Tallman said. "Your name is Ralph."

Alan nodded numbly and began to cry. He put his head in his hands and wept profusely, his body shaking with emotion.

Nancy patted Lorena and walked over to Tallman.

"What did you say to Alan?" she demanded.

"I asked him his name."

"You know his name. It's Alan."

"No, it's Ralph. Ralph Tallman. His mother, Esperanza, called him Rafaél."

Alan looked at Nancy. "I remembered," he said. "When he asked me in Spanish what my name was, I remembered."

Stunned, Nancy looked at Tallman, who smiled at her. He took her hand in his.

"It's all right," he said. "Don't worry. You found yourself a son, and so, it seems, have I."

Alan slid out of the saddle and embraced Nancy. Then he looked up at Tallman and began wiping the tears from his eyes.

"My mother?" Alan asked.

"I'll tell you about it someday, son."

"You know what happened to his mother, then?" Nancy asked.

Tallman nodded. Then, he turned to the boy and spoke to him.

"Alan, you'd better catch up all these spare horses and go get yours and your mother's. You're going to have some nice stock for your ranch when we get back."

"Yes, sir," Alan said, and climbed back on Pato's horse.

A moment later, blood bubbled up out of Redford's mouth. He gave one last sighing breath, gurgled in his throat, and died.

Nancy looked at Tallman, a wistful, loving look in her eyes.

"Thank you, Jon Tallman," she said. "Thank you for . . ."

She could not finish what she was going to say. Tallman leaned down and pecked her on the cheek.

"You've got a fine son there, Nancy," he said. "A mighty fine son. Are you ready to go home?"

"Yes," Nancy sighed and put her arms around Tallman in a grateful embrace, squeezing him until he could barely breathe.

Chapter
Twenty-Nine

The wagons were lined up neatly just beyond the fringe of trees that grew along the creek's mouth where it emptied into the Brazos River. Opposite the wagons, a cluster of white tents lay scattered among the trees on the other side of the creek.

Mexican soldiers sat on the grass and drank from goatskin *botas*, their rifles stacked in tripods just outside the tents. Some played cards and drank mezcal or tequila or smoked, while others stood guard or waved to soldier friends on the other side of the Brazos who were just setting up camp. The soldiers were jubilant, flushed with victory, and they laughed and joked among themselves, showed off their spoils of war, including Comanche scalps and scrotums, beaded moccasins and quilled pouches, buckskin shirts, eagle feathers, lances, war clubs, knives, bows and arrows.

The Americans with the wagon train talked among

themselves, looking at the Mexican soldiers with some trepidation because they could smell the alcohol and could not understand their language. But the Americans were in a jovial mood despite the heat, and the women clustered together with their fans while the men drank sugar water and stood in the shade of the trees. Some looked in the direction of the house, which was being guarded by troops belonging to Austin's Texas Militia, and spoke guardedly among themselves, some with nervousness, because they did not know what was happening or what was going to happen, though they sensed something momentous would occur that very morning.

Then the two Mexican scouts who had been sent north that morning came riding up on sweat-lathered horses and spoke to the leader of the troops across the river. The Americans stopped talking, and a hush fell over the wagon train.

Then one of the Mexicans signaled to those camped by the creek, and one of the soldiers jumped up and ran down to the house. Soon, Stephen Austin himself, his entourage, and some of his militiamen walked up to the mouth of the creek and stood around, smoking and chatting.

The commandant of the Mexican soldiers mounted a fine black horse, an Arabian, some said, and rode across the river to meet with Austin. A lieutenant and a captain rode with him.

American men came out of the shade and walked over to the women, and they all strolled down to the river like geese waddling to drink, and they asked questions among themselves, and, finally one of Austin's friends spoke to them and everyone started looking to the north with anxious eyes.

The Mexican camp on the creek stirred as an officer barked orders, and the men put away their cards and the *bo-*

tas, straightened their jackets, put on their hats, and grabbed their rifles from the tripods. Then they lined up in formation and marched to the river as a sergeant called cadence.

Austin pulled a sheet of paper from inside his coat, unfolded it, and scanned it for a moment before folding it back up and holding it in his left hand.

As the riders came into view, a deep hush fell over the assemblage at the Brazos. As they drew nearer, the Americans began to whisper among themselves. Austin leaned over and spoke to one of his aides and then to the Mexican commandant, Colonel Lujan.

It seemed like hours to some of the people as they waited. Finally, one of the women exclaimed out loud and pointed at the riders. "It's Nancy Stafford," she said.

Another one pointed and said loudly, "Looky, there's Sara and Lorena."

Mexican soldiers escorted the group of riders, and when they started down the bank, the people saw Jacobs and a boy leading a string of horses, and a tall man in the lead who stirred some recognition among them.

When they had crossed the river, the Americans could no longer contain themselves. They shouted "Hoorah!" and cheered wildly. Nancy finally waved to them, and the girls, too, began waving.

Jon Tallman stopped ten yards away from where Stephen Austin, Colonel Lujan, and the others stood.

"Jon," Austin said, "it's good to see you."

"Mighty good to see you, Don Estevàn."

"Set down, Jon. I want to meet Mrs. Stafford and the girls."

Tallman swung out of the saddle. He was covered with dust and sweat, but Austin stepped forward and shook his hand. Colonel Lujan saluted him, and Captain Montes grinned and saluted him as well.

Tallman helped Nancy dismount from the pinto while Jacobs and Alan helped Lorena and Sara off their horses. Tallman made the introductions as though it were the most normal thing in the world, but the girls were speechless, and Nancy's eyes were wide with wonder.

"Mrs. Stafford," Austin said, fingering the piece of paper in his hands, "I want to welcome you to Texas."

"Why, thank you, Mr. Austin. I'm honored."

"You are the kind of settler Texas needs. I have here a piece of paper that we found at one of the stakes that mark your property. I see you have horses and a cow and calf. That qualifies you as a rancher, and I am going to grant you the maximum amount of land under the terms of my agreement with the Mexican government."

"I . . . I don't know what to say," Nancy said. "I left no paper."

"No, but I recognize Jon Tallman's handwriting and he has already certified your acreage and started the process, so to speak."

Austin showed Nancy the paper that Tallman had left at her property stake. She looked at Tallman and smiled. "Thank you, Jon," she said.

"You and your son are perfect examples of the kind of Americans we want to settle this great land of Texas," Austin said. "I have looked at your home and marveled at your ingenuity and the hard work you put into its building. I hereby proclaim you a Mexican citizen by the authority vested in me and will send you a deed to your property by special messenger upon my return to San Felipe de Austin."

"Thank you so much, Mr. Austin," Nancy said.

"Now, perhaps you'd like to join your friends there, who were escorted by Colonel Lujan to your property just yesterday."

The Americans who had overheard the conversation yelled jubilantly and rushed to embrace Nancy and the girls. Even Jacobs was swarmed over by his former wards, and he grinned wide as he was swept away by men shaking his hand and slapping him on the back.

"Stephen," Tallman said when the crowd swept Nancy, Alan, Sara, Lorena, and Jacobs away, "how did you happen to come this far north on the Brazos?"

"A man you met, a friend I trust, saw to it that I was informed of what you were doing, what had happened to the wagon train, the kidnapping of two young girls."

"Who was that?" Tallman asked.

"You'll meet him shortly. He's waiting down at Mrs. Stafford's fine home for her."

"So, you just left all your business and traveled up here in this heat to welcome new settlers to Texas?"

Austin laughed. "I'm afraid it's more complicated than that, Jon."

"I expect it is," Tallman said dryly.

"We've had terrible depredations among our small contingent of settlers. The Comanches have murdered a number of my people, and I wanted to put a stop to it. I have been allowed to form a militia and given absolute authority over Texas's government north of the Rio Bravo clear to the Red."

"I'm impressed."

"I solicited the aid of Colonel Lujan and his fine troops, who, along with my militiamen, fought the Comanches who raided the wagon train and put those who survived to rout."

"I'm glad to hear of that. Cotton-Eye?"

"Dead, Jon. We have decimated the Comanche tribes along the Brazos, and I see nothing but growth and prosperity for my people. I have made treaties with the friendlier Wichitas and Tonkawas and driven the Karankawas completely out of my colonies."

"Whew," Tallman said. "You've been right busy."

"Come, let us walk down to the house and meet Mrs. Stafford's benefactor."

Puzzled, Tallman walked with Austin along the creek to the fort that Nancy and Alan had built. There another throng awaited them, militiamen and settlers Jon had not seen in months, people he knew from the southern part of the Brazos.

"You'll be glad to know we've founded another settlement south of here," Austin was saying, "not too far from this fine place. And these people from the wagon train are all going to settle here so that Mrs. Stafford and her son have plenty of fine neighbors."

"What's this new settlement, Stephen?"

Austin laughed. "I'm happy to say it makes our intentions quite clear to the Mexican government, in particular to Governor Martínez. The colony's settlement is called Washington on the Brazos."

"Well, I'll be damned, Stephen. You are even bolder than your enemies say you are."

Austin laughed heartily. "Enemies, Jon? I have no enemies."

"Stephen, you're the best politician the United States ever had."

"Ever will have, Jon."

A man finished hugging Nancy and turned to walk toward them. Tallman recognized him vaguely, but it was not until he raised his head as he drew near that he could recall his name.

"Virgil? Virgil Ottmers?"

"Tallman, good to see you," Virgil said, extending his hand.

Austin beamed as the two men shook hands.

"So, Stephen, this was the man who told you about Nancy and Alan?"

"And about you, Jon."

"I'm might grateful, Virgil," Tallman said.

"When I got back home, I went straight to San Felipe de Austin and ran into Don Estevan and told him the whole story. I told him I was going to come back up here and see how Nancy and the boy were faring and bring them some supplies. Practically the whole colony wanted to come."

Tallman looked at the large throng of people surrounding Nancy and Alan. "It looks like you did, Virgil."

"Did you hear the good news? Did you tell him, Don Estevan?"

"No, not yet, Virgil," Austin said. He turned to Tallman. "Jon, I've appointed you *alcalde* of this settlement, if you decide to move up this way. What do you think?"

Tallman drew in a breath. At that moment, Nancy turned away from her admirers and looked at him. She broke away and started walking quickly in their direction.

"I told Nancy," Ottmers said.

"Jon? I need an answer," Austin said.

Nancy rushed up then and curtsied to Austin and took Jon's hand in hers. She looked up at him adoringly. His face flushed, and he turned to Austin.

"I guess I will take that job, Stephen."

Austin grabbed Tallman's hand and shook it vigorously. "I won't ask you to do more than that, Jon. For the moment, anyway."

Virgil and Nancy both laughed.

"What do you mean, Stephen? As if I didn't know."

"Well, it is customary for my colonists to be married. I just thought . . ."

Nancy blushed this time and she dipped her head shyly. "Oh, Mr. Austin."

But Tallman put his finger under Nancy's chin and tilted her face up toward his.

"It's not such a bad idea, Nancy," he said softly. "If you'd have me?"

"Jon, please. Everything's happening so fast, I hardly know what to say."

Austin took Ottmers's arm. "Virgil, let's you and I walk down to the house. I believe your folks have refreshments for us."

"Yes, sir, we do."

Austin and Ottmers walked away, leaving Tallman and Nancy gazing into each other's eyes. Austin looked back and saw the two embrace. He smiled and squeezed Ottmers's arm.

"Virgil, tell me again what those people on the wagon train told you."

"They said that if everybody, Injuns and Mexicans and Americans, wanted land so bad they'd fight for it, they sure wanted to settle here in Texas."

"Virgil, someday Texas will be a part of the United States. That is my dream. That is my ultimate goal. You and Jon and all these people are the seeds that will grow a mighty state, the mightiest in the Union."

"I'll drink to that, " Ottmers said.

"So will I, Virgil," Austin said, smiling. "So will I. Shall we?"

The two men joined the throng of people and were swallowed up by them until they were all one group, friends and neighbors, allies in a common cause, willing participants on the very brink of history.

About the Author

Jory Sherman is the Spur Award–winning author of *The Medicine Horn*, *Song of the Cheyenne*, *Horne's Law*, *Winter of the Wolf*, and *Grass Kingdom*. In addition to *The Brazos*, he has written *The Arkansas River*, *The Rio Grande*, *The Columbia River*, and *The South Platte* for Bantam's Rivers West series. He currently resides with his wife near Belton, Texas.